DUST AND GLORY

Center Point
Large Print

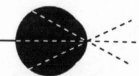

**This Large Print Book carries the
Seal of Approval of N.A.V.H.**

Dust and Glory

Michael Zimmer

CENTER POINT LARGE PRINT
THORNDIKE, MAINE

Lg Pt
Zim

This Center Point Large Print edition is published
in the year 2013 by arrangement with
Golden West Literary Agency.

The text of this Large Print edition is unabridged.
In other aspects, this book may
vary from the original edition.
Printed in the United States of America
on permanent paper.
Set in 16-point Times New Roman type.

ISBN: 978-1-61173-684-7

Library of Congress Cataloging-in-Publication Data

Zimmer, Michael, 1955–
Dust and glory / Michael Zimmer.
pages ; cm.
ISBN 978-1-61173-684-7 (library binding : alk. paper)
1. Large type books. I. Title.
PS3576.I467D8 2013
813´.54—dc23

2012042240

DUST AND GLORY

CHAPTER 1

There was no warmth in the low, melancholy tune Jesse Ross was whistling as he swung the old gray mule onto the rutted farm lane toward home, nor in the day for that matter. It was dusk, the sun long down and the western sky fading rapidly toward indigo, with a chill in the air that promised frost by morning. The deep, dense Missouri woods that bordered the lane was shapeless beyond the first fringe of trees, dark and silent, save for the echo of the wagon's rattling.

It was the silence that was bothering him, Jesse knew, that leeched the life from his song and made it seem so small. He kept remembering the thunder that had rumbled so unexpectedly around midmorning, and the way the sky had hazed over toward noon. Common enough at other times of the year but as unnatural as the silence here in November. Normally when he shucked corn in the narrow ribbon of the river field he would keep his pa's old Leman trade rifle handy for ground-hogs, and like as not pop a cap or two, but he hadn't seen a 'chuck all day, and the birds had kept to their roosts.

It all gave him a strange, shaky feeling deep in his stomach, like something he'd eaten earlier had turned sour, but he whistled anyway, forcing the same old nameless tune past stiff lips, as if in defiance of all that was wrong with the day.

Jesse was eighteen, tall and broad-shouldered, with brown hair and gray eyes and a quick, amiable grin that was a trait he had inherited from his ma. His hands were large and work-scarred: rough and calloused and blunt-fingered, but gentle too—when there was a need for it, deft and sure. He had always been that way, it seemed, quick and graceful in his actions, never clumsy or spilling like his brothers and sisters sometimes were. He had a way with animals, too, and sometimes made a little extra cash or traded for something the family needed by gentling mules to harness or horses to saddle.

He wore old but well-oiled brogan shoes over homespun wool socks, broadfall trousers and a sun-faded red cotton shirt under a canvas jacket. His cap was made of cloth, a hand-me-down like damn near everything else he owned or used. Hand-me-downs were a way of life on the Ross farm, as they were on most farms in that part of central Missouri, and about the only ones who ever got anything new were the oldest of each sex; that was Tom, on the boys' side, and Maybelline, on the girls'. There were seven Rosses, not counting his ma and pa, but since Tom and Eddie had gone off to fight with Beauregard in the East, that left Jesse the oldest at home.

Jesse sat in the center of the seat with his shoes propped against the footboard of the family's middle wagon, his elbows on his knees, the lines limp in his hands. Sam, the mule, trudged along with his head drooped low, too old for such work, Jesse knew, but all they had left since the Yankees raided their farm last August. Two fine teams of Missouri mules taken, and three saddle horses to boot, and he guessed they'd nearly taken Sam, too, until his ma had lied and told them Sam was night-blind. That was the first lie his ma ever admitted to telling, and he blamed that on the Yankees too, although, truth to tell, since August he was inclined to blame just about any hardship on the Yankees. Sometimes he'd mutter, "Damn Yankees," when a cold rain caught him in the fields, or a harness strap broke.

The whip'owill's call seemed loud and out of place after the long silence of the day, and the tune Jesse was whistling choked off and died. A piece of gray flitted across the road ahead of him, and he hauled up on the lines, waiting with his heart in his throat.

"I told ol' Denny you couldn't fool a country boy with a whip'owill's call." The voice came from the side and slightly behind him. Jesse turned slowly, recognizing the butternut gray uniform of the Confederacy even in the thickening shadows.

"Wasn't the call so much as that was the first

bird I'd heard all day," Jesse replied in a dry voice. The Reb was on foot, but he was carrying a big horse pistol and had it pointed more or less at Jesse's ribs.

"That a fact?" the Reb asked conversationally. "I hadn't noticed, but about all I've heard all day is a ringing in my ear. Your voice is as fuzzy as a caterpillar."

"Why ain't you fightin'?" This new voice came from the opposite side of the lane. Jesse turned back slowly and saw an older man with a black beard the size of a shovel bit masking his chin and neck, and a raw-looking scar on his forehead. He was hatless, and his long, uncombed hair fluttered softly in the breeze that nosed its way down the tree-walled canyon of the lane. He was carrying a rifle, Jesse noted, and had it cocked and aimed directly at him as well.

"You too young to fight, or just scared?" the younger man said. He had shifted his position while Jesse was studying the Reb with the rifle and now stood on the road bank, only a few feet away. Up close, this one also looked rough and uncurried, although the stubble on his face was only a few days old, and his hair was relatively short. Still, he looked ragged and tattered, his hands covered with scratches, like a man would get running heedlessly through brambles and such. His clothes were filthy with mud and ground-in dirt, one sleeve ripped to the elbow and half the buttons torn from his tunic. His face and hands were smudged with gunsmoke, and his eyes were red-rimmed, tearing. In his weariness he looked almost old, but Jesse suspected he wasn't much past twenty or twenty-five.

"Jim asked you a question, boy," the man with the rifle said. "Answer him."

"Got to get the crops in," Jesse said, still eyeing the one called Jim, who was aiming the pistol at him.

The man with the rifle snorted. "Reckon my crops have already gone to hell," he said. "What little I got out."

Jesse's anger flared unexpectedly. "I guess two brothers fighting with Beauregard is enough," he snapped. Then he added, "Unless one of you are planning to shoot me, get out of the way. I've got chores to do."

Jim's eyes widened some, and he laughed. "Full of fire, huh? Hell, don't mind ol' Denny there. We've been fighting goddamn bluebellies all day, and our tempers are some frazzled, that's all. Forget what I said about being scared, too. Didn't mean nothing by it."

Jesse was only half listening, though. He was staring toward the west, toward the thin, gauzy light still filtering through the trees. Softly, he said, "I thought it was thunder."

"Thunder from hell," Denny growled. He'd lowered the muzzle of his rifle some but hadn't dropped it all the way. "We need us some food," he said. "And we've got a friend up the road a ways that needs help."

Jesse felt an unfamiliar lurch of confusion. Save for the mules, which he viewed more as theft than a sign of the conflict, the war had always been a distant thing, read about in newspapers and on broadsheets. Now it had finally come home, and while he resented the weapons Jim and Denny brandished so readily, he couldn't deny a growing sense of excitement either. "Sure," he said, his voice tight. "We can put him in the wagon and Ma will fix him up. She'll likely have supper on, too."

"Supper?" Jim's face brightened. "I reckon it's been a spell since I've eaten home cooking. That sounds mighty fine."

"Up ahead," Denny said abruptly, scowling. "We've got Walt to look after afore we start worrying about our own bellies."

"Why, sure," Jim said mildly. "Wouldn't have it any other way."

Denny snorted and dropped down into the lane, trotting ahead until the dirty gray of his torn uniform disappeared ghostlike into the shadows.

Jim skidded down the bank and climbed into the wagon beside Jesse, settling back with a sigh. "Been hiking all day," he said. "My dogs is tired."

Jesse shook the lines out, clucked to Sam, and they started out with a small jolt. Jim made himself comfortable, but he didn't put his pistol away and his head kept swiveling from side to side, his gaze darting. Catching Jesse watching him, he grinned and said, "Them Yankees is tricky bastards. Best to always keep an eye peeled for 'em."

Jesse nodded, battled discretion for the better part of two hundred yards, then gave it up. "You said you've been fighting Yankees all day. Where?"

"Well, I ain't rightly sure," Jim admitted. "It was on the Osage River, I know that for damn certain. There was a big meadow on the west bank, and some chalky-looking cliffs back a ways."

"Big Meadow," Jesse said softly, picturing the place in his mind, the tall, lush grass, the verdant hills, the huge oaks and sycamores that tipped out over the river. Sometimes he and his pa, or his brothers, would ride that far just to hunt deer and turkey. It was a prime spot, though prone to flooding, he knew; that was why nobody had settled there yet.

"Yeah," Jim was saying. "A big one, a mile long or better, but not very wide. Know it?"

"That's the name," Jesse explained. "Big Meadow. About ten or twelve miles west of here. There's a shallow place to ford the river there, too, after August, anyway."

"Yeah, that there is," Jim said in a faraway voice. "We was fording it, all right, and never knew there was a bloody damn bluebelly about. Our scouts missed them entirely. They had a goddamn howitzer up on top of those cliffs and they was dropping grape right on our heads." He looked at Jesse, his face screwed up as if he might cry. "They waited until we were halfway across before they opened up. We didn't have a chance."

Jesse's breath caught in his throat. He remembered the first reports on Manassas, or Bull Run, and the claims that the water in the ditches had run red that day. And in his mind he saw Big Meadow that way, not rich and green as he knew it best, but as he had imagined Manassas—the grass and earth torn, cratered, the trees uprooted and the rivulets that twisted through the grass pink with blood.

"Reckon here will do," Jim said curtly.

Jesse glanced up, shaking the picture of Big Meadow from his mind, and saw Denny standing beside the lane.

Jesse whoaed the mule and set the brake, wrapping the lines around the lever. Jim jumped down and he and Denny faded into the woods. Standing, bracing the back of his legs against the seat, Jesse stared uncertainly after them. The funny feeling he'd carried in his stomach all day was back, although he couldn't say why. Nerves, perhaps, but just then Sam whinnied softly and Jesse knew the old mule sensed it too. There was something wrong with the evening yet, something out of kilter that he couldn't quite put a finger to.

A twig snapped, and a broad, gray shape heaved up from the woods and became three men—Denny and Jim, with the wounded Walt between them, struggling forward on a single, wobbly leg, with the other tied up to his belt. "Give us a hand," Denny hissed.

Jesse crawled over the seat and crossed the hard, shifting bed of shucked corn. Denny and Jim backed Walt against the side of the wagon and Jesse leaned over the sideboard to hook his hands under the wounded man's arms. "Easy now," Denny ordered, and together they hefted Walt into the wagon.

Against the gray of Walt's trousers the old, dried blood looked almost black, and Jesse had to swallow his lunch back at the way the foot flopped limply to one side—too far, Jesse thought sickly. Faintly, like the rustle of a gentle breeze through tall, sun-ripened grass, he heard the grating whisper of shattered bones. Yet Walt seemed beyond pain, or maybe only beyond the capacity to show it.

Jim scrambled over the sideboard and sank into the corn, cradling Walt's head in his lap. Jesse climbed into the seat, loosening the lines and releasing the brake. He paused for a moment, searching the woods, but Denny had melted into the darkness once more. Jesse hoped he was gone for good. The excitement he had felt earlier was gone now, completely, leaving him drained and half sick, the taste of his lunch still bitter against the back of his throat. There was something sticky on his left hand, and he kept twitching his fingers apart until it finally dawned on him that it must be blood. It was too dark to see now, but he knew the feel, and the smell. It reminded him of butchering hogs, and the thought sent his stomach to rolling again.

They entered a shallow creek bed, the wagon's iron-rimmed wheels bouncing roughly over the rocky trail, wringing a small, pain-racked cry from the injured man. Jesse could barely hear Jim's voice above the rattle of the wagon, but recognized the tone; it was the same voice Jesse used on green colts, or mothers used with frightened children, and it made Jesse inexplicably angry to hear it.

Sam started up the far bank, straining against the collar, his splayed hooves slipping a little in the mud. Jesse usually jumped down here for the climb to the top of the hill, where his house sat commanding a view down the far slope, but he decided against it tonight. With the woods full of panicky Confederate troops he thought it might be dangerous if someone thought he was trying to escape. He could feel Denny out there yet, keeping pace, watchful and distrusting. Still, seeing Sam's lowered head, hearing the thin, wheezing suck of his wind, Jesse's anger flared higher. Damn the Yankees, he thought, and the Rebs, too, for bringing their war to him.

"Say, hoss," Jim called quietly. "You never did tell me your name."

"Don't recollect you giving me much chance," Jesse retorted. Sam's right foreleg slid back and the old mule lurched against the collar, grunting loudly.

"You ought to get yourself a better mule," Jim offered then. "I noticed even in the dark this one is about played out."

Jesse bit his lip, held his temper. Sam got his footing again and leaned into the climb, dragging the wagon up the far bank. The grade was better after that, but it was still uphill, and he could see even in the shadows the sharply ridged blades of the old mule's withers humping with the effort.

"Say, your folks got any horses on that farm of theirs?" Jim asked.

"If you aim to steal horses, you'll have to be quicker about it," Jesse snapped. "Yankees have already raided our farm."

Jim chuckled. "Well, I ain't surprised, but you oughtn't look upon it as stealing. Not if the South does it. You got to look upon it as promoting a glorious cause."

Jesse grunted. The Yankees had made similar statements, his ma claimed, but their stock was gone all the same.

At the top of the hill Sam veered to the right,

toward the barn, but Jesse brought him back to the road. There was a lamp glowing in an upstairs bedroom and in the kitchen window of the tall, two-story frame house his pa and Eddie and Tom and he had built nearly ten years ago. There was a lantern sitting on the top step of the front porch too, and he could see Maybelline standing beside it, peering down the lane toward him.

Maybelline was his sister, sixteen and uncommon pretty for a Ross. Jesse had half hoped she would be inside when they arrived, and that she would stay there while they got the wounded man inside and Jim and Denny fed and on their way. It was worry enough to bring such a ragged bunch home, even if they were good Southern boys, without the added burden of thinking of Maybelline as a woman now, and needing looking after because of that.

"Jesse," she called, and came running down the steps as he wheeled Sam into the light. She was wearing her good, white Sunday dress, he saw, the skirt all aswirl, and he remembered the first time Billy Bob had seen her wearing that dress, and had gone bug-eyed the way he did at the whores down at Jefferson City. Billy Bob's folks farmed a patch down close to the river, and he was something of a friend, but seeing him looking at Maybelline that way had sparked something inside Jesse that he'd never felt before. He'd swung without thinking, right here in the yard, and knocked a tooth loose. Billy Bob never bugged his eyes around Jesse anymore, not even at whores, but the damage was done. After that Jesse never looked at Maybelline again and saw a knobby kid in overalls. Maybe Maybelline sensed something too, because shortly after that she'd taken to wearing dresses all the time.

"Jesse," Maybelline repeated, panting a little in her excitement, her bosom moving in a way that made him blush, thinking of Jim in back, likely peeping through the sideboards and thinking who knew what.

Shep came out from under the porch and trotted behind Maybelline, wagging his tail and grinning idiotically, heading straight for the nearest wheel to check out the news from the fields.

"There was a battle at Big Meadow," Maybelline informed him in a sort of hushed voice. "And some Johnny Rebs came to the back door. One of them was shot and Ma put him up in Tom and Eddie's room." She swayed closer, her voice dropping a notch. "Zeb wants to go with them when they leave, but Ma says no. Zeb's down at the barn, near fit to be tied."

"Ma's right," Jesse said, setting the brake. "Zeb's too young." Shep nosed the nearest wheel, wandered around to the off front wheel, where his hackles rose suddenly and he growled low in his throat. Scenting Jim, Jesse supposed. Thinking of Jim then, he said, "Why are you all dressed up like someone's getting married or baptized?"

"Why, because we've got company," she replied defensively. "Ma says we should treat Confederate soldiers like we'd want Tom and Eddie treated."

From the wagon box, Jim said, "Looks like we've come to the right place, all right."

Maybelline gasped, clutched at a small locket around her neck, and Shep sent up a frenzy of barking, dancing back and forth on the far side of the wagon. The front door opened and Jesse's pa stepped out, the double-barreled shotgun clenched firmly in his hands. "Maybelline," he called, squinting into the darkness. "Are you all right?"

Maybelline looked at Jesse, questioning, and Jesse nodded. "Yes, Pa," she called then. "I'm down here with Jesse."

Pa stepped to the edge of the porch, shielding his eyes from the lantern's glare. "Everything okay, son?"

"Yeah," Jesse replied.

"Put Sam up then and come to your supper. We've things to talk about."

Pa turned and went back inside, never having fully seen the mule and wagon, Jesse knew, or the way Shep had backed off with his tail slunk low; his pa's eyesight was failing, although he was too stubborn to admit it yet.

"Best go tell 'em I've got another out here that

needs patching," Jesse said to Maybelline. He wrapped the lines around the brake lever and jumped down.

"Johnny Rebs?" Maybelline asked, following him to the end gate.

"Why, yes, ma'am," Jim said, standing and bowing slightly at the waist. "Jim Thompson, ma'am, of Mobile."

"Alabama?"

"Yes, ma'am. At your service."

Maybelline curtsied—*curtsied,* for Christ's sake—and stepped back. "I am Maybelline Ross, Mr. Thompson. Pleased to make your acquaintance."

"Best be getting Walt inside," Jesse interrupted brusquely. "I'd hate to see a man bleed to death because of manners."

"Manners wouldn't hurt you much, Jesse Ross. It might be an improvement."

Jesse turned away, oddly embarrassed. Maybelline's anger was something he could handle, but he had seen the hurt deep in her eyes, and that bothered him. He wondered whether her new-found femininity was as confusing to her as it was to him. His gaze slid resentfully toward Jim, for what he had started with his bow, but Jim was looking down the front lane that led to the main road, his face twisted in horror.

Turning, Jesse felt his own fear swell in his

throat. In the dim light of the rising moon the lane was bristled with swaying and bobbing bayonets. A dark, sinuous line of advancing troops moved forward at a brisk trot, but eerily silent, without even the rattle of equipment or the sharp whisper of commands. Only Shep had heard them, and no one paid his barking any mind.

"You bastard," Jim cried. "It was just another dirty Yankee trick all along!"

Turning back, Jesse froze. Jim had lifted the horse pistol and had it pointed at Jesse's chest, the hammer eared all the way back.

"Mr. Thompson! No! Please!" Maybelline's voice seemed muted to Jesse, distant, a part of another world now. The dark eye of the pistol's muzzle looked suddenly huge, enveloping. Jim's finger was tightening on the trigger, the knuckle pale, and Jesse tried to protest but the words wouldn't come. The hammer snapped forward and Jesse swayed weakly, the dry click of a bad cap barely registering.

Gunfire lanced the darkness and Jim cried out, falling back against the wagon. He jerked there for a moment while his gray tunic blossomed crimson flowers, then tumbled sideways and sprawled inelegantly on the ground.

Shep's barking became frantic and he advanced toward the darkness, toward the flitting shadows, until a single shot reached out and Shep yipped shrilly and snapped at his flank.

Walt shouted incoherently from the rear of the wagon but Jesse ignored him. He took two quick steps, catching Maybelline around the waist and throwing her to the ground. He fell beside her and crawled over until he covered her body with his own. Gunfire raked the air above them, splintering the wagon's sideboards, shattering the windows in the house. A shotgun bellowed from the back porch, accompanied by perhaps half a dozen rifles and handguns—the Confederate troops Maybelline had mentioned, Jesse guessed. A controlled volley swept upwards from the woods, like a scythe passing overhead, and shook the house. There was a wild, hoarse cry from within, and desperate cursing. A hollow boom echoed from down the lane, followed by a long, piercing whistle, and then the night exploded in a flash of yellow flame and broken lumber.

It was over in less than a minute. Sam was braying loudly, walleyed with fear, his bloody ribs peppered with slivers of wood torn from the house. He had bucked and kicked and pulled the wagon half around, but the load was too heavy for him to bolt with the brake set. Now he stood with one rear leg thrown over the trace, trembling; his huge ears were laid flat along the roach of his mane. Beneath Jesse, Maybelline was also trembling, but she wasn't crying or hysterical, and he was strangely proud of that. She was a Ross, by God, and as tough as the rest of them, down deep.

Footsteps thudded dully behind them and Jesse looked over his shoulder, seeing half a dozen or so Union soldiers fanned out behind a small, ferret-faced corporal with darting eyes. The corporal offered a bucktoothed grin and motioned upward with a pistol as big as the one Jim had carried. "Okay, farmboy," he said. "Jump up and let's see what you've got covered there."

CHAPTER 2

Zeb, looking sullen and defiant, was already at the barn, under a private's guard. Locked in wooden stanchions, the cows—a pair of Guernseys called Sarah and Betsy—swung their tails in lazy circles; the tin bucket beneath Sarah's udder was partially filled with thick, yellowish milk, steaming slightly in the cool air. Relief flashed briefly in Zeb's eyes when he saw Maybelline and Jesse, but he didn't speak or make a gesture.

Jesse saw a lump on his brother's forehead, edged in blue, and he smiled. At fourteen, Zeb was the youngest of the Ross boys, but he was big for his age and wild as a bobcat.

"Over there," the corporal ordered, prodding Jesse toward Zeb with his pistol barrel. Maybelline started to follow, but the corporal grabbed her by the arm and said, "Not you, sweetcakes. You stay close to me."

Zeb tensed, and Jesse put his hand out, lightly touching his brother's arm. The corporal noticed, and grinned.

"She's our sister," Zeb whispered. "Touch her and—"

Still grinning, the corporal slipped his arm around Maybelline's waist. To the soldier who had been guarding Zeb, he said, "Have you checked the loft yet?"

"Anse is up there now," the soldier replied.

"Let her go," Zeb said tersely. His shoulders were hunched, rigid with anger, and Jesse let his fingers slide around Zeb's forearm and squeeze.

"He's a troublemaker," the soldier said, looking at Zeb. "Tried to brain Anse with a milk stool."

Zeb didn't say anything, just glared at the corporal. The corporal's cheek twitched once, and his lips thinned. He walked slowly forward, putting the muzzle of his revolver tight against Zeb's throat.

"Once upon a time I viewed this war as a noble effort to preserve the Union," the corporal said shakily, "but now I can see it for what it is. Just a silly little uprising staged by ignorant, inbred savages." He leaned forward, the revolver's muzzle sinking into the soft flesh of Zeb's neck, but Zeb didn't move, didn't flinch or blink or show fear in any way that Jesse could see. "Open your mouth again," the corporal whispered, "and I'll blow your goddamn head off."

"He didn't mean anything," Jesse said. "But there's no call—"

The corporal whirled, lashing out with the barrel of his revolver, and Jesse's vision exploded in a brilliant flash.

Maybelline's voice came dimly to him, the words muffled but clear enough, an anchor to slow the spinning. ". . . only trying to help me."

"Because you're a Southern-trash whore," the corporal replied viciously. "Because you sleep with pigs and sheep and dogs."

Jesse forced his eyes open. He was lying on his back, the cows on his right, the soldiers spread across the barn's entrance. Beyond, he could see the front row of trees and the lower slope of the yard, bathed in a yellow, flickering light that he realized dully was the house in flames. The corporal had backed Maybelline into an empty stall, and now he stood at its entrance, tipped forward, but with his feet braced.

"What about it, sweetcakes?" the corporal taunted. "Would you show the boys your titties for a chaw of tobacco?"

Zeb's fists were clenched, the knuckles as pale as fake pearls, but he hadn't moved. The soldiers were all tensed too, with their rifles trained on Zeb, but their eyes swinging rapidly between Zeb and the corporal. One of them, tall and blond and lean, said, "Aw, come on, Hayes. Leave her alone."

The corporal, Hayes, swung around; his eyes were bright and snapping. "Insubordination, Lowell? Is that what I heard?"

"Naw, it's not that," Lowell replied, licking his lips nervously. "But she's just a kid."

Hayes's throat worked convulsively, and his mouth opened as if he wanted to say more, to maybe scream it, but he finally just turned away, shouting toward the loft, "Anse! Did you find anything up there?"

"No." Anse's voice came muffled through wood and hay.

"Then get your goddamn ass down here, on the double."

Jesse heard the shuffle of shoes through loose hay, the familiar creak of the loft ladder when a man first swung his weight onto it. Slowly, with Zeb's help, he rose. He could feel the trickle of blood down the side of his head, soaking the narrow collar of his shirt. He'd lost his hat in the fall, and his hair was full of straw. He swayed a little, standing, but his head cleared soon enough and he shook Zeb's hand away. Watching him, the corporal laughed.

Footsteps pounded down the slope toward the barn and a button-nosed private in an oversized uniform burst into the barn. "Shit," he gulped, seeing Jesse and Zeb.

"What do you want, Goldwith?" Hayes growled.

"Lieutenant wants you up at the house if

you've secured the barn. He wants you to bring fresh mules and an empty wagon. Got us some Reb prisoners up there."

"We have some down here, too," Hayes said. He looked at Maybelline and grinned. "But I haven't searched them all yet."

Goldwith looked at Maybelline and swallowed visibly. "Shit," he croaked. He looked at Hayes, but the little corporal was leering at Maybelline and didn't see his glance. Goldwith looked at Lowell then, and Lowell mouthed, *Get the lieutenant.* Goldwith looked at Hayes again, then at Maybelline, and nodded. He began to back slowly from the barn.

Hayes's voice stopped him cold. "Where do you think you're going, Goldwith?"

"Uh, back up to the house. I'm supposed to help watch the prisoners."

Hayes advanced on the private as if he were stalking him, his face as hard as chiseled ice. "My ass," Hayes gritted. "You'll stay here until you're dismissed."

Zeb was crying silently, tears of frustration at his helplessness, and in the stall, Maybelline sobbed, terrified. Jesse stood weakly, listening to the throb of pain from the wound above his ear, his vision hazed from the blow and from anger, his fear growing and cold. Every time he looked at Hayes his fists would curl a little and he would think, *Pissant, a skinny little pissant,* but Hayes had the revolver, and with the parallel chevrons on his jacket, he had the men to back him.

To the soldiers, Hayes said, "Take these two seceshes outside and watch them. Just watch them. Don't do anything until I join you."

A couple of the soldiers exchanged worried glances, and Jesse's muscles tightened. Goldwith said, "Lieutenant said for you—"

"Shut up, Goldwith," Hayes said heavily. He let his gaze settle on the men, and they began edging toward the door. Lowell motioned for Jesse and Zeb to follow.

"This is wrong, Lowell," Jesse said desperately. A tremor shook his body, he felt wound tighter than a clock spring; the thumping in his head beat a quick cadence and his fingernails drew little crescents of blood beneath the flesh of his palms. "Goldwith," he cried. "Don't let this happen."

Hayes cocked his revolver, pointing it at Jesse, but he didn't speak.

"Come on, you two," Lowell said abruptly. "I've seen enough killing today."

"No," Zeb choked, shaking his head. "No." He took a slow, dragging step forward, and Hayes swung his revolver toward him.

"You know what he's going to do," Jesse pleaded to the soldiers. "What kind of men are you?"

Lowell looked at Goldwith, then shook his head. Zeb slid another foot forward, and Hayes's lips pulled back over his teeth. "Come on, you secesh trash," he whispered. "One more step, just one more."

Jesse reached out slowly, almost reluctantly, and grabbed Zeb's arm. "Don't, Zeb. That's what he wants, but it won't change anything."

Zeb looked over his shoulder, his face a stranger's, broken, defeated, streaked with tears. "I'd rather die," he said in a strangled voice.

"Ol' Zeb's a man, Jesse," Hayes mocked. "Let him come on. Let him die with good ol' Southern honor."

Jesse's fingers tightened on Zeb's arm. He could feel the tendons, muscle, rolling under them. "Zeb . . . don't," he said softly.

"Get these two jackasses out of here," Hayes snapped, his patience suddenly gone.

"Let's go," Lowell barked. He came forward and tapped Jesse's shoulder with the flat of his bayonet.

They went outside, stepping into the outer rim of light from the burning house. The fire was at its peak now, the flames towering into the black sky, dimming the stars. Gables sagged like old men, windows stared blankly and without glass, and here and there around its base, like tiny offspring, little hot spots of flames were growing in the dry November grass. Jesse couldn't see his ma and pa or the twins, but there were a lot of men standing around watching the fire, and a knot of

Confederate prisoners huddled well within its light. They looked hot, the prisoners did; their faces glistened with sweat and many of them had shed their tunics, but down here the breeze was like ice.

Glancing at Goldwith, Lowell said, "Rest of you boys go behind the house and check for some mules and another wagon. We'll watch these two."

"Ain't no other mules," Anse said. "Already checked."

"Check again," Lowell said coldly, and after a quick, startled glance, the others took off, leaving only the four of them. Taking a deep breath, Lowell said to Goldwith, "Are you with me on this?"

Goldwith looked doubtful at first, but just then Maybelline screamed, a shrill, terrified sound, severed abruptly. Goldwith sighed, nodded. Lowell looked at Jesse and said, "I'm sorry, hoss. Guess there's bad on both sides." Deliberately then, he turned his back on them and walked away. Goldwith followed. Jesse hesitated only a moment, then he and Zeb were sprinting for the barn.

Hayes was already in the stall with Maybelline, his body pressed roughly against hers, his hand clamped across her mouth, when Jesse burst into the stall and grabbed him by the neck. Hayes squawked loudly as Jesse pulled him back, spinning him into Zeb's arms. Zeb pinned Hayes's arms to his sides as Jesse stepped in, swinging with everything he had, swinging as if with one blow he could wipe the slate clean, could bury the entire evening and start fresh again.

Jesse cried out as his knuckles met Hayes's face, grabbing his wrist with his free hand and skipping back, falling against the side of the stall. Hayes and Zeb spun backward, their legs tangling, tripping to the floor. Blood spurted in a cherry fountain from Hayes's shattered nose, and his head rolled limply.

"God Almighty," Zeb howled, rolling free of Hayes's inert form. He came up spitting dust.

"I busted my goddamn hand," Jesse whispered fiercely, his face chalky, sheened with sudden sweat.

"Jesse?" Maybelline said quietly. "Zeb?" She came hesitantly from the shadows in the rear of the stall, her white dress smudged with dirt, her hair disheveled. She put her arms around Jesse's shoulders and buried her face against his chest.

Zeb came into the stall, putting his hand out and letting it hover about an inch or so above Maybelline's shoulder. Looking at Jesse, he muttered, "I want to kill the sonofabitch, Jesse. I want to break him with my hands."

"Do it," Jesse said wearily. He didn't care anymore. His knuckles throbbed and his whole fist felt swollen and hot, like half a dozen wasp stings across his hand. Sweat dripped off the end of his nose.

Maybelline stepped back, her eyes widening. "Jesse, are you all right?"

Suddenly, Jesse laughed. "I thought my head hurt," he said. "But now I can hardly feel it."

"It's his hand," Zeb said, drawing it away from the protective curve of Jesse's body. Maybelline gasped when she saw it, but Jesse didn't look, didn't want to. Zeb said, "Hell, it's not so bad. You just knocked a couple of the knuckles back. I can fix that."

"Then do it," Jesse hissed.

Zeb took the arm between his own and his body, braced Jesse's wrist with one hand and grabbed a finger with the other. "Hang on," he instructed, and gave the finger a sudden, forward jerk. Jesse grunted involuntarily, but the pain immediately diminished by half. A few seconds later Zeb had the other finger popped into place.

"Christ," Jesse said weakly, then smiled. He could feel the pain receding in waves, becoming bearable at first, then only an annoyance.

"We'd better get out of here," Zeb said then. "Down to the cave and hide Maybelline, at least. Then we'll come back for the others."

The cave was a nameless limestone sink with a small entrance almost hidden by blackberry brambles in the hollow behind the barn, with another entrance several miles to the west. There may have been more, but nobody knew of them. Jesse and Zeb had already explored some of the larger side passages, but they hadn't ventured much beyond that. It was a pretty woolly cave, with a lot of deep pits and slippery ledges, and a honeycomb of smaller passages that would make getting lost easy. But it would be a perfect hideout. Snugged down in there, Jesse figured Maybelline would be safe as long as necessary.

Without warning Maybelline screamed—Zeb whirled to see Hayes scurrying across the dirt floor on hands and knees toward his fallen revolver. Jesse cursed himself, then; in his rage he had completely forgotten Hayes's revolver, hadn't even seen it when he'd pulled the little corporal around.

Zeb raced Hayes for the pistol. Jesse grabbed a pitchfork and stepped quickly to the side. Hayes beat Zeb to the revolver, but now he rolled back, screeching shrilly as Zeb's shoe drew away from his already broken nose. He fumbled the revolver, almost dropped it, caught it again and fired blindly, the report deafening in the low-ceilinged barn, loosening a shower of dust and moldy hay from the loft. Zeb kicked again, catching Hayes in the shoulder.

"Zeb," Jesse yelled. "Stand aside."

Zeb looked over his shoulder, saw Jesse with the pitchfork cocked over his shoulder, and jumped back. Jesse heaved the pitchfork toward Hayes, leaning forward and putting everything he had into it. His aim was true. The triple-tined fork pierced Hayes's chest, burying itself all the way to the handle. Hayes groaned and rolled onto his back. He grabbed the pitchfork with one hand, grasping it close to its iron head, but he didn't drop the revolver. His eyes looked wild, crazy with pain and hate, and he thrust the revolver weakly toward Jesse, pulling the hammer back and squeezing the trigger before Zeb could kick it away.

Of all the shots Jesse heard that night, this seemed the loudest. It boomed toward him, an explosion of sound that seemed almost physical. He felt himself falling backward without any real sense of motion, felt the rear gate of the barn against his back, and then, as if jerked upward, the barn rose and his buttocks struck the floor.

For a while then, nothing made a lot of sense. Voices came dimly, as if heard through water, the words meaningless, and his vision fuzzed, fading in and out. He felt numb, but not without pain; like distant drums it pulsed along his veins, radiating outward from his chest. He could see his feet, splayed out vee-shaped and looking a mile away, but he couldn't feel them, or his arms.

Slowly, his senses began to focus. He could hear Maybelline crying and Zeb cursing, and he laughed to himself, thinking that nothing had changed much. He wondered idly if it would go on like this all night, one crying and the other swearing and himself taking all the falls.

He could hear shouting from the front of the barn, the thump of shoes; soldiers sawed back and forth, nebulous forms in Union blue. Zeb was talking fast, his voice high and edgy, but the words zipped past without meaning. Maybelline leaned close, her face a blurred moon against the barn's ceiling, whispering in a booming voice. "Go to the cave, Jesse. Hurry!" She pushed at him and he rolled under the rear gate, rolled a second time on his own, and then a third, until he was finally out of the light.

He rose, staggered and almost fell, then caught his balance and just stood there a moment. His head was spinning and his legs were wobbly as any colt's. But he knew the way and started instinctively toward it, the panicky sound of Maybelline's voice still ringing in his mind, goading him on.

He stepped clear of the barn's shadow, caught then in the soft light of the distant fire, but he didn't stop, didn't even look. He had seen it standing in front of the barn, but now the memory of it seemed too much to bear; he thought that if he stopped and looked again he might go mad. His world had been pulled down to a strange and frightening place, and only the cave seemed real, and his need to get there.

He crossed a small pasture on shaky legs, climbed a split-rail fence and started down the steep slope toward the hollow that hid the cave's entrance. He was weak yet, but gaining strength, and there were trees to hang onto now. He moved carefully from one to another, the crisp, dry leaves creating a racket that might have been heard at the barn if not for the cacophony of rushing, shouting soldiers, the braying of mules and the whinnying of horses. Still, he left a trail that he knew would be easy to follow come daylight, so when he reached the bottom he swung away from the cave's entrance, following a deer trail that skirted the spring in the middle of the hollow. He stayed on that until he reached the rocks at the far end of the hollow, climbed onto a small, squarish stone and stepped from there to a narrow, lichen-covered ledge that ran halfway around the hollow. He followed this almost to its end, then climbed down, staying on the rocks as much as possible until he reached the dense blackberry thicket that hid the cave's entrance.

He rested here a moment, light-headed and weak, half sick to his stomach. He could still see the reflection of the fire; it bathed the tops of the oaks and maples in a soft creamy light, but Jesse thought it might be fading some, too. He couldn't hear the crackle of the flames anymore, but he could still hear the soldiers, and a dog barking that made him flinch, until he realized that it was only Shep and not hounds. He felt an unexpected consolation at that; he remembered Shep's startled yelp when the Yankees had first opened fire on the house, and the way he'd rolled in the dust under the wagon, before slinking off. Jesse had thought he was dying then, and soft laughter bubbled to his lips. Rising then, he forced his way into the brambles.

They might never have found the cave if Eddie hadn't chased a hognosed snake into the thicket several years before. His ma had always picked berries here in July, claiming it seemed cooler than any other patch, but she'd never suspected there was a cave's entrance deep within its thorny embrace.

The entrance was small and Jesse had to stoop to enter, but it widened almost immediately and rose to a height of eight or ten feet. It felt warm inside, a sensation that puzzled him until he remembered that it was November now, and not the fiery days of summer. November, time to bring in the last of the crops, time to butcher a couple of hogs for frydown, and maybe a beef, and for Zeb to take the shotgun out for a Thanksgiving turkey. It was time to get the firewood cut and stacked for the winter, to clean the barn and spread the manure over the fields. Time to get the traps out and readied for the season, and to repair what harness they'd only patched over the summer. Time to get on with their lives, Jesse thought bitterly, and not have to watch everything they owned carted off or burned down.

Jesse put his back to the cavern's wall and slid

down until he was sitting cross-legged in the pitch blackness. In his mind's eye he saw the house engulfed in flames, heard Maybelline's terrorized scream. It had all happened too fast to absorb before, but he was letting it in a little at a time now, bits and pieces of the last few hours that he already knew would change the rest of his life, the rest of all their lives, until the enormity of it all swept over him and he cried out his protest, slamming his arm against the wall until the tears came.

Jesse awakened groggily, his head feeling full and feverish, his throat so dry he couldn't speak, could hardly swallow. There was a fire in a shallow pit at his side, its tiny, pulsating light nudging the cavern's blackness back some, and drawing the edge off its chill. Maybelline sat dull-eyed on the far side of the fire; her knees drawn up to her chin and her arms wrapped around them.

She still wore her white dress, but it was filthy with dirt and soot, pocked with little holes from falling sparks, soaked and nearly transparent over her shoulders. Her face was dirty too, streaked from tears and haggard-looking; her long wavy hair was matted flat against her scalp. She should have been shaking with cold, even sitting next to the fire, but she wasn't.

Jesse tried to rise but couldn't. His right arm moved all right but his left arm wouldn't flex at all, and his chest felt tight, stiff as rawhide. He thought for a moment that it was the wound that made him feel that way, but exploring his shoulders with gentle fingers, he discovered he was bandaged.

Maybelline looked up at his clumsy efforts, but she made no move to help, and after a while just looked away. When she spoke her voice sounded small, broken. "You've got to go," she said. "Pa says to go to Texas Crossing and stay with Gray Fletcher."

"Where's Pa?" Jesse croaked; he had to try twice to get the words out. "Where's Ma and the twins, and Zeb?"

"Ma and the twins are at the Richardses' place. Pa's gone to Jefferson City to see about Zeb."

"Zeb?"

Maybelline looked at him, the dullness finally receding from her face, washed away by tears. "They took him, Jesse. They took him off in chains for killing that nasty little corporal, and Ma's scared sick they'll blame Pa for it, too."

Jesse eased back, breathing deeply, staring at the rough contours of the cavern's ceiling, at the little cones of stalactites that clung there like bats. *Zeb!* They were blaming Zeb for Hayes's death, would hang him for it likely, and Jesse's throat closed suddenly, until he had to roll onto his side to get air. Panting then, his jaw set stubbornly, he braced his right arm under him and rose to one hand

and his knees. He rested there awhile, his head hanging, spots of light dancing before his eyes.

"Going to rescue him?" Maybelline asked, her sarcasm heavy. "Going to march right in and give yourself up so they can hang you for murder and Zeb for treason, and maybe Pa, too?" She half lunged toward him, pummeling her clenched fists into his right shoulder, his good shoulder. "You stupid, stupid oaf," she cried. "You stupid fool! Do you honestly think turning yourself in would change anything? Are you that thickheaded?" She broke off abruptly and sat back, resting on her knees with her fists, still clenched, in her lap, her head hanging. "They killed Sam," she said out of the blue, her voice small. "Killed him and ate him, and they butchered Sarah and Betsy to take along." She looked up, her cheeks glistening with fresh tears. "Oh, Jesse, they killed Shep, too. They found him this morning, crippled, and just bayoneted him." She sobbed, her shoulders shaking. "He cried, Jesse. When they stabbed him, he cried, and it sounded so pitiful, so terribly, terribly pitiful."

Jesse's arm bent, then buckled, and he stretched out full length. He felt numb again, drained of emotion and strength and will, a shell content to just lie for a while, but Maybelline wouldn't let it rest.

"They can't hang Zeb for killing the corporal," she said with unexpected conviction. "Maybe for treason, for helping Confederate troops, but not for murder. Pa's sure of that. That's why he went up to Jefferson City, why he wants you to go to Texas Crossing. Pa says they're going to make you an outlaw, Jesse, but there's nothing you can do about it. Not now, with the war on." She took a deep breath, then went on. "Pa says you're not to come home. Says when it's safe he'll get word to Mr. Fletcher. He says"—her voice broke, strengthened—"he says he loves you, Jesse. We all do." Leaning forward, she kissed his cheek, then rose and turned away from the fire.

He watched for a while, until her dress looked white and pretty again, away from the light. "Take care of yourself, Jesse," she called, her voice echoing slightly. Then she turned and was gone.

When the fire died to coals, Jesse rose, walking stiffly toward the cave's mouth. He stumbled once, on the incline, then forced his way through the brambles. Rain fell in a steady patter from low, gray clouds, and thunder, true thunder, rumbled in the distance. The hollow was empty, bleak and dripping, and cold, too; Jesse's breath, even at midmorning, puffed in thin clouds before his face. Hatless, his hair was soon wet, plastered to his scalp as Maybelline's had been, and he felt chilled. He was tired, weakened from the simple effort of leaving the cave, but he wasn't as light-headed as he had been earlier, and he thought it might be dangerous to rest too long. While he hadn't forgotten that there might be Union troops about yet, right now he was more concerned by the weather. Wounded, he didn't want to be out in a chilling rain any longer than he had to, so, turning the collar of his jacket up around his neck, he started slowly down the slippery deer trail.

CHAPTER 3

Looking back across the broad expanse of the river, Gray Fletcher studied the lone horseman he had just ferried over the Osage, trying to gauge the deputy's weariness against the remaining sunlight filtering through the dismal overcast. The deputy was tacking a dodger to the corner fence post of Kerwin's hog pen, and like as not he'd tack a few more up in town, if the dozen or so crude shacks and businesses nestled atop the low rise above his ferry could be called a town. Most local folks called the little burg Texas Crossing, in honor of the ferry, but that wasn't anything Gray took particular pride in. The population of Texas Crossing fluctuated with the seasons and never amounted to more than forty or so, mostly drifters and sharks of one kind or another, settling down for a few months, then moving on. Except for Gray and his daughter, Irene, there were no long-term residents; the people of Texas Crossing were like sunburned skin, always peeling off for someone new.

Not much to attract a man, Gray knew, except for the warmth of a fire or a meal and a drink or two. It was funny to think of Jesse's whole future hinging upon the whims of a stranger, his hunger or how cold he was. Well, nothing to be done about it now, Gray reasoned. He'd mosey on over in an hour or so and see what happened. Time enough then to decide the lay of Jesse's future.

Gray started up the gentle slope toward the low, square log cabin he'd built himself only eleven years ago. He was a big man, powerfully built, with arms that had to arch away from his body a little in order to swing freely. He had been a blacksmith most of his life, had developed his muscles that way, but working the ferry had honed them; dragging that stubborn craft across the bucking Osage current sometimes as often as half a dozen times a day had hardened Gray in ways that 'smithing never had.

He had a square, mouse-colored beard that he took pride in, thinning gray hair, and small, faded blue eyes—sad eyes, Irene always claimed, but she never asked why.

Jesse was studying the dodger tacked to the barn when Gray strode up, standing hunch-shouldered in his old, threadbare jacket, the flaps of the muskrat cap Irene had given him pulled tight over his ears. He looked thin yet, Gray thought, pale and drawn, with a guarded, delicate cast to his face that was easy enough to read. Defeat, in its simplest term, but defeat was never simple and its humiliation could brand like an iron. The night of the Federal's raid still ate at Jesse; Gray recognized its symptoms, remembered its pain.

March now, and Jesse had been with them since November, appearing out of a driving sleet storm in the middle of the night, half-frozen and nearly incoherent, racked with shakes, soaked clear through. The bullet wound in his left shoulder was bad enough, but in the end it proved only the nucleus. Fever set in by morning, sapping his strength further, and the shakes continued sporadically. A cough developed, but thankfully never settled solidly enough in his lungs to become pneumonia. Luck stayed at his side, and Irene. Still, it was only within the last few weeks that he had begun to get up and around a little. He'd been a long time recovering.

Jesse was Matt's boy and no stranger, although it had been a good many years since he'd seen any of Matt's children. He guessed Jesse must have been about fourteen or fifteen the last time he'd ridden up to Matt's place, tall even then, and gangling in looks if not action. He'd been with a green colt in a back corral, a two-year-old learning the saddle, Gray remembered, and he and Matt had stood for a while at the rear gate of the barn and watched silently. Gray had been impressed with the kid's skill and confidence, and had said as much as they left.

Matt had been naturally pleased with the compliment, but then his face had turned strangely pensive, and he'd said, "Jesse's different, Gray. He's special in a way I can't find the words for, but it's something I can feel in my heart. That's not a father's pride speaking either, because I couldn't say the same for the others, no matter that I love them all equally."

The intensity of Matt's words had surprised him a little, but Gray didn't doubt his conviction. He had known Matt for a long time—they had been like brothers once, when they were both a lot younger—and he knew Matt wasn't given to overstatement, not even with those closest to him.

"Not a very good likeness, is it?" Jesse asked, looking at the dodger. The question pulled Gray back from his ruminations.

"Not very," Gray agreed, eyeing the crude sketch that covered a big part of the dodger, but he thought it was close enough. The five hundred dollar reward for information leading to Jesse's arrest would be enough to prod a man into reporting that there was a stranger bunking at the Fletcher cabin. There wasn't much loyalty in Texas Crossing, but there was greed enough to fill any bucket.

Jesse sighed, looking toward the river, the little shelves of ice that arced away from the tiny, sheltered coves. Thinking of Zeb now, Gray figured. Zeb was in a Union prison somewhere in northern Illinois for his part in the corporal's death. It wasn't fair, but Gray knew inequities had no bounds during war. He thought Zeb was lucky to have escaped execution.

It occurred to Gray then that no matter what happened with the deputy he had just ferried across the river, Jesse would have to leave soon. There was a reward posted for him now, and word would get around one way or another. Jesse needed to leave the state at least, and Gray thought he would be wise to leave the East altogether, to go to Texas maybe, or California. But a trip like that would take money that neither of them had. Jesse would need horses, weapons, supplies. . . .

He thought of the buckskin then, secreted away just before the big Union sweep for horses and mules, and his heart beat a little faster. Could he? Irene would never consent, of course; she had raised the buckskin from a foal, but maybe he wouldn't have to tell her until Jesse was already down the trail. Gray tried not to think of his own dreams for the horse. He was too old, and there was Irene to consider. Rangering was a young man's game.

"You know you can't stay here much longer?" Gray asked abruptly.

Jesse looked startled. "I . . . yes, I realize that." He drew himself up. "If I've been a burden—"

"No," Gray interrupted, his voice gentler now. "Matt Ross's son could never be a burden. But I was thinking of the deputy. He'll find out about you sooner or later, maybe he already has. You need more distance between yourself and your pa's farm, son. I want you to go to California."

"California?" Jesse frowned. "I'm not going to California. I'm going east to find Tom and Eddie."

"East? No, Jesse. Two's enough for any family. No one would think any less of you for not fighting."

Jesse shook his head. "I appreciate your kindness, Gray, but I reckon I'm through running." He looked at the dodger and his lips thinned. "They're saying I'm a criminal, no better than a sneak thief."

Gray sighed, sensing Jesse's determination. A picture flashed into his mind, an image of Jesse on the buckskin, the old Walker revolvers blazing, and he irritably shook it away. California was the ticket he wanted to sell.

"They can say what they want, Jesse, but those who know you will know better. They'll always be beside you."

Jesse looked at him, his eyes cold, emotionless, a stranger's eyes, Gray thought, and felt a chill pass along his spine. "Will you walk with me down the main street of Jefferson City?" Jesse asked softly.

"Aw, Jesse . . ."

"They're saying I'm not good enough, Gray. They're saying I'm trash, scum off the river." He shook his head, his anger building. "I've got no choice, I have to fight now."

The buckskin again, and Jesse with the old Walkers, and Matt's face looming suddenly into view, then drifting back. He's going to fight anyway, Gray argued with himself. Taking a breath then, taking the final cold plunge, he said, "Why go all the way over the Appalachians to fight? There'll be plenty of fighting right here soon enough."

Jesse looked momentarily confused, then the confusion changed to doubt. Gray could read his thoughts. There had been a battle at Wilson's Creek, some minor skirmishes such as Big Meadow, but so far the hottest fighting had been in the East.

"I know a man," Gray continued quietly. "He's putting an outfit of raiders together. Good ol' Missouri boys mostly, protecting their homes. That's who you ought to be fighting with."

"Raiders?"

Gray could see Jesse's doubt growing, knew he didn't understand the effectiveness of small bands of skilled riders, hitting and running—he had never seen the Texas Rangers in operation.

"Sure, raiders, but they'll do more good for Missouri than half of Lee's army. That's what you need to be thinking of, Jesse. Missouri. Let Virginia fight her own battles."

Jesse looked at the river again, but Gray doubted if he saw it. Gray could feel his own excitement growing. Sometimes it felt like he'd been a smithy or a ferryman all his life, hammering and tugging and never looking any farther ahead than a mule's rump. Thinking back, his years with the Texas Rangers seemed like little more than a fleeting moment, the quick burst of a pumpkin blossom in the dawn's misty light that withers at the first touch of the sun's rays.

Jesse turned back, his brows furrowed. "Do you think they'd have me?" he asked quietly.

Matt's face again, his disapproval unmistakable, but Gray shunted it aside. "They'll have you," he said. "When you're ready, they'll have you."

The big revolver seemed unnatural in Jesse's hand, oversized and awkward, its weight dragging at his arm. It was an old Colt Walker weighing nearly five pounds, a saddle pistol Gray had carried in Texas. Its size made it obsolete, but it did the job and some besides, Jesse thought. Across the clearing the pale, barkless stump of a long-dead elm stood splintered and torn after only five rounds into its core.

"Good," Gray said, his voice muffled slightly by the ringing in Jesse's ears. He took the empty revolver and gave Jesse a second, another Walker.

"Powder's too scarce to waste today, but I wanted you to get the feel of these. Try something different this time, something farther away."

There was a dead limb caught in the lower branches of a live elm some thirty yards away, its butt about the size of a big man's forearm. Jesse hefted the Walker and sighted along the barrel. He pulled the hammer back, aimed, then squeezed; the Walker bucked heavily in his hand, threatening to spin out. Jesse couldn't tell where the ball went, but he noticed Gray's quick look of disappointment from the corner of his eye.

"You're flinching again," Gray said gruffly. "Your ball went ten feet high."

Ten feet! Biting the inside of his lower lip, Jesse brought the revolver back up, sighting carefully, determinedly, and fired; the Walker slammed back again, jolting him to his elbow.

"Better," Gray offered critically. "But you're still shooting high, and you pulled to the right on this one."

Jesse had fired revolvers and single-shot pistols before and knew they lacked everything that made him a good rifle shot. But it was the way he kept wanting to flinch that bothered him. The Walker's heavy powder charge was the culprit, he knew— forty-five grains of coarse powder behind its .44 caliber ball—but it was a fault he would have to correct if he was ever going to master revolvers.

Raiders. Volunteers who chose their own leaders

and fought their own unique war. Jesse thought Gray might be right: in the long run it would be raiders who might make the difference for Missouri. Still, he had hesitated. Guerrilla warfare was nothing new. Indeed, Gray had learned it fighting the Comanches in the forties, but it was Kansas's bloody soil that had tempered Jesse's enthusiasm.

Kansas long had been aflame with the old and damnable issue of slavery, with riders in the night who burned barns and crops and homes. Since the Kansas-Nebraska Bill of '54 it had been the abolitionists versus those who supported slavery —and no middle ground for anyone. The war between the states had been going on for nearly a year now, but the war along the borderlands had raged for a lot longer. In the Missouri back-woods, raiders were already legends, but they were legends tainted in Jesse's eyes. He wanted no part of petty, personal quarrels, of hoods and flickering torches; there was a grander scheme to this war than that, a scheme he couldn't even see clearly yet, but he wanted to see it, and maybe to be a part of it.

Grimly then, he pulled down on the dead limb a third time, concentrated, squeezed the trigger, then stepped aside, away from the billowing cloud of powder smoke. He had missed again, but this time the limb was swaying slightly. He looked at Gray for an explanation.

"Close," Gray said, a smile playing at his lips. "Right above it this time." He looked at Jesse in a quick, appraising manner. "Just lift the revolver this time," he said. "Don't aim."

Don't aim? Jesse wondered how he was supposed to hit something offhand that he couldn't hit with careful aim. Then Gray's voice cut swiftly through his doubts, challenging, urgent.

"Do it now. *Now!*"

Jesse lifted and fired from just above his hip, stepping quickly to the side. The dead limb was swinging slowly, twisting a little, giving up its grip with small jerks before finally dropping.

Gray laughed loudly, his blue eyes twinkling. "I knew it. Goddamn, I knew it." He came close, clamping a hand to Jesse's shoulder and squeezing affectionately. Then his voice dropped and the twinkle left his eye. "You're going to shine, Jesse. You're going to make them all sit up and take notice."

Gray's praise sounded good, but Jesse remained uncertain. He hadn't hit the limb, he noticed, but had put the ball into the branch holding it. He was still shooting high.

"Try the stump again," Gray said. "From the hip."

Jesse lifted and fired, and they both stepped to one side. The stump, his first target, was cratered dead center.

"Yeah," Gray said softly. "You'll do."

They walked quietly through the deep, somber woods. Gray was in the lead, moving swiftly yet silently along the spongy trail. From time to time he would pause, cocking his head this way or that, listening, looking, sensing like a wolf. Then he would go on, his broad frame like a hawk's shadow upon the land that disturbed nothing, while Jesse humped it to keep up.

Jesse couldn't figure Gray, never had really, but lately he had been more puzzled by him than ever. Around the cabin or working the ferry Gray seemed like any other backwoodsman, big and strong and leaning toward work-simple, slow-talking and ambitionless. But roaming the forest, he became a different man, different in a way Jesse found enigmatic. It was more than just his obvious comfort in the woods—hell, farmboy over the age of five had that—but something deeper, more subtle. Watching his quick, sure passage through the woods, Jesse was reminded again of the image of a wolf, as much the hunted as he was the hunter, and keener for it.

That much could be attributed to Texas, Jesse knew. Gray had gone early, one of Stephen Austin's colonists, and settled on the Brazos River with a wife and three daughters. He'd opened a black-smith shop and done all right for a while, but Texas was always a turbulent place, and harmony was always short-lived. Some said that Texas in the thirties was like an open keg of gunpowder at a Fourth of July celebration, but then, a lot of people said it still was.

A thrown shoe on a roan mule kept him from dying a hero at the Alamo, but he'd fought aplenty after that, fought all the harder for knowing what he'd escaped, maybe.

A man would have thought that after San Jacinto things would have settled down, but they didn't. Before the decade ended Gray's youngest daughter died from a snake bite, and the rest of his family perished from the yellowjack. He'd come back to Missouri for a spell in the forties, married a grass widow, then departed for Texas again, settling this time about a dozen miles south of Victoria. The Comanches had sacked Victoria once, but no one really expected them to return after Plum Creek. They had, though, skirting the town and raiding the isolated farms surrounding it. They attacked while Gray was in Victoria overnight on business. They killed Gray's son, pinning him to the door of their crude cabin with a lance, and an infant daughter by throwing her against the log walls of Gray's home, and missed Irene only because Gray's wife had dropped her unceremoniously down a half-dug well. His wife was taken captive.

Gray discovered Irene late the next day, dirty-faced but too frightened to cry. He never recovered his wife.

For a while then, Gray left Irene with friends while he rode with the rangers, fighting the Comanches on their own terms, hitting them where it hurt the worst, on their own ground. He'd been a demon for a spell, but a hate that hot soon burned itself out. Then, too, there was Irene to think of, growing like a weed, needing a family, so they'd come back to Missouri, to stay this time. They'd settled on the Osage and Gray had given up 'smithing to build his ferry, calling it Texas Crossing, in honor of the state he loved. The town, such as it was, came later.

Jesse had learned all this from his pa, who was old friends with Gray. Gray seldom mentioned Texas at all, and never spoke of his past there. It sobered a man, though, Jesse thought, knowing what Gray had seen in his life, what he'd been through, and made him kind of proud, too, seeing the way Gray had gone on. It reminded Jesse that tragedy wasn't a recent thing, and that a good man could survive even if he did scar.

But if Texas could account for Gray's skill in the woods, it certainly didn't unravel the rest of the mystery. Most of the time Gray seemed to cultivate an air of ignorance that Jesse knew was false. That he was collecting information was obvious, but was he a spy on payroll, or simply a loyalist?

Once or twice a month strangers would come in the middle of the night, sitting their horses well back from the cabin. Gray would rise as if expecting them and slip into his coat and disappear outside. After a while Jesse got to where he could predict a night visit by Irene's nervousness, her quick, jerky actions and her sharpened tongue. Those nights, Gray seemed like a different man, too. Not the work-simple bumpkin he portrayed so readily, nor even the quick, confident woodsman Jesse knew from past years, but a deeper man, a fountain of hidden, conflicting wisdoms. Sometimes, seeing him in that light, Jesse wondered if even his pa had ever really known Gray.

Jesse followed Gray out of the woods and paused, staring down the long slope to the cabin, and the ferry beyond, snugged to the pier with its butt end swung around in the current. There was a small, yellow froth caught at its side, punctured here and there by the slim black fingers of twigs; the Osage wasn't in flood yet, but it was close, its swollen, muddy waters littered with winter's debris, a startling contrast to the green mist of the forest rolling gently to the west. It was cool yet, and damp, the way Missouri always was in early spring, but there was a warmth on the breeze that couldn't be denied. It was April now, and if winter came again it would be short-lived.

On the far side of the Osage a man in a light-colored duster sat on a stump, smoking, waiting for the ferry while his horse cropped the new grass just sprouting. He was a small man, wearing a big hat, and Jesse could see a rifle jutting from a scabbard on his horse. A stranger . . . Jesse thought again of the deputy Gray had ferried across the river. It had only been a few weeks since he'd passed through, and even Gray admitted it was only a matter of time now.

"Maybe I should stay up here," Jesse said. He was carrying one of the Walkers in his belt, but he suddenly wasn't so sure he could use it against a man, even a Yankee.

"Naw, he doesn't look like a lawman to me," Gray replied. "Besides, he's on the wrong side of the river to give us any trouble we don't want."

Slim logic, Jesse thought, but he scanned the far bank and didn't see anything out of the normal, and the only thing moving in town was one of Kerwin's hogs, rooting in the mud beside the saloon.

They walked down the slope together, but at the cabin Gray handed Jesse the second revolver and said, "Keep this handy, but stay back, too. No use in taking any chances."

Jesse took the revolver, but he didn't belt it. He climbed the three steps to the porch and moved back into its shadow. Gray was walking easily toward the ferry, his arms swinging back and forth in small arches, but Jesse noticed that his fists were clenched. The stranger had risen when he spied Gray, and now he flipped his cigarette into the river and stooped to unhobble his horse.

"You ought to be down there with him," a voice pronounced from behind him. Jesse winced. He hadn't seen Irene at the window. "If there's trouble, you'll likely be the cause of it," she added.

"Your pa told me to come up here," Jesse countered, without looking around. "Unlike some, I don't argue with everything he says."

"Shoo, he just wants you out of the way, is all," she said.

Jesse bit his lip, wondering briefly if she had always been this way, or if it was just something in him that was always setting her off. Sometimes, thinking back to these long, dark days of his recovery, he thought he could remember her as demure and caring, but he could never be sure. His memory of those days was fuzzy, at best.

Irene Fletcher didn't look much like her pa, which Jesse figured was to her advantage. She was slim, willowy, taller than was fashionable perhaps, with reddish-gold hair and blue eyes a shade or two darker than her father's. She never tried to hide her height the way some women did, by stooping or hunching her shoulders forward. Just the opposite, in fact; she stood so straight and ramrod stiff, with her shoulders thrown back just a tad, that a man would have to be blind not to notice the full swell of her breasts. Jesse wasn't blind, but sometimes he wished he was. From time to time he would catch himself just staring. Or she'd catch him, which was always worse—

she would look at him quicklike, with a knowing smile that always made him blush. It bothered him, the blushing. He saw it as a weakness, but it always happened so fast he was never able to prevent it.

"Papa's not afraid," Irene continued after a short pause. "And he doesn't have a big pistol about to pull his pants down."

Jesse flared. "Someone ought to pull your pants down and blister your butt." He blushed then, at the image, and wanted to bite his tongue.

Irene didn't say anything for a moment and Jesse began to wonder if he'd finally edged a last word in, but then she laughed loudly and he cringed. "And I'll bet you want to be the one to do it, too, don't you?"

"Well, hell," Jesse said, and stepped closer to the edge of the porch. It was always like that, he thought. He remembered an incident from his childhood, on one of Gray's rare visits. Irene in the old apple tree behind the barn, gangling and tomboyish, but daring, climbing higher for one huge red apple. And himself, scrambling up a nearby branch, both of them after the same prize. He had scratched and clawed, sweating in his struggles, and won, eventually, reaching out and snatching the apple scant seconds before her. But even now he could still hear the sharp *crack* of the limb, and see Irene's laughing face as the limb cracked again, then broke, tipping him into a headlong fall through slapping branches. He remembered Eddie snickering from the barn: "He beat her to the apple, but she still won the race."

Would she always win? he wondered.

Jesse watched Gray slip the noose free of the anchor post and launch the ferry. It slid awkwardly through the muddy waters, bucking small but choppy waves, dipping roughly as it reached the main channel. Jesse heard Irene's sharp gasp, felt his own throat constrict unexpectedly. The cable was stretched taut now, popping little beads of moisture from its fibers that caught and reflected the light. The river broke against the side of the ferry, tipping it some, and threatening to wash over the deck. Gray's feet were braced against the cleats nailed to the deck, his shoulders bunched to the strain of quartering the clumsy craft across the powerful current.

"The river's too swift," Irene said. "You should never have let him try it."

"He knows what he's doing," Jesse replied, but he could feel a knot of worry tightening.

Slowly, Gray began to gain on the river, and as he slipped free of the main channel the cable slackened somewhat. Jesse leaned back, off the balls of his feet, and breathed easier. The stranger walked down to the end of the pier and, as the ferry edged alongside, stepped aboard. He and Gray grasped hands, pumping wildly.

"Well, I guess we aren't going to need you after all, two-gun," Irene mocked, and closed the window on her soft laughter; but Jesse had heard the relief in her voice, too.

The stranger led his horse onto the ferry without any trouble, which surprised Jesse a little; stepping onto a bobbing craft wasn't the kind of thing many horses would do without coaxing. The cabin's door swung open and Irene stepped outside, coming up so close beside him he could feel her elbow against his own. He thought briefly about shifting his arm or stepping away, but decided against it. He kept his face to the river, though, and wouldn't look at her, not even when she made a quick, small sound of delight.

"You can put that pistol up," she said. "He's a friend."

Jesse wondered if the stranger was a Texan, although he wouldn't ask, wouldn't give her the satisfaction of another rebuke. From time to time Texans did stop on their way through, though, and Gray would always be a different man for a while afterward, cheerful and more content. Gray had been born a Missourian, but Jesse knew his heart was still with Texas. There was a sort of bitter irony in that, he thought, knowing Gray had left Texas largely to shield Irene from frontier violence, only to land smack in the middle of a civil war.

The stranger tied his horse to the downstream rail so the ferry wouldn't dip as badly, and came over to help Gray on the cable. Irene stayed by Jesse's side until the craft left the main channel again, then laughed suddenly and dashed off the porch, running like a small child to the pier. Slower, frowning some, Jesse followed.

Irene waited on the pier, laughing yet and raising up on tiptoe now and again, as if waiting were almost more than she could bear. The stranger was grinning too, and when the ferry had approached to within a few feet of the pier he left Gray to the cable and jumped onto the pier, catching Irene and lifting her, spinning her around until her long hair came loose and spread like a golden fan. Gray, Jesse noted sourly, was grinning hugely.

"How's my number-one girl?" the stranger asked, setting her down finally and stepping back without releasing his grip.

"Dewey," Irene cried happily. "Nobody told me you'd clean up to look like this."

Dewey laughed, hugged her to him, pushed her away. "Still the same old spitfire," he said cheerfully. He looked at Jesse then, the smile slipping but not fading completely. "This the one you were telling me about, Gray?"

"Jesse Ross," Gray said, stepping ashore and dropping the anchor line over its post before the current could tug the ferry back. Hitching at his pants then, he said, "Jesse, this is Dewey Harker, an old friend."

Jesse nodded and shook Harker's hand, noting

the stranger's intense stare boring into him, measuring.

Harker was a short man, slim and wiry, his old, lined face brown as mud, his dark eyes hooded beneath bushy brows. There was a huge, drooping mustache that covered his upper lip, and his hair, peppered with silver, was combed back over his collar. He wore a blue suit under his duster, with a snug-fitting vest over a white linen shirt, and a string tie, of all things. He was wearing a brace of revolvers, too, Jesse noticed, that rode low on his hips, the way only a man intimate with pistols would carry them. His grip was brief but firm. "Good to meet you, Jesse," Harker said. "Any friend of the Cap'n is a friend of mine."

Captain? Jesse glanced uncertainly at Gray, but Gray was still watching Harker, still grinning. Jesse wondered suddenly what Gray had told Harker about him, and why.

"Can you stay, Dewey?" Gray asked. "Sure like to catch up on old times."

Harker hesitated, then shook his head. "Not this time, Cap'n. Wish I could, but I've got business up the road." He looked at Irene, his eyes twinkling. "As I recall, this little lady can turn a fine breakfast egg. I'll be thinking of that, eating my own cooking in the morning."

Both Gray and Irene looked disappointed. "That's too bad," Gray said. "Maybe on the way back?"

"Could be," Harker agreed, then, curiously, turned his gaze on Jesse. "Could be," he said again.

"A cup of coffee?" Irene suggested. "Surely you have time for that?"

"Reckon I could take time for that," Harker concurred.

"Good," Gray said, the smile returned to his face. He clamped a hand to Harker's shoulder, turned to Jesse. "Fetch Dewey's mare along and give her a bite of grain," he said. "Rub her down, too." He and Harker started toward the cabin, but Irene hung back for a moment, her blue eyes blazing.

"There he is, Jesse Ross," she whispered fiercely. "There's the man you think you'll be someday."

She turned abruptly, hurrying after them, slipping in beside Harker, who put his arm around her waist. Jesse's heart was hammering. As far as he knew, Dewey Harker was the first honest-to-God raider he'd ever met.

CHAPTER 4

Away from the river the air seemed warmer, the promise of spring more real today than it had been all year. Less than a mile from the ferry Dewey pulled his mare off the road and slipped out of the cream-colored duster, folding it once and lashing it atop his bedroll. He rode on then, keeping the sorrel at a quick jog along the center hump of the narrow road, only now and again glancing down at the fancy new suit he wore and smiling self-consciously. It was less than a week old, bought with money out of the Colonel's poke and not rightly his, of course, but he still felt a certain foolish pride in wearing it. He was fifty-five, long past an age for vanity, but the suit and a fresh shave and oiled hair had tapped feelings he'd never suspected he had.

Dewey couldn't remember his parents, had never met anyone who did. Sometimes it seemed as if he had never rightly been born, but had just rolled out of the bushes somewhere around the age of five and taken up life from there. Taken that way, he could appreciate the humor in old Dancing George's quip: *"Born with a pitchfork in your hand."*

Dewey had been more or less adopted by a man named Harker and his spindly wife, but that had only been a formality. He couldn't remember ever spending more than a dozen nights at the Harker's small frame house on the edge of Angus McCullough's great plantation south of Louisville, Kentucky. Harker had apprenticed him out as a stable boy almost immediately and after that Dancing George became all the father Dewey ever wanted.

Dancing George was McCullough's head

groom, an old, wizened and white-haired Negro with a perpetual smile, despite the arthritis that crippled his knees in cold or damp weather. George's cheerfulness was always something of a puzzle to Dewey, who had spent enough time among the slaves to be accepted as a friend. Most of the slaves on the McCullough plantation seemed content enough and seldom spoke of the free states so temptingly near. There was laughter and songs and good-natured pranks among them, and all would feign a certain dull-witted sunniness when McCullough came around, but there were tears, too, and tempers that flared, and moods as gray as March. Only George's happiness seemed constant. Dewey had asked him about that once, and George had chuckled and patted his head, saying, "You only gets out of life what you puts in, so a smart man puts in only the best."

George's words hadn't made a lot of sense to Dewey then, and they probably wouldn't to a lot of people now, but Dewey never recalled them without immediately remembering his last night on the McCullough plantation.

It had been close to Christmas, a date remembered only because of the evergreen wreaths that hung upon the broad double doors of the mansion, and McCullough's prize racing mare was about to foal. George had sent one of the youngsters up to the main house with the news before Master Angus retired for the night, then had squatted patiently outside the stable door. This would be the mare's first colt, sired by a Tennessee stud for an outrageous fee, and everyone knew how much Master Angus was counting on the foal.

But something went wrong and the colt breeched. McCullough arrived just as Dancing George was slipping out of his coat and shirt, and his lips tightened around an expensive cigar. George and Dewey eased into the stall. Dewey moved slowly up to the mare's head where he could comfort her with a steady hand and soothing words, or throw himself over her neck if she panicked, while George approached her tail. Dewey couldn't see much of what George was doing, but he'd been around horses long enough to know what had to be done. The colt was lying wrong, and if it was to ever pass through the birth canal alive, George would have to slip his arm into the womb and straighten the colt into the proper position.

Dewey knew now that the entire chore hadn't taken fifteen minutes, but at the time it seemed to drag on forever. He remembered glancing up occasionally throughout the operation to see George's face above the mare's hip as he probed blindly at the colt; George's broad, ebony face had been slick with sweat, despite the cold, and he had worked with his lower lip caught unconsciously between his teeth.

Dewey remembered McCullough, too, standing just outside the stable door, short and fat, with the cigar in his mouth gone dead, and his eyes, like pieces of dark flint, boring into George's back. And then his voice, soft as a whispered breeze, cold as the night: "Fail me, George, and I'll sell you downriver to grub in the swamps."

Dewey had gone bug-eyed, staring at McCullough. He could hardly believe what he had heard, but knew from the way the others were backing away from the fat plantation owner and rolling their eyes fearfully that he wasn't mistaken. George neither answered nor acknowledged McCullough's words, but continued to sweat over the mare until he finally pulled his arm free and rocked back on his heels. "Good 'nough, I 'spect," he said, and rose slowly, his old, swollen knees popping loudly in the quiet stable. "Come on, Dewey. Reckon she can do the rest her ownself."

They'd exited silently and a short time later the mare delivered a little stud colt. McCullough had been all smiles then, his cheeks dimpled and his squinty eyes almost lost. He'd run his fingers roughly through George's white hair, saying, "You aren't fooling me, you old nigger. That hair's as black as you are." To the others, he added, "Trouble is, 'ol George is so slow the crows just naturally mistake him for a fence post."

McCullough had laughed hugely at that, and

the others had too, though softer and without appreciation. Even George had chuckled some, a familiar sound, but Dewey saw something in the old groom's face then that had changed his life, a rage as powerful as any he had ever seen, there and gone in the blink of an eye. Dewey had turned away in shame, of himself and others of his color.

By dawn Dewey was on the Ohio, rowing toward its northern shore, but Indiana was only a temporary stop. By spring he was jockeying for a horse breeder outside of New Orleans and doing all right for himself. In those years he had nurtured for a long time the idea of someday riding back to the McCullough plantation and buying Dancing George his freedom, but somehow he had never found the time or the money. He knew that there was more to it than that, but even today he never dwelled too long on those other, deeper excuses. He thought some doors were better left shut.

Age, not skill, had eased Dewey out of jockeying, but by then he had built a solid reputation as a trainer and he knew he could have found work just about anywhere in the South. Instead, he'd gone to Texas like just about everyone else seemed to be doing, riding a sorrel stallion and leading three fine brood mares. There was a market for good horses in Texas and Dewey intended to tap into it, but goddamn the Comanches. He'd lost everything the first full moon of spring, and like so many others who lost to the Indians, he'd joined the rangers, thinking, erroneously, that he might recover his horses that way.

Rangering was his first job outside of breeding and racing thoroughbreds, and to his surprise he discovered that he liked it. Always something of a drifter, he enjoyed the long, hard forays into the Comanche's heartland, the sweet thrill of victories and the camaraderie of the rangers. The life suited him and he stayed with it for about six years, a Fletcher man for most of that time. But when the Cap'n quit, he'd quit too, not really sure why but sensing that with Gray gone things wouldn't be the same.

Josiah Slaughter had taken over the reins, and Dewey heard through the grapevine that he was an effective if colorless leader. Dewey could remember the day Slaughter had ridden into their camp on the San Sabo, a tall, rawboned kid with a shock of dark, curly hair and angry eyes that Dewey had always suspected might hide a weakness only Slaughter knew the depth of. Still, Slaughter was a fair hand with horses and pistols, ruthless in a fight, though sometimes brash, inclined to tackle a problem head-on rather than approach it from a flank. To Dewey's way of thinking that made Slaughter a good ranger but a questionable commander.

Dewey had gone back to Louisiana after quitting

the Rangers and taken a job with his old boss north of New Orleans, but after Texas he found plantation life as boring as fishing. Then last fall word had drifted down through a network of old rangers that Slaughter was in Missouri, recruiting men to fight for the South, and despite Dewey's doubts he had ridden north to join.

Slaughter had changed considerably from the quick-tempered, fiery kid Dewey remembered. He had become a quiet, brooding commander, a man given to long silences and harsh discipline, intolerant and demanding.

There were less than a dozen men bivouacked in the broad, slightly sloping meadow lost in the hill country southeast of Springfield when Dewey arrived; old rangers mostly, come up to apply their skills against a new enemy. But that had changed quickly once word of Slaughter's new unit spread across southern Missouri. Where once nearly the entire company had been composed of ex-Texans, now only a small part of the Colonel's eighty-plus men had ever ridden Lone Star soil. The rest were largely Missourians, hill people for the most part, fighters to the core and as tough as they came, but stubbornly independent, too—sullen and resentful of any command and next to impossible to discipline. They came in old, ragged, and patched clothes and occasionally barefoot, toting squirrel rifles and shotguns and riding thin, wormy mules or horses, those that didn't walk. All but a few were illiterate, scratching a crude "X" behind their names that the Colonel had listed in a leather-bound journal. Dewey had been half surprised at the Colonel taking them in, but Slaughter had adamantly shaken his head. "They can learn," he said, although Dewey had his doubts.

The Colonel had hopes of recruiting one hundred and fifty men eventually, but Dewey had doubts about that, too. Still, he hadn't objected to swinging wide on his trip to Jefferson City to check out the new man the Cap'n was training. It had been a spell, and he was hoping he'd have time to visit a day or so on the way back.

To Dewey, Jesse Ross didn't seem much different from any of the others who had recently wandered into Slaughter's camp. Just another uncurried farmboy thinking that all he had to do was scratch a line in the dirt with his toe and dare a Yankee to cross, before sending him home like a whipped pup. They had no concept of *war,* of the overall picture. They couldn't grasp the idea of two entities fighting for principles or moral con-viction. For most of them it was a lark, an opportunity to escape the plow or the ax; for others it was a personal matter, revenge maybe, or a debt they felt they needed to pay. They didn't know, as Dewey did, that this wasn't a matter to be settled in a battle or two. They hadn't accepted yet that some of them, or perhaps many of them, would die before the fighting was finished.

Could be they soon would have to confront that fact, Dewey knew, depending on what he found out at Jefferson City.

Dewey had never been to Jefferson City before, and its size amused him some. He had expected something bigger and gaudier of the state's capital, a hint at least of decadence. What he found instead was an air of quiet industry, a subdued energy that flowed along the city's broad, tree-lined streets, a sense of waiting.

Jefferson City was a community in quandary. It was the capital, if not the largest city, of a slave state, and its loyalties, like much of its commerce, were tied to the South. But state government had voted against secession despite majority feelings, and the Confederate defeat at Pea Ridge only a few weeks earlier seemed to assure the Union's hold over Missouri. The result was uncertainty and nagging fear. Life went on, but slowly now, and a day's work might be interrupted half a dozen times by rumors and false alarms.

A little decadence might have helped, Dewey thought wryly.

He was searching for a merchant named Copeland, first name unknown. Dewey had been in Jefferson City several days already, making the rounds of every business in town without success. In the meantime he had registered at the

Capitol Hotel on Broadway under the name of Jack Roswell, an alias Slaughter had suggested. His guise was as a horse trader up from Texas to scout the market, a role he fell into with ease. He had already talked with a number of prospective buyers, discovering that, with the war on, there was a flourishing market for horseflesh.

He was standing in the shade of the Capitol's wide veranda with one shoulder propped lazily against a whitewashed pillar, legs crossed at the ankle, when a surrey approached from down-street, the bay horse in its traces tapping a quick, sharp cadence against the cobblestones. Dewey recognized the man handling the lines but hid his aversion behind a neutral mask. Oscar Jellico was a speculator, a heavyset man with a florid face and huge muttonchop whiskers that failed to hide the excess flesh that hung like bunting beneath his chin. Jellico had been one of the first to approach Dewey about Texas horses, but he had become quickly bored with Dewey's opinions of blood-lines and confirmation. Jellico was interested in quantity and would buy sight unseen, he claimed, adding with a twisted smile that he would probably sell them the same way.

Now, spotting Dewey on the veranda, Jellico swung close and stayed the bay with a heavy hand. "How do, how do," he called loudly, bowing slightly at the waist. "A fine day, sir, is it not?"

Dewey nodded politely and ignored the twinge of uneasiness he felt at Jellico's broad smile.

"Tell me, Mr. . . . Roswell, was it? Do you still have those Texas horses for sale?"

Dewey's uneasiness swelled, but he didn't stray from his cover. "For the right bid."

Irritation flickered across Jellico's face and disappeared. "Well, has anyone topped my offer of six dollars a head yet?"

"Now, Oscar, you know I can't reveal my top bid until they're all in," Dewey chided.

Jellico laughed. "You may be a fine stockman, Mr. Roswell, but you'll never be a businessman with those principles. Look me up when all bids are in. I might just top a close offer." Jellico lifted a buggy whip, then paused as if a thought had just occurred to him. "By the way, Mr. . . . Roswell? I mentioned you to Major Jamison, the local Quartermaster, and he also seemed interested in your horses. He was surprised that you hadn't already paid him a visit. Frankly, so was I. I would have thought the army would have been your first consideration."

Dewey's throat constricted, but he forced a friendly grin. "I reckon you're right about my not being much of a businessman, but I was preparing to call on Major Jamison within a couple of days."

"Is that right, Mr. Harker? Mr. Dewey Harker?"

A nerve jumped in Dewey's cheek, but that was

all. "I'm afraid you're poking under the wrong rock, Oscar. Dewey Harker is a well-known trainer from Louisiana, but I've never heard of him in Missouri."

"Hmmm, maybe," Jellico said. "But if you should change your mind in a hurry, I'm staying at the Riverfront Hotel, on the upper end of Main. Room twenty-four." He popped the whip then, without waiting for Dewey's reply, and the surrey clattered up the street and around a corner.

Dewey held his smile until Jellico disappeared, then let it slide off. He had been found out, his cover pulled back like the heavy curtains of a theater to reveal everything on stage.

Jellico's motives were easy enough to understand. He wanted the horses he thought Dewey was holding somewhere within the borderlands, and discovering, perhaps even by chance, that Dewey was using an alias, he'd gone to Jamison to pressure Dewey into a quick sale at what he was sure would be a reduced price. It was a smart, ruthless gamble on Jellico's part, and despite his dislike for the pudgy speculator, Dewey felt a grudging admiration for his pluck. If Jellico hadn't underestimated the depth of Dewey's charade it might have worked.

But no matter what Jellico thought, his deed had put Dewey in a precarious position. Major Jamison would have to investigate and Dewey knew his fabrication would quickly unravel. He needed to get out of town immediately, to ride hard and fast back south and lose himself in the Ozarks.

So where the hell was Copeland?

To leave now would mean defeat, and Dewey wasn't ready to accept that yet. But he couldn't stay here any longer either, so turning, he walked quickly into the hotel, loosening his tie as he did.

There wasn't much traffic along the St. Louis road—the steamboat trade handled most of that— but it gave Dewey a direction, as exercising the sorrel gave him purpose. It was late afternoon, the sun low in the west and throwing slanting shafts of light through the forest, like transparent columns of an ancient city falling into ruin. It was warm enough to ride in shirt sleeves but not hot yet, and the road was dry, firm and unrutted; only gnats and an occasional greenhead kept the ride from perfection.

The road paralleled the Missouri River, though keeping back from it some, above the flood plain. Still, it was close enough for Dewey to catch sight of its muddy waters from time to time, and the spray of green on the hills beyond. Dewey's mood had been low when he left town, but it had risen soon enough. He could never stay despondent for very long when he was riding, and the sorrel was horse enough to lift any man's spirits. She was a four-year-old, young and cocky sometimes, but smart, too, able to sense Dewey's moods through the reins, to know when he might allow a bit of feistiness, or when he would bear no foolishness at all.

A rattling grew on the road ahead of them and the sorrel lifted her head to snort her disapproval. Dewey halted at the side of the road and rubbed her neck, grinning suddenly as he recognized the din of a peddler's wagon. It hove into view soon enough, an old dearborn, gray with age and warped in places, but solid looking for all of that, the iron tight to the wheel rims and the patched harness shining under a coat of oil. Tin pans and wash basins, cups that hung in clusters like peppers strung on twine, and copper and brass kettles created a loud, jangling discord that was the peddler's trademark. It was his advertisement, that which brought the farmwives to their doors and the children in from the fields and barns. It some-times brought the men, too, if they were the jealous type, for peddlers enjoyed two kinds of reputations and only one of them was for cheap wares at high prices.

The peddler was handling a single team, a tall mule with a broken-down ear and a sorrel horse several shades lighter than Dewey's mare. The peddler pulled up as he drew alongside Dewey, a tall man, incredibly skinny, with slack jaws furred with stubble and ears that were too big flanking a melancholy face. He wore a gray suit with sleeves that rode above his bony wrists, and there was a dented stovepipe hat on the seat beside him, slick with wear on its narrow, curled brim. Dewey had been struggling with his memory ever since his first clear look at the peddler, but it was the stovepipe that completed the picture. Dewey's lips twitched.

"Go ahead and say it," the peddler said in a woebegone voice that matched his face. "But I've been wearing a stovepipe hat for twenty years before anybody ever heard of Lincoln, and I'll be damned if I'll change now."

Dewey allowed a smile. "I'd consider it," he said. "Folks around here don't much cotton to the railsplitter."

The peddler sighed and lifted the hat, turning it to exhibit a pair of small holes near the crown. Poking a finger into one, he said, "You're right, of course. A mere lad did this with a forty caliber squirrel rifle. He said he thought I was 'that damn Republican,' and when I asked him what he thought the president of the United States might be doing driving a peddler's wagon through Missouri, he could only shrug his young shoulders and allow that he supposed even a president had to make a living somehow."

Dewey laughed, knowing the story was probably true. People thought differently in the back country, and many, he knew, resented

Missouri's involvement in a war begun by others.

"Could you tell me, friend, how far it might be to Jefferson City?"

"Five, six miles back," Dewey replied. "No more than that."

"Ah, an honest bed for weary bones. I shall look forward to it. Well, a good day to you, friend. May your road be smooth."

Dewey nodded, tipped his hat. The peddler clucked to his team and started on his way. As the wagon rolled past, Dewey looked, blinked, looked again, closer this time. The paint was faded now, nearly illegible, but it had been a bright blue once, full of hope and promise. It arched across the entire side of the wagon in eight-inch letters, like a pair of bleached rainbows, reading: ZACHARIAH COPELAND, and below that: FINE WARES.

Dewey watched for a moment more as the wagon lumbered up a small grade, then grinned and reined the sorrel after it.

CHAPTER 5

It was a little past dusk now, the pale light fading rapidly toward full dark, with bats flitting crazily overhead. The broad, sloping meadow was freckled with firelight, palled by woodsmoke. The day gone, and Freddy too.

Gilbert Banks lugged his saddle from the grove of trees at the top of the meadow where his bay horse was tethered for the night. He dropped the saddle beside the small fire Roscoe Hammer was nursing and flopped beside it. Gil was short, broad through the shoulders, bullnecked and powerful—blunt, like his pa had been before the fanatics hung him from the lowest bow of an S-shaped cottonwood limb outside of Baxter Springs, Kansas. It seemed strange to Gil that he felt more sadness for Freddy, whom he had only known for a few months, than for his pa, who had raised him single-handedly from a pup, but that was the way it was. Of his pa's death, Gil remembered only a cold rage, a need for revenge that had blotted out everything, even sorrow.

That hadn't been so long ago in time, but it seemed like it. It seemed like a lifetime ago, and Gil supposed that in some ways it was. The killer who had ranged across eastern Kansas last year was gone; Gil was a different man now. But what scared him the most was the stranger he'd become since then. If the killer was gone, so was the old happy-go-lucky Gil, the jester of the freighters' camps. He didn't recognize this new Gil, didn't even know where he'd come from, knew only that he was here, in this body, in this meadow, signed on with Missouri Rangers to fight the Yankees.

Roscoe squatted across the fire from him, sprinkling coffee from a limp cotton sack into the palm of his hand, dropping that into a battered tin pot. Roscoe's face looked blank, and Gil figured he was thinking about Freddy, too. Nudging the pot into the flames, Roscoe wagged his head. "I didn't think it was going to be like this," he said softly, the tone of his voice saying as much as the words.

Earl said, "I liked to piss my pants, seeing them goddamn sabers come a whirlin' after me. Damn!"

"Man, did you hear 'em *whistle?*" Pete asked.

Pete was a kid, fifteen maybe, towheaded and freckled, but he didn't act like a kid. Pete's old man had died young, leaving Pete the head of a family of three girls and a ma who seemed lost after her husband's death, incapable of anything except the simplest chores. It was a responsibility Pete had taken readily, but when his ma had gradually recovered and begun to show some interest in a balding clerk in a nearby store, Pete had cut his pin.

Chance threw him in with Roscoe Hammer. Roscoe was on his way north to join the Yankees, but in Cape Girardeau he got into a row with a couple of Union privates and had his little finger busted. Six weeks later Roscoe joined Slaughter's command. Roscoe was the oldest of the bunch, pushing thirty at least, but Gil thought Roscoe was backward in some ways, too—not dumb but not a man to take charge, either. Roscoe was tall and skinny and generally gloomy, no matter how bright the day, and a death just seemed to put him in his element.

Earl was the stranger of the group. Quiet, withdrawn, only now and again breaking loose with a little information about himself, his past. Earl might have been handsome if not for his ears. Like small flapjacks, they hung low on the side of his head, canted away from the skull as if pushed there by cupped hands. His ears were the only thing Earl was touchy about, but they were an uncommonly sore subject with him. He wore his hair long, with a floppy-brimmed gray hat with a chin strap that he kept pulled low over them.

They were partners of a sort: Gil and Roscoe, Earl Dickson and Pete Bottoms. And Freddy Spence, who Jubal Butler sometimes called Freddy Four-eyes because of the wire-rimmed spectacles he wore. But Freddy was two days gone now, and Gil was wondering how things would ever be the same.

As if sharing his thoughts, Pete said, "Poor ol' Freddy. He never knew what hit him."

Roscoe grunted, his face looking gloomier than usual in the firelight. "He knew. Don't think he didn't." Roscoe sounded almost angry, but Gil knew it was an anger without direction or source, other than the overwhelming helplessness they all felt.

"That bastard Chadron," Earl said, but added no more. Jack Chadron had been commanding, but it wasn't his fault. Hell, it wasn't anyone's fault, Gil reasoned.

Slaughter had commissioned Chadron a lieutenant and ordered him to take a detail of ten men into the hills west of their camp and comb them for stray livestock. The Colonel's Company of Missouri Rangers, as he'd taken to calling the ragtag group of backwoodsmen he'd gathered with the promise of Yankees to fight, had nearly exhausted the small herd of cattle and hogs he'd purchased last fall, and rumor was that the colonel's purse was getting thin. Slaughter's orders had been to hunt for strays only, but to Gil's way of thinking that was coming mighty close to theft. He knew a lot of the men riding for Slaughter had been more or less neutral until the Federal's big sweep for horses and mules last summer. But grub had been scarce the last few weeks, too, and Gil discovered that hunger had a way of changing a man's perspectives.

The Yankees caught up with them north of Cassville, probably thinking they were only chasing cattle thieves. There had been twenty-five or thirty Union troopers jogging along sleepily behind a youthful lieutenant, but despite the numbers, Chadron had ordered them to form for a charge. That had surprised Gil some, and it must have surprised the Yankees too, because they scattered quickly under attack, leaving behind half a dozen wounded or thrown men. Maybe

Chadron should have ordered them executed, but he hadn't, and no one brought it up. They confiscated a few horses and all the weapons they could find, gathered the cattle that had scattered and pushed north again, but maybe not hard enough. Federal forces caught up with them once more, just as they were about to leave the Cassville road, and this time it wasn't a small patrol under a green lieutenant they faced, but a seasoned troop with drawn sabers.

For all of that, Chadron hadn't panicked. He'd pulled his men behind the cattle and stampeded the herd into the advancing Federal forces, taking time for one devastating ride along the eastern flank of the Yankee column before disappearing into the rough terrain that bordered the road. Everyone came through unscathed except Freddy, whose horse stumbled once and lunged up just in time to put Freddy into the cutting path of a saber. Gil shuddered, remembering the wet, tearing sound of Freddy's severed arm, and the way his chest had kind of sprung suddenly to one side as muscle and sinew were cut. Freddy had gotten a funny, wide-eyed look on his face for a moment, until it suddenly went slack and he toppled from his horse. Thinking about it, Gil could hear that sound now, could see the bright sheet of blood fanning back over the soldier who'd killed him and the sudden paleness of Freddy's face, a distant thing, though, muted by time; it was while he slept that the sights and sounds returned with a startling intimacy and he would awaken to a soft whimpering that he knew, with shame, came from his own throat.

"Wish Sarge was back," Pete said, out of the blue. "Things would have been different with him here."

Maybe, Gil thought, and maybe not. But like the others, he wished Dewey was back too. Everybody liked Dewey, but more than that, they trusted him and felt safer with him than they did with just about anyone except maybe Slaughter, and there were a few who trusted him even more than the Colonel. Gil doubted if Dewey's presence would have changed anything for Freddy, but he knew the air of guilt, the feeling that *something* should have been done differently, would have been diminished significantly.

From downslope a mounted man approached slowly and silence drifted over the small fire as they all turned to watch. It was Chadron, his shoulders slumped and his face haggard in the thin light. He halted some distance back from where they sat and regarded them thoughtfully. Of them all, Gil thought guilt hung the heaviest on Chadron.

"Light and sit," Gil offered. "Coffee's on."

Chadron shook his head. "Go on down to the Colonel's fire and get yourselves something to eat," he said in a worn voice. "Then ready your horses. We leave in half an hour."

"Huh?" Earl stood, scowling. "We just got in, goddamnit. I ain't riding out no more tonight."

Chadron eyed him wearily, then straightened his shoulders with effort. "Private, we ride out within half an hour. If you aren't with us I'll list you as deserted." That said, Chadron backed his horse away from the fire and rode away.

"That bastard," Earl muttered, but Gil knew he'd be ready. A quarter-breed Indian named Harvey Quint had refused an order once, and slipped away in the middle of the night to avoid Slaughter's punishment of digging fresh latrines. Slaughter had him run down the next day and brought back to be flogged. It had been a sobering thing to witness, but not without results—since then, no one had attempted desertion.

"Well, it's the Colonel behind it," Pete said, as if to placate Earl's temper. "You know the Lieutenant wouldn't be taking us out on his own hook."

Earl just grunted. He had been angry since Freddy's death, and Gil sometimes thought he blamed Chadron for it, although he hadn't come out and said it yet.

Roscoe pulled the coffeepot off the fire with a quick, irritated motion. "Well, hell," he said. "Let's go eat something before the other hogs get to it first." He started downslope and Pete trailed without comment. Earl hesitated, then rose, kicked once at the fire, and followed quietly. But Gil stayed hunkered close to the flame, staring past it, though, and past a score or more of other fires, past the irregular rows of tents and crude brush and canvas shelters and the horses still on picket lines, and blankly into the trees that rose abruptly on the far hill. He was thinking of Quint, who had tried to desert once, and of himself, and his own chances.

For a while it seemed Jesse had peaked with the stump. He was shooting without aiming all the time now, either from straight on or standing broadside to the target, twisting at the waist to quickly cock and fire. And he was hitting regularly, too. Probably half of the stump was gone, chewed to chips by the heavy slugs, and by their knives, prying the old lead out to be recast. But outside of the clearing, away from the protective circle of the forest, his shooting went to hell.

Gray's annoyance grew with each cloud of burnt powder smoke scattered by the breeze, and he would become thin-lipped and silent as Jesse's two hours of daily practice drew to a close. It was more than just the wasted powder, Jesse knew, or the seemingly impregnable wall of his progress. Gray had stuck his neck out pretty far with Harker, and Jesse feared letting him down. So he practiced grimly, doggedly, never questioning where Gray found the powder and caps that kept the old Walkers firing until his arm ached from the pounding recoil and the back of his head throbbed in protest of the thunder of the mammoth revolvers.

In between, he worked around the place, cutting firewood, tilling and planting in the garden, splitting shakes for the corncrib Gray wanted to put up that summer. He worked with a zeal that had been absent only a week earlier, feeling fit and whole again, healed for the first time since the November raid, drawing strength from anticipation.

Jesse only worried at night, lying awake until late, his arm twitching and his trigger finger slowly squeezing, seeing in his mind's eye the explosion of wood, hearing the cracking boom of the report. At night, doubt nagged. Was he good enough? Would he ever be? Gray thought so, or had at one time, but Jesse wondered what he thought now. Even Irene's derision had softened into something akin to pity, a sure and frightening sign of failure.

On the seventh day, before dawn, Gray roused him, tugging the blankets back and ordering him in a gruff tone to get dressed and shag his butt outside. Remembering the deputy and the dodger folded under his pillow, Jesse quickly skinned into his clothes, but outside he found only Gray, calmly studying the dawn's spreading light. Gray held both revolvers in one big hand, with the thumb wrapped around the straps of a small pigskin shooting bag.

"Now?" Jesse asked, puzzled. They usually practiced later in the day, or sometimes in the evening.

"Now," Gray grunted, and descended the steps and took off for the river.

Jesse followed uncertainly. In the past they had always gone deep into the woods, putting a sharp ridge and nearly a mile of forest between them and town. Letting one of the Walkers off now, this early and this close to Texas Crossing, seemed to Jesse a little like marching a band down the town's single street with his name painted in bright letters across a big bass drum.

The Osage slid past swiftly, its surface dark, muddy with run-off, but dropping daily after a crest three days before. There wasn't much debris in its current anymore, but there was quite a bit on the banks, uprooted trees and broken limbs and pieces of trash snatched from farmyards built too close to the river's unpredictable banks. About fifty yards downstream, wedged against the trunk of a sycamore, Jesse spied the padded, ripped seat of a buggy, sodden and twisted and spilling clumps of dirty cotton wadding like flesh torn from the dark hide of a carcass.

"It's time you quit farting around," Gray said suddenly. Slapping one of the Walkers against

Jesse's stomach, he added, "Load up and let's see if I'm wasting my time."

Silently, gritting his teeth, Jesse loaded five cylinders. When he finished, Gray thrust the second revolver at him. "Think you can load two without shooting your foot off?" Gray asked.

Jesse's eyes flashed, but all he said was, "Reckon I can." He set the first revolver aside and quickly loaded the second. Finished, he stared defiantly at Gray, saying nothing.

"Today's your last chance," Gray said harshly. "Start hitting what you aim at or get off my place."

Jesse's vision hazed in red anger but he bit back the retort that came to his lips. He owed Gray, but he had to tell himself that twice to keep his mouth shut.

Spotting his fury, Gray laughed mockingly.

"Bastard," Jesse hissed.

"Then shoot, damn you." Gray pointed at the river, at a dark, bobbing object in its middle, above them yet, but closing. A keg, Jesse saw, riding low in the water, its lid torn off. "Shoot!" Gray said.

Jesse shot, wheeling, earring the big hammer back as he did and snapping from the waist. The solid report of the Walker rolled across the river and echoed back from the buildings of Texas Crossing. A geyser of water lifted just short of the keg, and above the revolver's echo he heard

Gray's curse. He fired again, missed again, and Gray's voice penetrated the ringing in his ears. "Again, damnit! Use both guns! *Shoot!*"

Jesse straightened from the half crouch he had dropped to, snapped a shot with the left-hand revolver that missed, followed with another round with the right-hand revolver that splintered wood and sent the barrel spinning and bobbing, tried another with the left, firing quickly then, but without haste as the keg drew abreast, about thirty yards away, right, left, right, left, while the barrel jerked and spun and finally floated out of range.

Jesse's breath came slowly and the Walkers felt like deadweight in his hands, hanging at his sides. Out of ten shots he'd hit the barrel six times, three with each revolver.

Gray sniffed, stepped close, clamping a hand roughly to Jesse's shoulder. "I knew you could do it," he said. "I knew it all along." He shook his head, added, "Jesus, left-handed, too."

"Yeah," Jesse said softly, but without elation. He was staring at the spot where the keg had disappeared, and a chill shook his body.

Gray disappeared after the midday meal and Jesse thought at first he had taken the skiff across the river to Texas Crossing. But when Jesse walked down to the pier he spotted the small craft overturned on the bank above the ferry.

He asked Irene but she refused an answer,

turning her back to him and kneading dough for bread with an abrupt roughness. He checked the barn but that was empty, and at a loss then, wandered around back to where a pile of splintery shakes waited to be planed and shaped for the corncrib roof. He worked in the sun for a while, then shifted to the barn's shade, whistling a popular tune now and again, with long stretches of comfortable silence between. He was still there late in the day when Gray walked around the corner of the barn and surprised him.

"You're a good man, Jesse," Gray said, stooping and hefting a slim pine shake. "Topnotch in everything you do."

"Missed you this afternoon, Gray. Figured you must have walked off the pier and drowned."

Gray chuckled and tossed the shake aside. "Come on, I've got something to show you."

Curious, Jesse followed. It had been cool that morning, with a small, icy breeze off the river, but the air seemed thick now, humid, as the sky clouded up in the west with April showers.

There was a horse hitched to the rail in front of the cabin, a big, well-muscled buckskin with a broad blaze running down its forehead. A stud, Jesse thought at first, but drawing closer he saw that it was a gelding, but cut late. The buckskin threw its head up as they came close, whickering softly, and Irene, standing by the bit, scolded in a gentle voice.

"What do you think?" Gray asked, halting several feet away.

Jesse threw a quick, wondering glance toward the cabin, then began to slowly circle the gelding. Coming back around, he whistled his admiration, then stepped close to the buckskin's head, extending his hand for the animal's inspection. Jesse had seen a lot of good horses over the years, but he couldn't ever remember seeing anything that impressed him more than this big buckskin. The horse sniffed, blew, and Jesse let his hand slide along the gelding's neck, up until he could scratch the coarse mane hair across the bridle path. The buckskin snorted then, twisting his head sideways, closer, while Jesse's fingers dug deeper.

Gray laughed, a quick expulsion of air that Jesse recognized as relief. "You've made a friend, Jesse. A good one, I'd say."

Irene whirled suddenly, racing up the steps and inside without a word, slamming the door after her.

"She was hoping you wouldn't," Gray explained to Jesse's puzzled glance. "He's got a mean streak you have to watch for, and he won't take to just anybody, but I was hoping he'd take to you."

"Then he's yours?"

"No, son, he's yours," Gray replied, stepping close and rubbing the buckskin's forehead.

Jesse stepped back as if burned, shaking his head. "I appreciate the things you've done for me, Gray, but I couldn't accept this. He's . . . my God, he's the best horse I've ever seen."

Gray nodded soberly. "He may be the best horse I've ever seen too. But he's yours, Jesse. Not for you, but for your pa, and the South, too, if that makes the taking any easier."

Jesse didn't know what to say to that. Gray was putting the buckskin into the same light as the Walkers, not a gift so much as a contribution. He remembered the Johnny Rebs he'd picked up in the woods after the battle at Big Meadow and the certainty he'd felt in deciding to take them home. He nodded then, and said, "Okay, Gray. Thanks."

"He's an eight-year-old," Gray said. "The grandson of my old Rangering horse. He's a good horse if you treat him right, but you'll always have to watch him for biting or striking or kicking, and don't ever cross him, because I think he'd kill you. There aren't many I'd trust him with, but I guess if Jesse Ross can't handle him, no one can."

"We'll get along," Jesse said. He moved around to the side, eyeing the heavy saddle loosely cinched to the buckskin's back.

"It's a Hope saddle," Gray said, coming back to run a hand along the thick, smooth *mochilla.* It had a broad, flat horn, a high cantle and neat tapaderos fitted to bentwood stirrups. Gray touched a pouch sewn onto the *mochilla*, flanking the cantle. "Like saddlebags," he said, and let his hand drift forward to a narrow pocket flanking the horn. "Holsters. Same on each side. This is where you'll carry the Walkers. They're too damn heavy to carry on your belt."

Jesse nodded, fingering the thick leather, the pockets, running his hand down to the broad cotton cinch. It was a good rig, solid and well made, beat up some, sure, but still sound.

"I rode this in Texas," Gray said softly, almost reverently. He touched a scar in the rawhide covering the fork, patched with strong linen thread. "Comanche," he said. "An arrow." In the *mochilla* he fingered half a dozen tiny holes. "This was Comanche, too, an old flintlock trade gun loaded with shot. There's another scar on the off-side, put there by a Comanche lance that near took my leg off. We had us some wild sprees down there, Jesse, though I'm thinking you'll have your share before this is ended."

Gray stopped speaking and stepped back as if suddenly embarrassed. "Well, I guess you'd rather be giving this horse a ride than standing here listening to an old man. Hop on up, son, and put your face into the wind for a spell."

That evening Gray fetched a burlap sack from the corner and set it on the floor next to the kitchen table. From it he pulled a tin plate and cup, fork and spoon, a small tin boiler, a quart-size coffee-pot, four one-pound cans of good Miami gun powder, two tins of caps, twelve pounds of lead in slim one-pound bars, a mold and ladle, a sack of rice, another of beans, and a third of coffee. There was a corked bottle of salt, too, and needles and thread and an awl for repairing leather, a brush for the buckskin, two pairs of good wool socks, a single pair of gloves, and a small, leather-backed mirror about the size of a half dollar. There was a razor, too, but no soap or mug for lather.

"Some would say there's not much there," Gray said, setting the empty bag aside. "But there'll be more here than you need when you get used to traveling light."

Jesse picked up the razor and poked at the socks with it. "Same as the horse and pistols, I reckon?"

Gray nodded. "Plus the blankets you're using, and I'll give you my coat, too, the caped one. You'll need it more than I will."

"I'll have to pay you back some day, Gray. I couldn't accept this otherwise."

"Worry about it then. After the war."

The war. Jesse fingered the razor, pulling the blade out, then gently folding it again. On long deer hunts and such he'd never bothered shaving, but now, holding the ivory-handled razor, the enormity of what he was about to do began to sink in. He was going off to fight strangers, among strangers. He was going off to war.

Gray picked up the spoon and tapped the fork

with its handle. "No knife. Use your jackknife for now, but first chance you get, pick up a butcher knife. Or better, a good Bowie. Only a belt ax comes in handier around camp than a good Bowie. There's lye soap here you can use for shaving. Not much lather, but better than dry-scraping."

Jesse nodded dully. "You figure Harker will be back soon, then?"

"Just a hunch, but yes. Seven days gone now. That's plenty of time."

Irene's door swung open and she came into the main room wearing an old woolen robe Jesse had only seen her in once or twice through the winter. One cheek was reddened, tracked by the pillow, but she didn't look like she'd been sleeping.

Gray rose. "Think I'll go check Buck," he said.

"I'll do it," Jesse said, pushing his chair back. "It's time he started getting used to me."

Gray's hand clamped onto his shoulder, forcing him back. "Time enough for that later," he said. "I'll see to him tonight."

Gray went outside and Irene clucked her tongue. "Sometimes he's easier to read than a newspaper," she said.

"Who is?"

Irene shook her head and went to the stove. "There's coffee left. Want another cup?"

Jesse was tempted to refuse. It seemed like every time they were together they ended up in an argument, but she so seldom offered anything he decided to accept. "Sure," he said, and tentatively nudged his cup toward her, masking his surprise when she took it without comment, without laughing and telling him to get it himself.

She filled two cups, put his on the table before him and took her own to the spiceboard, turning and leaning against it. She held her coffee in both hands, close to her face, and from time to time would tip it slightly to drink, but even drinking, she never took her gaze off him.

They looked big, her eyes, and in the dim light of the room's single lamp they looked innocent, too. Her hair, combed out, gleamed richly and her robe, belted tightly at the waist, emphasized the flare of her hips and breasts in a way that made him suddenly choke on his coffee.

"What's the matter?" she asked, laughter in her voice, and her eyes, too. "See something too big to swallow?"

"Hardly," Jesse said darkly, then something inside snapped and he added, "I doubt if you've got anything I'd ever want to see."

Irene stiffened, the cup coming down and her cheeks blossoming red, but there was flame in her eyes, and her voice came as sharp as the crack of a whip. "I guess that's a lie, Jesse Ross. You've done nothing but drool over me ever since you came here."

"Maybe if you learned to cook we'd all drool a

little less." That was a lie, of course; only his ma turned a better meal than Irene.

"If you don't like the accommodations here, try another hotel."

"Can't you ever talk to a man without laughing at him, or cutting him down?"

"Show me a man," she countered bluntly.

Jesse stood suddenly, tipping his chair backward. "Fancy talk for a backwoods harpy," he shouted. He might have said more, had not the look of shock upon Irene's face abruptly silenced him.

"My words aren't the only ones that cut, Jesse Ross," she whispered fiercely. "You might remember that sometime." She set her coffee down carefully then and walked swiftly from the room.

Jesse stood immobile, staring at her closed door. It struck him after a while that he had finally won one, that victory was his, but it was a shallow thing that left him feeling miserable.

Discounting the weeks he had laid wounded with Irene as his nurse, it didn't seem like they'd ever gotten along. Lately though, things had become steadily worse. They hardly spoke to each other at meals, said even less in the evenings. It was as if they hated each other, although Jesse knew they didn't. They were like two dominant mules hitched to the same wagon, he thought, heading in the same direction but constantly working against one another. He wondered then if it wasn't time to leave, to pack up his things and ride south alone, without Dewey. He had a horse now, and weapons and an outfit, and maybe with him gone things here could slide back to normal.

The outside door swung inward and Gray came inside, taking in the scene at a glance, the spilled coffee and Jesse's chair on its back and Irene gone, and with a stony cast to his face went directly to his room without speaking. Sometimes Jesse wondered what Gray thought about all this —his relationship with Irene—but Gray never spoke of it. Remembering the look on Gray's face tonight, though, Jesse decided that this had been their final confrontation. He would leave before noon tomorrow, alone if he had to.

Dewey arrived before breakfast, looking jaded but pleased. He jogged his sorrel down the long slope from the Jefferson City road and dismounted stiffly, shaking hands with Gray, hugging Irene, nodding to Jesse.

"Breakfast?" Gray asked, after the greetings were finished.

Dewey shook his head. "No time, Cap'n. Sorry."

"It won't take long," Irene protested. "The stove's already warm."

"Sorry, honey," Dewey replied. "But I'm afraid I'm rushed this time." He looked at Jesse. "You set, Ross?"

Jesse looked at Gray. He was set if Gray said so, if he was still willing to give up the buckskin and the revolvers.

Gray nodded and said, as if reading his thoughts, "They're yours, Jesse. Saddle up."

Jesse took time for a deep breath, then rushed down the steps and toward the barn, not running like a kid, but wanting to. Inside, he brought the buckskin into the aisle and tied him to a post. He ran a brush over the animal's back and down his legs, then quickly saddled and bridled him.

A shadow flitted across the door, a quick finger of shade passing over the hard-packed dirt floor, and he turned, expecting Gray or Dewey Harker, but not Irene.

She held the *mochilla* awkwardly in her arms, its saddlebags bulging with what Gray had given him last night, and the roll of his blankets—a heavy green one and a light, patchwork comforter —perched precariously atop that. She had paused at the entrance, but when Jesse looked up she made a small gesture with the *mochilla* as if to draw attention to it. "I brought your things," she said.

Jesse nodded uncomfortably and hurried to lift the *mochilla* from her arms. Setting the bedroll aside, he draped the *mochilla* over the saddle's tree and smoothed it into place.

"Papa sent his coat, too. It's the greatcoat Mama's family gave him when they moved to Texas."

"Your pa's done enough for me," Jesse said. "You keep the coat for him."

"Papa wants you to have it," Irene replied. "It means a lot to him, but you do too, being Matt's son. I . . . I want you to have it too."

"I've got that old jacket of mine. That'll do, I reckon."

Irene's lips thinned suddenly, and there was an edge to her voice. "Just take it, Jesse. Take it for Papa's sake."

"I ain't looking for charity," Jesse replied with a stubbornness he didn't understand.

"Funny, I was thinking we ought to rename Buck Charity. It seems to fit."

"Was it your horse to rename," Jesse said stiffly.

"Why do you always have to be so stubborn?" Irene cried in exasperation. She came forward, pulling something dark from around her neck and slipping it over his. Then she grabbed his ears in her hands and, twisting harshly, pulled him down until his lips met hers. A kiss, his first ever, and his head swam and his vision blurred while his ears burned like coals under her grip, until she pushed him back, turning and fleeing before he could speak.

Jesse swayed, caught his balance, staring at the white glare of the barn's entrance, rooted and speechless until the buckskin, bored with standing cross-tied, nudged his shoulder. Numbly then, he strapped the bedroll behind the cantle, the greatcoat across the pommels, and mounted clumsily, riding out of the barn into full sunlight.

Dewey was already mounted and Gray stood on the porch, a Walker in each hand, but Irene wasn't in sight. As Jesse rode up, Gray came over and slipped a revolver into the off-holster, strapping it in, then did the same on the near side. Giving the buckle a final tug, he looked at Jesse and said, "Are you okay, son?"

Jesse only nodded.

Hesitantly, Gray said, "A woman isn't like a horse or dog or goat. They ain't really like anything I can think of, but a good woman can enrich a man's life, Jesse. That's straight talk, son." Gray put a hand gently against Jesse's leg, then lifted it. "You're Matt Ross's son, and Gray Fletcher's friend. The time ever comes, remember that. It might help."

"Thanks, Gray. I won't let you down."

"Hell," Gray said gruffly. "I knew that all along."

"Best be getting across the river, Cap'n," Dewey said. "There's a chance I might've been followed."

Gray looked at Dewey, then nodded and started toward the ferry without asking any questions. Dewey looked at Jesse and smiled. "Let's go, Jesse. You'll see her again."

"Who?" Jesse asked foolishly.

"Why, whoever gave you that scarf, I'd guess,"

Dewey replied, and reined his horse after Gray.

For a moment Jesse didn't know what he meant. Then he remembered the circle of black Irene had draped around his neck, and he reached up and pulled the loose ends out to where he could see them. It was a scarf, all right, black silk and almost new—a Christmas gift from Gray to Irene, Jesse remembered. She hadn't worn it much, just on special occasions, Christmas day and New Year's Eve and Gray's birthday in February. It seemed strange that she would give it to him now. But then, remembering the kiss, he supposed it wasn't, and turning the buckskin he rode after Dewey.

CHAPTER 6

Springfield bustled in the afternoon heat, the streets crowded with spring buggies and buckboards and rattling old farm wagons near to falling apart, while horses stood hock-deep in mud at the rails and switched their tails at flies. The boardwalks were crowded with men and women and shouting children, and here and there blacks scurried quickly and with lowered faces on errands for their owners. The number of people on the street puzzled Dewey until he remembered that this was Saturday, market day for the farmers.

Jesse kept the Cap'n's big buckskin close as they rode slowly down National Street, dodging people and wagons and the deeper mud holes. With a dodger out on him, Jesse was nervous about riding openly into town, Dewey knew, and kept the slick leather bill of his old muskrat cap pulled low. In the two days it had taken them to reach Springfield, Dewey had come to hate Jesse's cap. It represented all that he despised about Missouri, the poverty and backwardness of its hill people that so readily provided the fodder for Slaughter's Rangers. Dewey had had a bellyful of raw-boned, gawking farmboys in clumsy shoes and ill-fitting hand-me-down clothing, and he'd decided last night Jesse would be different, that Gray Fletcher's recruit deserved that much. He had ten dollars and some change and figured that would buy the basics.

They reined up at the rail in front of the National Mercantile and Dewey stepped down and waded mud to the store's steps. But Jesse remained mounted, and Dewey looked at him with a grow-ing irritation. "You coming?" he asked, sharper than he had to.

"Maybe I'd better wait outside town," Jesse ventured.

"Maybe you'd better haul your ass out of the saddle and bring it inside. We've got business to attend to."

Jesse hesitated, then dismounted and joined

Dewey on the boardwalk, carefully scraping the mud off his shoes.

The National was a long, dark, high-ceilinged room with ladders affixed to rollers that slid along the walls to reach the upper shelves, and saddles and buckets and ash-split baskets that hung like decorations from the heavy oak beams overhead. There were several people inside, with clerks hurrying among them, but Dewey had frequented the National before and knew his way around. He led Jesse down the far aisle to a table piled with used clothing, with boots and shoes lined neatly beneath, and a shelf above stacked high with hats.

A clerk appeared as if from nowhere, short and slight of build, wearing thick glasses that seemed to magnify his pupils somewhat, and asked, "May I be of some assistance?"

"I want to outfit my friend here," Dewey replied. He pegged Jesse with a hard glance, stilling his protest before it was voiced. "Boots, jeans, maybe a shirt," Dewey went on. "And a hat. Something broad-brimmed."

The clerk studied Jesse critically, as if mentally measuring him for a new suit, then bobbed his head. "Yes, of course. It won't take long."

"Good. I'll be back in a few minutes," Dewey replied, and turned on his heel and walked away.

There was a long glass case near the front of the store and Dewey made his way to it. Inside, a dozen handguns resided on a gaudy Mexican blanket, with brass powder flasks, bullet molds and bars of lead scattered between. Most of the pistols were the old single-shot variety, big-bored and awkward, but there were several revolvers near the front of the case and Dewey bent down to eye them closer.

"Needing some help, sir?" A middle-aged man with thinning hair hovered over the far side of the case. He glanced at the two revolvers belted at Dewey's waist questioningly and said, "Looking for something lighter, perhaps, easier to carry?"

"Maybe looking for a friend," Dewey said. He was packing Navies at his waist, with a LeMat in a shoulder rig under his jacket, and felt like that was enough for him. But Jesse needed a side arm. Gray's old Walkers were fine for horseback, but they would be sharing camp with some pretty rough company after tomorrow, and a man could never tell when a revolver, handy to reach, might slide him past trouble.

"What did you have in mind?" the clerk asked.

"What's that one right there?" Dewey asked, pointing at a New Model Remington Army in the center of the display.

"An excellent choice, sir." The clerk reached into the case and brought the revolver out, placing it gently on the counter. "This is the Army model, somewhat rare on the civilian market right now. A very sturdy, serviceable weapon."

Dewey hefted it, admiring its balance. He tried the action and found it quick and smooth. Letting the hammer down, he eyed the muzzle. "Forty-four caliber?"

"Yes sir."

"How much?"

"That one would be twenty-five dollars, including mold, worm, and screw. For that price I'd also include a capper." He reached into the case and brought out a slim, brass cap dispenser.

Dewey winced inside but kept a horse-trader's face. Pointing at a short-barreled revolver in the corner, he said, "Let's see that one."

The clerk's face took on an immediate look of pain. He lifted the Army and replaced it carefully, taking his time, while Dewey resisted the urge to grab him by his lapels and drag him over the counter. Setting the smaller weapon on the counter, the clerk said, "This is a '51 Dragoon, somewhat worn. I can let you have this for twelve dollars."

Dewey lifted the Dragoon. Though smaller than the Army, it was heavier, and the trigger felt sloppy to the touch. "Not the pistol the Army is, is it?" he asked casually.

"No sir," the clerk replied as if bored.

Dewey felt the slow burn of anger, held it back. Putting the Dragoon down, he said, "That pistol isn't worth twelve dollars. I don't think it's worth five."

"Very well, sir." The clerk put the revolver away. "Will that be all, then?"

Dewey sighed. "No, let's see that Bowie knife down there. The one in back."

The clerk retrieved the knife and a riveted leather sheath and set both before Dewey. Dewey picked it up and knew immediately that he wanted it. It was a big knife, maybe twelve inches overall, broad-backed and keen-edged, with an iron hilt that curled like a gambler's fancy waxed mustache. The handles were slabs of curly maple, slightly concaved to fit the hand, and the blade had been left dark and rough by the smithy who made it. Testing its edge with his thumb, Dewey thought a man could shave with this knife if he wanted to, or cut down a small tree.

"There are those who prefer the knife to the pistol," the clerk said. "I can let you have this for six dollars."

"Five's best I can do," Dewey countered.

The clerk studied the knife for a moment, then shrugged. "Okay. Union scrip or gold coin?"

Dewey smiled thinly. "Coin," he said, and dug the money from his poke. Before he could sheath the knife and slip it into his belt, Jesse showed up, looking self-conscious, but proud, too, and Dewey stepped back and nodded his approval. Jesse had chosen well—good tan boots reinforced at the heels, canvas pants, a blue chambray shirt, and a broad-brimmed, cream-colored fur felt hat.

Irene's scarf knotted at his throat added a touch of flash. "You'll do, by God," Dewey said, grinning, and handed Jesse the knife.

"What's this?"

"Side arm," Dewey replied. He turned to the clerk with the glasses. "What's the damages?" he asked.

"Five and a quarter. The boots were a steal at two dollars."

Dewey grunted and shelled the money out. He didn't count what was left but knew it was less than half a dollar, and that he'd have to start rationing his smokes for a while.

Jesse had examined the Bowie while Dewey paid the bill, and now he looked up, his eyes shining with a gratitude that Dewey knew he would never speak, and he grunted again, softly, wondering if there was hope for the kid after all. "Come on," Dewey said shortly. "Let's swing past the farmer's market and pick up a chicken for tonight's supper."

Jesse nodded, slipping the knife into the sheath, the sheath into his belt.

"What about these?" the near-sighted clerk asked, lifting Jesse's old clothes like some kind of offering, and Dewey was about to tell Jesse to bring them along, that they might come in handy someday, but Jesse spoke first, saying, "They're farmer's clothes. Give them to a farmer," and Dewey grunted his approval once more.

•••

They rode south and east after leaving Springfield, abandoning the main road and following a
network of trails that wound through the knobby
hills of the borderlands, skirting small hollows
and rocky ledges and bubbling springs nearly
hidden by soft green ferns. Now and again they
passed small clearings carved grudgingly from
the dense forest, rocky patches of poor dirt sowed
in corn or beans or tobacco, with like as not a
small cabin or crude shack at one end, seemingly
deserted except for maybe a thread of smoke
rising from the chimney. They never saw any
people, but they sometimes saw a few hounds and
maybe some hogs or cattle running loose nearby.
Dewey dreaded the cabins; around them he
always sensed an air of distrust that bordered
hatred, and he felt vulnerable when exposed to it,
and was always relieved to put them behind.

Gnats bothered them incessantly, and green-
heads, and sometimes passing still pools of clear
water they would disturb clouds of mosquitoes
that rose in dark, swirling masses from the rushes
and cattails bordering the water.

Near noon of the second day out of Springfield
they crossed the headwaters of the Gasconde
and Dewey began to recognize landmarks he
associated with the colonel's camp. Through a
break in the trees he spotted Possum Knob, and
knew that the camp wasn't far on the other side.

Maybe Jesse sensed its proximity. Pausing at the bottom of a hill to let their horses drink from a stream, he said, "How much farther?"

"An hour, maybe. No more."

Jesse looked around him, at the thick wall of forest, dark with shadow. "Doesn't seem like you could hide an army in here."

Dewey shrugged. "There's a good-sized meadow we've been camping at through the winter."

"Maybe now's the time to tell me what I'm riding into," Jesse said softly, without looking at him.

Life, Dewey wanted to say, and all the uncertainties that went with it, but he knew Jesse couldn't understand that yet. Dewey wasn't sure a man ever could. He said, "The Colonel's a transplanted Texan, like me and the Cap'n, although he ain't so sawed-off. He come up from the Lone Star last summer when it looked like this shitaree was here to stay a while and started putting together an outfit of rangers. Most are Missourians like yourself, but there's a few from Texas and Arkansas and even a couple of farmers from Kansas that nobody trusts too much just yet. We're a pretty mixed lot, with some rough customers I wouldn't want to turn my back on, although there's more good than bad among us. I'll give the Colonel credit for that. He's maybe signed on some I wouldn't have, but he won't harbor a known murderer or thief."

Jesse looked suddenly uncomfortable. "Reckon maybe you've taken a long ride for nothing, Dewey. I thought you knew, but there's a dodger out on me, and a pretty hefty reward too."

Dewey chuckled, gathering his reins and lifting the sorrel's head. "I know about the dodger, Jesse. But that's a federal warrant, for crimes against the Union. Hell, I'm guessing before summer's out half the men riding with us will have dodgers on them, and the others will be wanted under John Does. Naw, that ain't the kind of man I'm talking about. It's the one that would knife his own partner over a card game, or maybe someone who enjoys killing, like some I've run across, that the Colonel wants to keep out."

Jesse looked relieved. "That's good, Dewey. I know you think I'm green, and I reckon I am, but I can fight. Even green and scared, I can fight."

Odd words from a kid, and Dewey felt a guarded respect take root. "Well, I reckon that's good, too, because I have a feeling you're going to get the chance real soon."

Dewey gigged the sorrel across the stream and up the far bank, thinking back to Copeland and what he'd learned from him. Then he thought about the men waiting on the far side of the Knob and a little shiver of dread ran through him.

After the winter, when every day seemed a week long because of inactivity, Dewey was almost shocked by the hustle he saw in camp. He sat his horse at the edge of the trees, the long, sloping meadow before him alive with men hurrying here and there, pulling down tents, saddling horses; even as he watched a great ball of white steam rise from the cookfire at the meadow's base, extinguished for the first time in months.

"Busy place," Jesse observed quietly.

"Yeah," Dewey replied, and urged the sorrel down the slope. He had spotted the Colonel's big gray gelding standing hipshot in front of the red-trimmed marquee tent at the lower edge of the meadow, but he angled away from that now, toward a small camp just below the fringe of trees. He could see Gil Banks there, poking at something in a cast-iron skillet, and Roscoe Hammer squatting nearby with a tin cup dangling empty from a long finger. Earl Dickson was there too, his hat pulled low and trapping the blue smoke from a stubby corncob pipe, and there was someone with the horses in the trees, but he couldn't tell if it was Pete Bottoms or Freddy Spence. In the whole camp of antlike hurry, their small, open camp was an island of serenity.

Gil looked up as Dewey approached and a slow grin spread across his face. "Well, goddamn, look what finally rolled in."

Roscoe and Earl grinned in unison, then Earl stood and called, "Howdy, Sarge."

Roscoe added dryly, "Gil made the coffee,

116

Sarge. Come on in and you can chew the fat and drink it too."

Dewey smiled. Coming back late one evening last winter from an unsuccessful hunt, Gil had absently trimmed the fat from a piece of pork and dropped it into the coffeepot instead of the lard can. It was a small thing, looking back, but it had grown steadily in retelling and now hardly a week went by without someone bringing it up one way or another.

"Howdy, boys," Dewey greeted, halting but not dismounting. "What's all the commotion about?"

"Moving on," Gil said. "But no one knows where."

"I'm thinking the Colonel's got a hair crosswise to his ass and thinks a fresh log to squat over might help," Earl drawled softly, chuckling alone afterward in solitary appreciation of his words.

Roscoe said, "Just got in ourselves, Sarge. The Lieutenant said to fix us a bite, then break camp and be ready to move when everybody else is."

"That goddamn Chadron has been running our asses ragged the last few weeks," Earl added with a scowl.

"Freddy got killed, Sarge," Gil said soberly.

In the drift of conversation, Gil's words flowed with the rest at first, without meaning. Then Dewey's breath snagged in his throat and he looked at Gil as if he thought it might be a joke. Lifting his gaze to the top of the slope then, he saw Pete Bottoms come out of the trees and start toward them.

"About a week ago," Gil added. "Over on the Cassville road."

"Yankees?" Dewey asked.

Gil nodded. "We was scouting for stray stock and run smack into two bunches."

"Two?"

"Small patrol and a troop. We ran once but they ran twice."

"Colonel thinks they're scouting for a bigger outfit somewhere close by," Roscoe added. "Rumor has it we're going after 'em."

"That suits me," Earl growled. "We been squatting here too damn long already."

Dewey nodded. Small patrols of scouts made sense, coupled with what Copeland had told him. Abruptly, he said, "Boys, this is Jesse Ross of near Jefferson City. He's new and I want him to bunk here. Show him the ropes, huh?"

"Here, Sarge?" Pete asked, stopping nearby. "We've kind of already got a group here."

"It just grew," Dewey replied curtly, reining the sorrel away. He didn't bother with introductions, figuring Jesse could work that out on his own. It probably wouldn't be easy if they were still hurting over Freddy's dying, but Dewey knew that the easy part of Jesse's life was likely behind him now.

Dewey halted close to the Colonel's gray

gelding and swung down. An orderly wearing homespuns, patched brogans, and a Confederate kepi looked up from where he sat cross-legged in the dirt next to the marquee's entrance. "Howdy, Sarge," he greeted, the words slurred some by a wad of tobacco tucked into one cheek. "You an officer?"

"More or less," Dewey replied.

The orderly rose and arched tobacco in an amber stream at a tent stake. "Well, if you're an officer I gotta take your horse around back with the others," he said. "But if you ain't, I ain't gotta. I ain't a goddamn stableboy for every ass-scratcher that wanders up."

Dewey tossed him the reins. "Take my horse," he said brusquely, ducking past the startled youth and into the tent.

Inside, the conversation of half a dozen men speaking at the same time came to an abrupt halt; all eyes turned blankly on Dewey, then Slaughter smiled and said, "Welcome back, Sergeant. You had a safe trip, I hope?"

"Yes sir," Dewey said. He shook hands with Captain Prescott and Lieutenants Borden and Chadron, nodded to Ted Miles and Eli Davis, sergeants like himself.

"And a fruitful one?" the Colonel pressed.

"Yes sir, I think so."

"Good," Slaughter said with a barely contained enthusiasm. "If the rest of you gentlemen would

119

momentarily excuse us, I'd like to have a word with Sergeant Harker."

Most of them exchanged glances, but except for Chadron and Miles, they were Texans, old rangers, and they didn't grumble. Dewey stepped aside as they exited, then approached the small table near the rear of the tent. Slaughter nodded toward a camp chair next to the table and said, "Have a seat, Sergeant. A drink?"

Dewey shook his head and sank gratefully onto the chair. It felt good to sit on something that didn't rock again.

"Tell me what you've learned," Slaughter said, leaning forward and putting his weight upon the table. He looked eager, almost young, and Dewey thought back to the kid he had known in Texas. Always tall, Slaughter had filled out some over the years, was slim yet, but not skinny anymore. He had grown a beard at some point that he kept carefully trimmed; the beard, flecked with gray, together with the gaunt, weathered face and brooding eyes seemed to have added years to his countenance.

"I brought back a recruit," Dewey began. "Left him up-slope with some of Chadron's men."

"Captain Fletcher's man? Good, I want to meet him later. But what about Copeland? Did you find him?"

"I found him," Dewey said. He briefly related his experiences in Jefferson City and the events that had led him out the St. Louis road to his encounter with Copeland. Then he got down to business. "There's a General Hugget commanding three thousand infantry marching south along the Kansas line. If Copeland's information was correct, they ought to be at Fort Scott by now, or a day or two south of there."

Dewey stood and walked to a map suspended from the guide ropes along the tent's side wall. Slaughter followed. "They're going to make a sweep right through here," Dewey said. He traced a finger down the Kansas-Missouri line, then curved it through Arkansas. "Fayetteville, right through the Ozarks to Little Rock, then up to Memphis. Other federal troops will come down the Mississippi and the plan is apparently to hitch double-trace just outside Memphis. Who knows from there."

"Is that all?" Slaughter asked, unable to hide his disappointment.

"No sir. I was saving the best for last. There's a supply train on its way from St. Louis. Food stuff, mostly, even a small herd of cattle, but Copeland says they're also carrying weapons and ammunition. Several wagons of it, he thought."

Slaughter smiled, slapped the side of his fist into the palm of his other hand. "A supply train. By God, Sergeant, that is a prize. Where?"

Dewey stabbed Missouri on the map with his finger. "Rail it as far as Rolla, then freight it on a civilian contract to a rendezvous somewhere along the Buffalo River in Arkansas. He didn't know where, but hell, Colonel, there's only one decent road leading south from Rolla—they'll have to take that."

"An escort?"

"Copeland thought a small one, fifty or seventy-five men. Maybe twenty wagons."

Slaughter leaned forward, devouring the map with his eyes. "Yes," he breathed softly. "That would explain the increased federal activity west of us." His gaze flitted erratically across the map. "And the Rolla road lies to our east. A perfect setting, Sergeant, perfect." He leaned back, his eyes bright. "By God, Dewey, the Company of Missouri Rangers is about to enter this damn war at last!"

"Yes sir," Dewey replied hollowly. "I believe it is."

CHAPTER 7

The bay shifted restlessly under him and Gil jerked roughly on the reins, regretting his action almost immediately. It was nerves that gave him such a heavy hand, he knew, but he could no more change that than he could stop the steady drip of rain that fell from the leaves above him.

He had once thought that, after Kansas, nothing would ever worry or frighten him again, but he had been wrong. Death frightened him. It turned his skin clammy and his bowels to water, it strummed his muscles like banjo strings under the curious fingers of a crawling babe. In his mind now, every day, he could hear the rip and tear of Freddy's flesh and his mouth would go dry and his head light. It had been a tremendous surprise to discover that he was a coward, but oddly, he felt no shame—only a nagging desire to escape.

Thunder rumbled low in the distance and faded away, but there was a brightness in the western sky that hinted of blue. Gil hoped so. He hated the thought of fighting in the rain, of damp powder —no matter how well a man greased a chamber —and misfires. In his mind he kept seeing himself, dismounted, facing a charging Yankee with a flashing saber while the old Remingtons he carried misfired one chamber after the other. Such thoughts were enough to make a man consider running, but Gil didn't think he could do that. He supposed there wasn't much logic to his thinking, but he knew there were times in a man's life when he had to think of his pride, too, and Gil figured that in the long run he'd probably prefer death to being branded a coward.

It was funny, the directions a man's life could take. Two years ago he was swamping for his pa's freight outfit, handling the brakes on grades, harnessing mornings and unharnessing in the evenings and throwing meals together when on the road—all the small, menial chores that were beneath the skinner. That was about all he knew of life, mules and freighting, all he'd done since he was around six years old. Then two summers ago jayhawkers had killed his pa.

There had been no obvious reason for their killing him, and little conversation preceding it. His pa had contracted to freight a load of mostly mercantile goods to Baxter Springs and had been forced to deadhead back. The jayhawkers caught up with them just north of town, riding into camp with their revolvers drawn. The leader, a big man on a roan horse, had asked his pa two questions: Where was he from and what was his opinion on slavery? Gil knew his pa had never supported slavery but he supposed working with mules all a man's life led to a natural stubbornness. His pa told the big man to go to hell and someone slipped up behind Gil about then and laid him out cold with a piece of firewood. When he came to he'd found his pa hung from a cottonwood tree. Shortly then, he'd learned that sometimes hate was all the motive a man needed for killing.

He never did find the men who had killed his pa, but staunch jayhawkers were easy to find in eastern Kansas and he'd led a bloody career for almost a year, burning and looting and killing without much discretion. He'd come out of his rage abruptly last summer and rode west, onto the prairie, with two bottles of cheap whiskey. Afterward, he rode into Missouri and stumbled onto some of Slaughter's rangers. He'd joined on impulse but soon discovered that killing—even Yankees—held no attraction for him anymore, and that supporting the South was supporting a cause he didn't totally agree with.

It put him in an awkward position. It didn't seem like there was any middle ground in the East anymore. You either supported the North or the South, or you hightailed into the West to look for gold. Gil didn't figure he would make much of a prospector, but he often thought longingly of going West. He figured a good mule man could do well freighting supplies into the gold fields of Colorado.

The bay lifted her head and Gil grabbed up the slack in the reins, ready to yank if it looked like she might nicker. Other animals up and down the line had lifted their heads too, and Gil wondered if it was Dewey's sorrel they scented returning, or the freighter's mules.

Slaughter had split the rangers into two groups, leaving Chadron here with about twenty men and taking the rest with him to a small meadow flanking a ribbon of water called Cow Creek. Rumor had it that Slaughter intended to take the brunt of the battle, but he wanted Chadron to close the back door. It seemed like a fair enough plan to Gil, but he couldn't help wondering what might happen if the Yankees attempted a retreat.

Gil waited near the rear of the group and from time to time he would glance over his shoulder at Jesse Ross. Ross sat stiffly atop his big, ill-tempered buckskin, a huge Walker resting butt-first against the flat horn of his saddle. He didn't show much fear, not like a man would expect to see in a kid about to enter his first battle; he fidgeted some with his reins and now and again licked at his lips as if they were dry, but that was about all. It struck Gil that he didn't know Ross very well, and he regretted that suddenly. They'd been pretty hard on him this past week, with Roscoe and Earl doing most of the carping, but they'd all done their share. Earl claimed it was Ross's inexperience that bothered him, but Gil knew that was absurd; only Chadron's men had any real experience fighting Yankees, and that no more than a couple of minor skirmishes.

Gil knew it wasn't Ross's lack of experience that was bothering them; it was Freddy. Dewey had dumped Ross on them too soon after Freddy's death, and they resented that, and took it out on the kid. But it wasn't the kid's fault, and of a sudden Gil reined his horse around and rode back to where Ross waited alone, halting when the buckskin laid its ears back.

Ross nodded and Gil whispered, "How."

"Waiting chews on you like a dog on an old boot, don't it?" Jesse whispered in return.

"Sure as hell," Gil agreed. They sat in silence for a few minutes, watching the rustle of movement that passed among the men and horses, knowing others felt as they did. After a while, Gil said, "Your first raid, right?"

"Yeah."

"I've been on a couple. Wondered if you'd want some advice?"

"Sure," Jesse said promptly.

"Tie your reins together, in case you drop them, but leave enough loose that you can hold them in your teeth if you need to. Gives you a little control and still lets you use both pistols. Best to have 'em both fully loaded too. A couple extra rounds might come in handy."

Jesse quickly knotted the reins and let them drop against the buckskin's neck. From a pouch he carried strapped to the saddlehorn he pulled out a powder flask, balls, patches, caps, and grease. Gil watched silently as he loaded the two chambers generally kept empty under the hammer. Jesse worked swiftly, efficiently, and Gil felt a prick of admiration; it wasn't an easy task to load a revolver from horseback, but Jesse made it seem that way.

Finished, Jesse dropped the off-revolver into its holster and said, "Thanks."

A murmur soft as the breeze passed through the men, and turning, a bearded Missourian named

Joe Boone said, "Come on, Banks. We're moving out." Gil looked once more at Jesse and nodded curtly, then he turned his bay mare and rode after Boone.

They wound their way slowly, single file, through the dense woods, keeping to a shallow depression that looked like it might occasionally run water for most of the way to the road. At a spot some distance back from it they halted again, until Harker appeared from ahead, riding his sorrel fast through the trees, speaking quickly to Chadron, then whipping around and spurring back toward the road. With a forward wave of his hand, Chadron led them on, coming quickly onto the broad, hard-packed road from Rolla.

They halted again, briefly, then turned south. The rain had tapered off some but it hadn't quit yet. The dirt in the road was surface-slick with mud, tracked by uncountable hoofprints, with small, inch-deep ruts flanking the center hump. Gil wasn't a tracker but a blind man could tell these prints were fresh. He could smell tobacco, too, and the pungent odor of wet cattle.

They followed the road at a walk, loosely grouped and scarcely talking. The horses were skittish, tossing their heads and blowing, and in the lead Chadron kept twisting in the saddle to peg one or another of them with a glare. The road wound along the base of a forested hill, descending gradually toward Cow Creek and the meadow on this side of it. Gil knew it was only a short distance ahead, but he was still surprised when they rode into it.

Chadron halted his command with an uplifted hand. Before them Cow Creek Meadow stretched for several hundred yards, split through the middle by a column of Yankee blue uniforms and white humped Conestoga wagons, a brindled patch of cattle milling to one side. Gil counted eighteen wagons, each pulled by a twelve-mule hitch, and estimated there were probably fifty or sixty federal troopers massed near the head of the column, with a small detachment of no more than eight huddled near the last wagon. So far no one had spotted them; their attention was riveted on Slaughter and his sixty-plus men neatly blocking the road as it dipped toward the creek.

A lieutenant and two troopers broke from the Union ranks and rode forward at a fast jog, halting about fifty yards from where Slaughter had stopped his own men and calling for someone from among the Rangers to meet them. Slaughter sent Prescott. Charlie Prescott was an old friend of the Colonel, second in command of the rangers. Gil thought Prescott might be a captain, although he wasn't sure; among the rangers rank seemed more a title than a position.

Prescott didn't waste much time; within two minutes of meeting with the Yankee lieutenant he wheeled his horse and loped back to Slaughter's side. The lieutenant did the same and a minute later the Yankee bugler blew "Charge," and all hell broke loose.

Wild, echoing rebel yells broke from among them, and Gil's bay bolted just as Chadron shouted, *"Let's go!"*

Gil couldn't hold the bay. She lunged past Chadron and those in the lead, fighting for the bit. At first Gil fought the bay, but then he let her have her head and drew one of his Remingtons, a shrill, startling yell breaking unexpectedly past his own lips. He could hear the others close behind, the pounding of hooves that kept time to his hammering heart, and the frightened shouts of the small detachment they surprised at the rear of the column. Cattle bawled in sudden alarm as their herders fled, mules brayed, kicked, bit at their mates. Gil's Remington barked and jumped, and he breathed in the acrid taste of spent gunpowder as the bay raced forward. He heard the shrill purr of lead, saw in his mind the flash of a saber, and pulled wide, bending low along the saddle.

Gray clouds of powder smoke blossomed among the wagons, and bullets buzzed angrily after him. The bay squealed and kicked out wickedly with her rear legs, and Gil's thumb slipped off the Remington's hammer, sending his second shot high. Others pulled even, coming between him and the wagons. Chadron, Boone, and Jesse Ross, riding erect and firing the old Walkers methodically. A soldier appeared from among the wagons, racing past the others, toward him, a bayonet fixed to his rifle, and Gil snapped a shot and watched him spin away. Toward the head of the column gunfire made a steady racket as Slaughter's men met, merged with the Federals. Gil took time for a quick look, then grimly turned the bay back along the column, closer this time, where the air was peppered with lead and cloudy with gunsmoke.

Nothing made sense now. He saw riderless horses scampering through the melee, saw others rearing and whinnying shrilly, walleyed in fear. Bodies tumbled from horses and were dragged or trampled, while others crumbled afoot. A bullet tugged at his sleeve, another smashed into the pommel of his saddle and stung him with splinters of wood and rawhide. He saw Jesse again, the big buckskin dodging like a yellow demon among the wagons, ears back, teeth bared. A team of mules stampeded, lurching like drunks against the braked wagon. He saw Chadron on his knees in the tall grass like a man praying, clutching at his chest with a hand that still gripped his revolver. Dewey slid his long-legged sorrel to a halt near Chadron, and Gil reined the bay roughly in their direction. Dewey bent close to Chadron just as a teamster stepped away from his wagon and ran into the field with an old single-shot cap-and-ball pistol in his hand.

Gil yelled, "Sarge," loud enough to hurt his throat, but his voice was lost in the din of the battle. The teamster skidded to a halt a few feet behind Dewey and leveled his pistol. Gil screamed, *"Sarge!"* and snapped a shot that went wide.

Then Jesse appeared from between a pair of wagons, the buckskin squealing angrily, his hooves flashing dangerously as he reared. Jesse fired twice, once with each of the old Walkers, and the teamster jerked, spun, and fell.

Dewey looked up as Gil pulled his horse to a rough stop, then behind him, taking the situation in at a glance. When Dewey let go of Chadron, the lieutenant fell forward, dead, Gil saw. "Follow me," Dewey barked and, swinging onto his horse, led Jesse and Gil toward the rear of the column where a knot of soldiers still fought.

Gil sat on a rock at the edge of the creek and dipped his bandanna into the water, raising it to press against the spot where the lobe of his right ear had once been. The cold water stung at the touch but he didn't pull it away. It was a small thing, the wound, a stretch of ruffled but unbroken skin along his neck and the missing lobe. It barely warranted attention, considering Earl, with his spine shot away.

In the meadow the rangers were scrambling

over the wagons like kids, shouting and laughing as they dumped boxes and barrels and crates over the sideboards to split open and spill their contents on the ground. Close to the lead wagon nearly a score of prisoners sat in the shade, taking quite a bit of abuse from the handful of rangers watching them. There were a few Yankee soldiers among them, but most were teamsters. There were quite a few soldiers lying dead in the grass, among the larger mounds that were horses, but most of the troopers had escaped, scattering into the woods, routed by the overwhelming firepower of the rangers. Gil figured it was a hell of a victory for their first real confrontation, but he didn't feel like cele-brating.

He heard the slow approach of a horse and looked up to find Dewey riding along the creek. Beyond, at the edge of the road, Jesse Ross sat his buckskin alone. Gil nodded as Dewey came up, but didn't speak.

Dewey took in the wet bandanna and the blood that ran slowly down Gil's wrist and said, "How bad is it?"

Gil shook his head and slid a glance toward the wagons.

"Quite a haul," Dewey offered. "Twenty some crates of spanking new Colt Armies, enough to outfit every member of the company with at least a pair, plus powder, lead and caps, food and medical supplies, rifles if anyone wants one. The

Colonel's about to go cross-eyed trying to fit everything into one wagon."

"He ought to just take it all."

Dewey shrugged. "Rangers need to travel light," he said, then sighed and added, "Six dead. Jesus."

"Earl was one," Gil said quietly.

"Yeah, I know. Roscoe took a ball in the elbow that played hell with the joint, too."

Gil looked up, blinking. He had seen Roscoe briefly after the battle, sitting with his back to a wagon wheel, but he hadn't known he was wounded. "Bad?" he asked.

"Enough to send him home. My guess is even if he doesn't lose that arm, he'll never use it for anything again."

Gil dropped his gaze and shook his head. "Ain't nothing good going to come out of this war, Sarge. I know that, but I'm damned if I know what to do about it."

Dewey didn't answer immediately and Gil began to wonder if he would, but finally Dewey said, harshly, "Get on your horse, Banks, and quit feeling sorry for yourself."

Gil looked up, then rose with his fists clenched, letting the bandanna fall into the water. "Earl's dead, goddamn you, and Roscoe's maybe crippled for life, and you don't care. You didn't care about Freddy and you don't care about Earl or Roscoe." Tears came to his eyes and he rubbed at them with the back of his wrists; he hated himself for letting Dewey see him like this, but couldn't stop.

In a softer voice than Gil expected, Dewey said, "I rode with the Texas Rangers for a long time. Death doesn't surprise me anymore. Get on your horse, Banks."

Gil almost balked but didn't have the energy. The tears dried on their own. He felt weak, half sick, but went to his horse and mounted without complaint. He could hear Slaughter barking orders in the meadow, and looking that way, saw a dozen mounted rangers surrounding the prisoners. Jubal Butler was forcing his horse among them, separating the soldiers from the teamsters. Gil frowned and looked at Dewey.

"That's none of your concern, Gil," Dewey said. "Colonel wants us to scout a trail back to camp."

Gil didn't understand at first, then he did, and he looked again at the prisoners while a cold horror filled him. "Jesus Christ," he whispered.

Dewey said, "Just the soldiers, Gil. He'll let the civilians go."

Gil reined the bay around numbly, urging her to where Jesse waited in stony silence. He could hear Dewey behind him but he didn't look back. He supposed it was only fair; he knew that if he was ever captured by federals a rope would likely be his fate, also. But that didn't make it any easier.

From the big oak tree that towered atop the high bluff, scarlet leaves fell in a dry, clattering shower. They struck the low-humped caprock where Dewey lay belly-flat and spun past him like flaming cartwheels. A few lodged against his body but most of them rolled on, tumbling off the rock and drifting lazily toward the valley far below.

It was funny the way the seasons changed. Up here the old oak was completely transformed, a flaming ball with a crimson skirt, while in the valley where the Mississippi flowed sluggishly, the forest was almost all pale green yet, with only a few spots of bright red or yellow. Still, fall wasn't so far off anymore. Far across the river, in Illinois, the wheat fields undulated in a brisk breeze like tawny waves upon a yellow sea, and there was a crispness in the air too, an absence of humidity that made everything seem brighter and more alive. September was nearly behind them now, and the horses were turning shaggy for winter.

Dewey pushed backward off the caprock and rolled onto his back, shutting his eyes against the glare of sunlight. The wind wasn't so bad here, and he stretched his legs, basking for a moment in the penetrating warmth of the sun. But as much as he wanted to relax, his mind couldn't let go of what he'd seen through the lens of his telescope: the low, turtle-backed shape of the iron-clad that was steaming down the Mississippi beneath twin clouds of roiling smoke, and the sidewheeler that followed.

He would report them to Slaughter, of course—

duty demanded that much—but he dreaded it. An iron-clad would make a hell of a coup and he wouldn't put it past the Colonel to make an attempt. These past months Slaughter had become hell-bent on recognition, eager to separate the rangers from the other bands of irregulars raiding throughout the borderlands. To Dewey's way of thinking it had been an expensive objective. In more than two dozen skirmishes over the summer they had lost nearly twenty men, either seriously wounded or killed.

"We're trimming the fat," Slaughter sometimes said, and Dewey figured that was true enough as far as it went. But Dewey could never see it that dispassionately. Every time he thought of the Colonel's words he would remember Freddy and Earl and Roscoe, and the horseplay around last winter's fires.

He heard the thud of hooves, the jingle of bits and spurs and the creak of saddle leather, but didn't open his eyes. He didn't need to.

"Sarge has got the right idea," Dewey heard Gil say.

"See anything?" Jesse asked. He and Gil dismounted nearby.

Dewey smiled, picturing them in his mind: Gil, easy-going and quick to laugh; and Jesse, somber, reflective. As different as night and day in some respects, but they'd taken to each other, and Dewey had taken to them, and the three of them made a good team. Nowadays, when Slaughter sent men out on a scout it was generally Dewey and Jesse and Gil that he sent, and that suited Dewey just fine.

"P'shaw," Gil snorted. "Sarge ain't a man to soak up sunshine if there's anything to get excited about."

"Dewey ain't a man to excite too damn easy," Jesse replied. To Dewey, he added, "I been thinking they might send the troops downriver on a steamboat. Be the quickest, was they rushed."

Without opening his eyes Dewey handed Jesse the telescope, listening to the low scuff of his boots, the tiny musical sound of his spurs, as he climbed the caprock.

Rumor had drifted into Slaughter's camp on the Whitewater River a couple of days back that the Federals were moving troops south from St. Louis to Cape Girardeau. Dewey and Jesse and Gil had haunted the river road since then but so far hadn't spotted anything in blue.

He heard Gil settle close by, yawning loudly, and he wanted to smile, remembering Gil as he had been last winter, and Jesse, too, wide-eyed and annoyed as he lifted Irene off the pier at the Cap'n's. They had come a long way, he knew. Gone were the two greenhorns he had picked almost at random that day on Cow Creek, and in their places stood two skilled rangers, both of them quick and capable.

Gil said, "Ol' Jesse's het up to fight once more, but I'm set on wintering."

"You've been set on wintering since June," Dewey countered, and Gil laughed. Above them, Jesse whistled softly, then slid back from the skyline. Dewey sat up, waiting for Jesse's word, his reaction.

"What?" Gil asked, spitting a stem of grass from his mouth.

Jesse handed Gil the telescope and looked at Dewey. "You figuring to tell the Colonel about this?" he asked.

"That's our job."

"Well, hell," Gil said, and scrambled up the rock.

"They're moving fast. We'd never catch up," Jesse said.

"Do you think the Colonel'd want to try?"

"That bastard might," Jesse said bitterly.

"Gil says you're hot to fight."

Gil laughed from above. "Not no iron-clad, he ain't. Jesse ain't a fool." He slid back from the caprock and sloped down close to Dewey. "Ain't no soldier boys on that sidewheeler that I could see," he said. "That's what the Colonel sent us scouting for—soldiers."

Dewey took the telescope and dropped it into its rawhide case. He looked at Jesse and said, "What about you?"

"Hell, I ain't afraid of a fight, I guess you know that. But I didn't see any troops either, and I can't see rangers against an iron-clad. You know that old bastard would order a charge into midchannel if he thought we stood a snowball's chance."

Dewey laughed suddenly. "He might at that, but like Gil says, we were ordered to look for soldiers. Hell with iron-clads."

"Hell with fighting," Gil whooped loudly. "And hurrah for winter quarters."

Dewey laughed again, feeling an old vitality creeping back that he had thought was gone for good. He felt a sudden anticipation for winter quarters himself; it had been a long summer.

CHAPTER 8

Jesse tipped his hat to the swirl of snow, cold all the way through now, his feet numb in the stirrups. He rode hunch-shouldered, the broad, heavy collar of Gray's old greatcoat pulled up high around his neck, creating only a small window of exposed flesh beneath his hatbrim. Still, the snow found its way in, settling like frost against his beard and turning his nose red, chapped and hot to the touch, a sense of warmth he knew was a lie. From time to time the buckskin would angrily shake his head and attempt to put his butt to the wind, but Jesse would haul him back, forcing him on.

There were six of them, riding north from

Slaughter's winter camp along the Current River toward a spot on the Missouri somewhere between Jefferson City and St. Louis. Harvey Quint led, the trip largely his idea, and Pete Bottoms followed Jesse, bringing up the rear. Between rode Dan Black and Bob Wilkes, both Borden men, and a shuffling bear of a man called Curly Barnes. Quint was taking them to a friend he thought might have cattle for sale. Quartered in a permanent spot for the winter, Slaughter's old problem of supply had immediately reared its head again, and he had been quick to accept Quint's offer to go after the cattle.

It had seemed almost warm when they left the huge, shallow caverns that fronted the Current, but Wilkes had glumly predicted a change. He had trapped muskrat and raccoon as a boy, and he suffered greatly from rheumatism because of it. Jesse's ma always said there was no better weather gauge than a rheumatic joint, that it was the marginal good the Lord always saw fit to tag to any bad; winters, his ma would go through two or three jugs of Ivan Richards sour mash to ease the pain of her rheumatism.

The change hadn't been long in coming, the sky clouding over the first day and the temperature dropping to below freezing. Toward nightfall it began to snow, and by morning eight inches blanketed the ground, with no let-up in sight.

The snow slowed them down some, but it didn't

stop them, and by noon of the next day they came out of a deep woods to find themselves on a broad, trackless highway. They halted their horses in a loose group, and Quint looked at Curly Barnes and asked, "This is it, ain't it?"

Curly looked up and down the road, doubt as plain on his face as his big nose, but Curly wasn't a man to admit uncertainty on anything, and he said, "Yeah, east of here, if you followed the right trail."

Quint didn't bother to look irritated. He only grinned and turned his horse to the east. Quint was a lanky man, dark and usually reticent, a quality he credited to his Cherokee heritage. Quint was a puzzle to Jesse. He seemed like a good man, cool, levelheaded, deadly in a fight, and a top horseman, which was always important in the rangers. He never shirked his duty or hid from work, although he never did more than his share either. He should have been a well-liked man, but he wasn't. Quint had tried to desert once, and that single, impulsive act had marked him like a brand. He was a coward, they said, and untrustworthy when the chips were down; they didn't actually shun him—the rangers were too small a company for that—but they didn't go out of their way for him, either, and in the end he had drifted into the Jubal Butler and Curly Barnes crowd.

Jubal and Curly, Marsh Tanner and John Martin and three or four others, mostly hardcases with shadowy pasts, always shared the same fire and rode together when they could. They were the scum of the Rangers, the bottom of the barrel according to some, although as Dewey pointed out, if they were that bad the Colonel would have run them out a long time ago.

Quint's association with Jubal and Curly didn't surprise Jesse, but his casual acceptance of the situation did. Quint should have been bitter toward Slaughter and the others, he should have resented their treatment and opinions and fought them with mockery and contempt. He didn't. Nor did he fawn and attempt to curry favor. Instead, he drifted with the flow, took each day as it came and treated others as if their animosity toward him didn't exist. It infuriated some and frustrated others, but it only baffled Jesse.

The others weren't such a puzzle. Curly Barnes was a barrel-chested man with a mass of beard and a surly temper. He was merciless in battle, though often clumsy, and a poor shot to boot. Barnes was only a marginal asset as a ranger, but he never balked at the dirty work. It was Barnes and Butler who had handled the ropes when Slaughter hung the federal prisoners captured at Cow Creek, but only Butler had staggered off afterward and vomited. Barnes was a trouble-maker and a bully, more tolerated than accepted.

Dan Black was another story. Like Curly, he was a big man and he sported a fair-sized beard, but

Black had an easygoing manner that everyone liked. In the early days, before the weariness of constant riding and scanty sleep had taken its toll, there had been a lot of wrestling around the fires at night, and not too many ever beat Dan. He was quick on his feet, lithe as a cat in fact, but Jesse knew that wasn't what gave him the advantage. Dan fought with his head as much as he did his back, and that made the difference, made the men he fought laugh easily at their own clumsy attempts to best him. A lot of men couldn't have pulled that off—whipping those he wrestled so soundly and then laughing with them about it, but Dan could, and that made a difference too, Jesse knew.

Jesse didn't know Bob Wilkes very well. He was a new man, had joined in August, but he seemed like a steady hand. Wilkes had farmed in Kansas for a spell, but jayhawkers had run them out, and in the running his wife had accidentally pricked her thigh on a pitchfork tine. Wilkes had mentioned that only once, and laughed a little and shook his head, adding that it seemed like such a tiny puncture to die from, but that's what she did, with tetanus.

Using the road made Jesse nervous. From time to time the forest would thin a little on their left, revealing gray skies and a sense of emptiness that he knew would be the Missouri's valley, but the road never led close enough to the bluff for them to see the river itself. Still, Jesse knew the road, knew it was a popular route for those who couldn't afford a steamboat passage, and he couldn't shake the memory of the federal dodger tucked into the *mochilla*'s pouch, with the crude image of his face and its five hundred dollar reward in bold print. He was a wanted man, used to keeping to the backtrails now, and riding in the open tied his stomach in knots. He wasn't alone in his status of course; in fact, both Barnes and Wilkes carried dodgers on themselves for crimes against the Union, as well as ten or fifteen others among the rangers, but it made Jesse edgy, nonetheless.

They rode in an easterly direction for a couple of hours, riding single file mostly, and silent, although now and again someone would drop back or jog forward to exchange a few words. The snow had tapered off until only a few flakes drifted down, but it remained overcast and gloomy, and miserably cold. It seemed to go on forever, the gray and cold and dogged plodding of their horses, so that Curly's sudden whoop of joy startled them all. Looking ahead, past the others, Jesse saw a low, rambling house of stone with a smudge of yellow lamplight glowing in one small, glassed window, like a piece of the sun broken off and fallen here. A roadhouse, Jesse saw.

"All-goddamn-right," Black growled. "Whiskey."

"Whiskey and hot food and a fire to prop my

boots in front of," Wilkes added. "Damn, let's go!"

They rode into the yard and dismounted. Jesse felt stiff from the cold, uncoordinated and awkward as a pup, and he took a minute to stomp some feeling back into his feet—and to unbutton the greatcoat to free the pair of Army revolvers he carried butt-forward in a gunbelt. Most of them carried Armies now, confiscated in the Cow Creek raid, but most of them still carried their old weapons, too; Gray's Walkers were still holstered on the buckskin's saddle, and Jesse carried the Bowie behind the revolver on his left hip.

Quint led them inside, where they paused for a moment to allow their eyes to adjust to the dim light. The place seemed smaller than Jesse would have guessed, with a low ceiling that gave it a cramped, closed-in feeling. There was only one big room, divided into four obvious sections by the furniture placed there. On their left, just upon entering, was a short bar with a row of bottles that gleamed dully in the light on a single shelf behind it. Next to the bar was a kitchen, crowded with a butcher-block table and a big cast-iron cook stove. The dining room was on their right, with three long tables flanked by low benches scarred and gouged by bored patrons with sharp knives. Beyond the dining room, in the far righthand corner, six bunks sagged on rope springs covered by buffalo robes. Folded at the foot of each bunk was a single wool blanket and a thin pillow.

Directly opposite the front door was the biggest fireplace Jesse had ever seen. It was made of stone, like the house, and it arched from a flagstone hearth to a height of nearly five feet and looked as deep as a closet. There was a good-sized fire blazing inside, throwing a yellow, pulsating light across the wavy wooden floor. Except for the small window and a candle lantern behind the bar, the fireplace offered the only light.

There were three people inside when they entered; a short, caved-in man of fifty or so, stubble-cheeked and balding; and a young couple sitting together at the far table, the man tall and well-groomed, the woman dark-haired with a creamy complexion, wearing an expensive traveling outfit of robin-egg blue.

"Welcome, gents," the caved-in man greeted, walking around to the business side of the bar. His gaze lingered on Quint and Barnes, but he didn't show any sign of recognition until Curly shouted, "Silas, you greasy old horse thief, I thought you were going to take a bath this year?"

"Did," the barkeep grinned, exposing half a dozen teeth as black as sin. "Last spring," he added, and laughed.

"I God, it didn't take, and that's a fact," Quint said.

Silas chuckled and pulled a bottle off the shelf. "Drinks?" he asked.

"Goddamn right," Black said, pushing past the others and taking center stage at the bar. Wilkes laughed and joined him, and the others crowded close. Jesse nodded to the couple at the rear of the room, as did Pete and Bob Wilkes, and Curly tipped his hat to the woman, a gesture of politeness canceled by his hungry leer.

"Colder than hell froze over, boys," Silas announced, lining six glasses into a neat row and tipping the bottle. "Weather like this, the first round's on the house."

"Is that supper I smell?" Jesse asked, sniffing.

"That it be," Silas answered. "Fat possum and fritters, and there's nothing better on a day like this."

Possum and fritters. Jesse's mouth began to water. He took the drink Silas offered and said, "Mud," and tossed the whiskey against the back of his throat. It went down like liquid fire, making his eyes tear and his nose run, before settling like molten lead on his empty stomach.

"Christ," Pete choked, setting his drink down and coughing hoarsely.

Silas and Curly laughed, and Silas refilled those glasses that were empty. Custom demanded a second drink that they paid for, and Jesse dug his poke out, wondering what the evening would cost him. He had close to three dollars picked up here and there—patching saddles and shoeing horses for those not handy at the task, but he knew roadhouse prices usually doubled what a man would pay in town.

"Pete," Quint said loudly, but without looking around. "Go put the horses up."

Pete looked surprised and Jesse thought for a moment that he might refuse, and he would have backed him if he had, but then Pete slammed his glass on the bar and stalked out. Barnes chuckled into his glass as the door slammed behind Pete and said, "A kid comes in handy."

"You should have kept yours, Curly, instead of drowning them," Silas said.

Curly chuckled again, louder this time, but didn't reply. Black said, "Pour us another round, Silas, and set out some of that possum, if it's ready. My belly's near rubbed raw against my backbone."

Silas poured and left the bottle to fetch bowls and spoons and half a loaf of hard bread, setting it all out on the table. When Pete returned they sat, and Silas introduced the young couple, Lyle and Ellie Brickman, of St. Louis. Afterward, Ellie sat on the edge of the bunk nearest the fire and brought out some knitting, but Lyle joined Barnes and Wilkes and Black and Jesse and Pete at the bar, while Quint and Silas wandered into the kitchen to talk in hushed tones. Curly tended bar like he was familiar with the job, dropping their dimes into a tin box without hesitation.

"You and Silas must be old friends," Pete said, but Curly ignored him.

Black said, "You're a long way from St. Louis, Mr. Brickman."

It was a question, Jesse knew, one that Brickman could either respond to or let slide, and no hard feelings either way. But Brickman elected to reply.

"My wife and I are on our way to Independence where her uncle is contemplating the disposal of his mill. If conditions permit, I hope to purchase it."

"You'll do well," Black said. "A mill is always a good venture.

"People enjoy their bread," Brickman acknowledged.

"Soldiers, too," Curly added shortly.

Brickman looked momentarily confused, sensing, perhaps, what wasn't yet seen. Then he said, "Yes, I suppose they do."

"You aim to help the soldiers?" Curly prodded. Beside the fireplace, Ellie Brickman looked up.

"I would be happy to contract with the army for milling, provided we buy," Brickman said stiffly. He lifted his glass and sipped daintily. Something was bothering Curly, but Jesse couldn't decide if it was Brickman's city manners, or his wife.

"Which army?" Curly asked bluntly. He seemed to be growing madder by the minute.

Brickman's eyes flashed. "Why, either army,

sir. I'm sure you understand the economics of free enterprise."

"I ain't so sure about that," Curly replied. "But I reckon I know a goddamn carpetbagger when I see one. Do you know what a carpetbagger is, Brickman?"

Brickman didn't answer.

After a moment, Curly went on. "A carpet-bagger is a goddamn thief that talks out of both sides of his mouth."

Brickman's face reddened. "I will have satisfaction for that remark, sir," he whispered in a tight voice.

Curly laughed and downed his drink, set his glass on the bar, and took his next swig straight from the bottle.

"Sir, I demand satisfaction."

"Lyle, no!" Ellie Brickman stood, the knitting spilling from her lap.

Curly let his gaze slide across to the woman, and he deliberately licked his lips. "How long you two been married?" he asked. "Beggin' my pardon, ma'am, but you don't hardly look broke in good yet."

Brickman gasped, reared back. "Now, you filth," he said, and reached inside his coat as if for a weapon.

Ellie screamed and Curly pushed away from the bar, grabbing for his revolver, but he was too slow. So was Brickman. Jesse palmed his revolver and laid the barrel neatly along Brickman's scalp and the dandy dropped to the floor with a little grunt of surprise.

Ellie screamed again and rushed to her husband's side. Curly stared uncomprehendingly for a moment, then lifted his gaze to Jesse, letting it linger only briefly on the still-drawn revolver pointed at his stomach. Then his lips peeled back and he snarled, "I'll kill you for that, Ross."

"No, you won't," Wilkes said tonelessly. He stepped closer to Jesse's side and put his hand on the butt of his revolver. In a wired voice, Pete added, "That goes for me too, Curly."

Curly growled low in his throat and looked at Black. "Well, are you backing 'em too? Will I have to take you all on?"

Black looked at Brickman, lying in a heap on the floor with Ellie sobbing over him. Then Black set his glass down and nodded once.

"Best let it slide for now, Curly," Quint said, coming to the bar. "Silas knows where there's a herd of about twenty Holstein heifers and I figure we ought to get them tonight."

"You go ahead," Curly taunted. "I think I'll stay and have another drink or two. Me and Ellie here." He looked down at the woman's horror-strickened face and grinned.

"Reckon not, Curly," Quint said softly. His thumbs had been hooked behind his gunbelt, but now he let his hands drop close to his revolvers.

"Well goddamn," Curly exploded. "You too?"

"Be a dark night, cloudy as it is," Quint said. "We'll need all the hands we can get."

Wilkes scowled. "Wait a minute, Quint. What are you talking about?"

Curly laughed loudly. "He's talking about driving a herd of cattle back to the caves. You don't want to starve to death this winter, do you, Wilkes?"

"No, but I ain't interested in stealing like a goddamn jayhawker, either."

"Bob's right," Jesse said. "I didn't join the rangers to become a thief."

Below them, in a voice harsh with hatred, Ellie said, "You're all guerrillas, that's all. Just back-woods trash. Wait until I see the United States Army about you! Just you wait!"

Ignoring Ellie's outburst, Quint said, "You wouldn't mind stealing from a copperhead, would you, Bob?"

"Copperhead?" Wilkes grunted. He looked at Jesse. "That puts it in a different light."

Jesse shook his head, but deep down he began to sway. A copperhead was a northerner sympathetic to the South, yet unwilling to take a stand either way. Jesse hated a copperhead worse than a Yankee and didn't know anyone who didn't feel the same way. At least a Yankee stood behind what he believed in.

Ellie rose and backed away, her eyes wide with

disbelief. Looking at Silas, she said, "You can't condone this. These men are outlaws discussing theft. You must fetch a sheriff."

"Ma'am, I ain't putting my nose into my customers' business. If you was smart, you wouldn't either."

"*But you helped them!* You told them about those cattle."

"Idle conversation, Miz Brickman. We was just talking."

"What's a copperhead doing in Missouri?" Black grumbled. He had gone back to his drink, though warily, keeping an eye on Curly.

"An Iowan," Silas said. "Down to buy milk cows but hard luck gave him a late start back. He's got pastures rented all over north of the river, but this one is on the easy side."

"Goddamn, Jesse, I agree with Bob on this," Black said. "A copperhead gets none of my respect."

"What the hell do we care what Ross thinks?" Curly Barnes said. "This ain't his show."

Jesse wavered, steadied. He didn't respect a copperhead either, but he wasn't as convinced as the others that it made theft acceptable.

"That's five for and only you against," Quint said softly.

"I ain't said I'm for it," Pete protested.

"Shut up, kid," Curly said casually. His gaze was on Jesse like a challenge, a dare.

154

With uncharacteristic impatience, Quint said, "Come on, Jesse. It's getting on toward dark. Let's go."

Did it matter, Jesse wondered? Was stealing from a copperhead any different than stealing from federal troops? He looked at Curly, still glaring back at him, and said, "What about it? You want a ruckus?"

Curly laughed, sneered at the revolver that had never wavered from him. "Ross," he said, "someday you will pay for what you did. So will the pilgrim. But not today. Today I'm gonna go steal some cattle." He slammed the bottle on the bar and headed for the door. Quint followed.

"Goddamn," Silas muttered softly. "You guys are a hair-trigger bunch."

"Oh, we ain't so bad," Black replied, grinning. "Now, Ma, she was some when she got mad. I wouldn't want to mess with her, but us boys are just funnin' around some."

Silas laughed, but softly, as if he wasn't really sure if it was a joke or not.

Black looked at Ellie Brickman and tipped his hat. "Ma'am, my name is Dan Black, a soldier in Josiah Slaughter's Company of Missouri Rangers. I ain't got me a dodger what says I'm a genuine outlaw to the North yet, so I'd appreciate you remembering my name to the Yankee officer you report us to."

"You are an animal, Mr. Black, as are your

155

comrades, and you may rest assured that I will report every name I heard tonight to the nearest Union officer."

"Thank you, ma'am," Black said. He briefly eyed the bottle Curly had slammed onto the bar but left it with only a sigh.

On the floor, Lyle Brickman moaned and his head rolled limply to one side. Jesse joined Black at the door, slipping into his heavy coat. They walked outside together, slowly, their eyes searching, but Curly and Quint were leading their horses from the barn and paying them no mind. It was snowing heavily again, bullet-size flakes that danced gently on the breeze, making small tapping sounds on their hats. "Reckon we're lucky to have this snow," Black said. "It'll help hide our trail if it keeps up."

"Yeah," Jesse mumbled, pausing to pull his gloves on. It struck him that he had been a wanted man for about a year now, but tonight was the first time he felt like an outlaw.

CHAPTER 9

It wasn't far to the small, square pasture that held the twenty Holsteins, but it continued to snow heavily all the way, drifting deeply in those spots where the breeze that always followed the river swept without interruption, so it was full dark by the time they arrived. Quint and Curly Barnes made short work of pulling down a section of the low, split-rail fence, and they rode in and made a quick gather, pushing the reluctant heifers back through the fence and edging them south, into the hills.

It snowed most of the night, although the wind eased up as soon as they left the river and there wasn't much drifting. If they had followed a trail they might have made good time, but Quint led them straight into the woods and by morning they hadn't made a dozen miles.

Dawn came with a pearl cast, waxing the rolling hills surrounding them in a light that seemed fake, slashed by a thousand tiny scars that were only tree trunks; in the false light the trunks were all that Jesse could see, the bare, spidery limbs still invisible. It was snowing a little yet, tiny flakes floating out of a gray sky, with maybe a foot on the ground, but it seemed to Jesse that the end might be near. In the east, where the light was already growing and becoming real, the sky seemed higher and only thinly clouded.

It was cold, though, dangerously so. He thought longingly of stopping and building a fire for its warmth but knew he wouldn't, and that the others wouldn't either. They had to push on, goaded by a sense of guilt they couldn't shake.

Cattle thieves, Jesse thought, and wondered what his ma would think of that.

On the south slope of a tall, broad-based hill, Jesse pulled the buckskin away from the herd and halted to watch it pass. It wasn't a tight group—a man couldn't keep a herd close in a woods even in daylight—but they hadn't lost any through the night, which was a pleasant discovery. He could see Harvey Quint up ahead, leading the way; and Wilkes on the far side of the herd, beginning to tighten the gather; and Dan Black and Pete riding drag. But he didn't see Curly anywhere, and he looked twice before letting his fear grow. Pulling the buckskin around, he plowed a path back up the slope to where Black was. Seeing him, Black halted and looked around; he was cursing by the time Jesse joined him.

"Where's Curly?" Jesse asked.

"I don't know," Black said grimly. "But I'd bet my saddle I know where he's heading."

"He's gone to kill the pilgrim," Jesse gritted. "Goddamn that bastard."

"Hell, it ain't the pilgrim he wants," Black replied. "You know it ain't. You saw the way he looked at her."

Jesse knew. He had known all along. But Brickman wasn't a match for Curly; he wouldn't stand a chance, and neither would Ellie. "I'm going back," Jesse said suddenly.

"Can you find your way?" Black asked.

Jesse understood what he meant. They had come north in a storm, had trailed south again under the cover of darkness. Now, in the spreading light, the whole land looked different, bigger and more sprawling in a way that only fresh snow could make a country look.

"I'll find it," Jesse said. He touched the buckskin with his spurs, following the broken trail of the cattle back up the slope and down the far side. Barnes couldn't fly over the land; he'd leave a trail somewhere. Jesse would only have to look sharp.

He cut Curly's sign within half an hour, angling to the west. Within fifteen minutes they dropped onto a narrow, twisting road, but here Curly picked up the pace, and Jesse lifted the buckskin into a trot. The sun was pushing up in the east now, big and brassy, and the clouds began to break apart before it, but there was no warmth in its rays, only a brilliant light. Jesse rode with his face pulled low inside the collar of his coat, his breath fogging his vision, freezing to his mustache and creating a stubble of hoarfrost along the brim of his hat. The sound of snow crunching under the buckskin's hooves was loud in the frozen silence of the woods, and he saw no sign of either fur or feather—not even tracks—and wondered if the wildlife sensed what he couldn't, but looking to the west he saw only high, thin clouds, ripped by the wind, with a pale blue sky beyond.

He kept the buckskin at a steady jog, more lost than not but keeping to the trail and coming, after an hour or so, back to the roadhouse. He wasn't surprised, either by that or to see Curly's horse hitched to the rail out front.

Jesse slowed but didn't stop. He rode forward at a walk, his gaze shifting from the small stable to the house, from there to the woodpile and the forest behind it. Nothing moved, not even Curly's horse, and the thin column of smoke above the chimney seemed motionless in the still air, as if that too had frozen.

Jesse dismounted and looped the reins around the rail. He could dimly hear voices from inside, a deep, masculine voice that he recognized as Curly's, and a woman's sharp cry of objection, severed abruptly. Still, he didn't rush. He shrugged out of his coat and hung it on his saddle horn, then pulled his right-hand revolver and checked the caps, the action; he did the same with the left, then holstered them both. He approached the road-house slowly then, his gaze fixed on the door. He paused a final time on the stoop, drew a deep breath, then lifted the latch and stepped inside.

He'd forgotten the gloom. After the sun's glare the big room seemed as murky as river water. He quickly elbowed the door shut and stepped to one side, breathing shallowly and listening for the telltale clicking of a revolver being cocked. But except for the pop and crackle of the fire, no sound greeted him, and it only took a few seconds for his eyes to adjust.

Curly was there, bent over Lyle Brickman, who was sitting limply on top of the farthest table, his hands bound behind him and his head tipped forward. Silas stood behind the bar with his hands in plain sight, looking frightened. Ellie Brickman sat sprawled on one of the bunks, her dress ripped away from one shoulder to expose a part of her chest. She looked stunned, her eyes big but blank, and even in the dim light from the fire Jesse could see the splash of color across her cheek where Curly had slapped her, and a trio of raw-looking welts where he had ripped away her dress. Yet for all that was obvious, there was something here that didn't make sense. Then Lyle groaned and stirred, his head rolling back and forth, and it all came together.

"Jesus Christ," Jesse croaked. "You were going to make him watch."

Curly straightened and stepped clear of the table. "So what?" he asked belligerently. "They ain't nothing to you."

Jesse thought of Maybelline and flexed his fingers. "No," he said. "I won't let you do it."

"I ain't gonna fart with you, Ross. You want a piece of her, that's fine. Otherwise, turn around and walk out of here."

Jesse took another deep breath, whispered, "No." He wished now that he had kept his revolver in hand before entering, but had hoped vaguely it wouldn't come to this. He had heard of gunfights of course, of fast draws and snap shots, but it wasn't a thing he was really familiar with. Duels were still the more accepted mode of settling an affair honorably, or shotguns from the bushes, if a man didn't stand too tall on honor. So he hadn't worried much about speed when he'd rigged his holsters for a cross-belly draw, opting instead for comfort when riding.

Curly let his hand brush the butt of his revolver. "Goddamn you, Ross, go ahead, then! Go ahead and try your goddamn luck, you meddling sonofabitch!"

Curly's hand dove, then rose, and firelight glinted off the long barrel of his revolver. Time seemed to stand still for Jesse, and his draw seemed slow and incredibly awkward. But in the end, it didn't matter. He was fast enough.

Curly grunted and seemed to draw into himself as his pistol slipped from his fingers and clattered to the floor. He took a half turn and fell sideways into the fireplace, creating an explosion of cherry sparks that soared quickly up the chimney's draft.

Jesse whirled as the sparks still climbed and snapped a second shot at Silas, who had been groping under the bar with his left hand. Silas howled and jerked his right hand back, off the bar, and clutched it to his chest. On the bar, in a small pool of dark blood, his pinky finger jumped once, then lay still.

Jesse had dropped to a crouch when he spun;

now he straightened slowly, anger turning his voice harsh. "You were going to let it happen," he accused. "You were just going to goddamn watch!"

Silas glowered. "Ain't my affair. Man can't defend what's his, he aint' got no business having it."

"Like that finger?" Jesse asked tightly.

"Yeah, like the finger," Silas growled, thrusting the crippled hand toward Jesse.

"Bastard," Jesse muttered, and walked around the far end of the bar without lowering his pistol. Motioning for Silas to step back, he bent and located the short, double-barreled shotgun cradled there in a muleshoe rack. Lifting it, he cocked both barrels and holstered the revolver. "Get him out," Jesse said, jerking his head toward Curly. "Before he starts to stink."

"I want a drink first."

"I said get him out."

Silas studied him for a moment, as if gauging his determination, then shrugged and walked toward the fireplace. Little flames danced along one sleeve of Curly's coat and his hair was singed and the flesh along one cheek was blistered, but he wasn't burning yet, and Silas grabbed his ankles and dragged him into the room. "Now what?" Silas asked, dropping Curly's boots loudly to the floor.

"Untie the pilgrim."

Silas glanced briefly at the woman, curled on

the bed with her face buried in a buffalo robe she'd pulled over her, then went to Brickman's side and fumbled with the knot. Brickman had been maintaining a sort of slumped position, but untied, he began to tip forward and would have fallen if Silas hadn't caught him and laid him back on the table. Walking to the fireplace then, Silas spit into the flames as if to rid his mouth of a bad taste. "Never could abide a pilgrim," he said. "It's like they was born without bark on."

"Let's go bury Curly," Jesse said in sudden weariness. He'd been pushing for several days, through long hours and sapping cold, and he felt so tired now he could hardly keep his eyes open.

"Hell with Curly. I want to doctor my hand," Silas said.

"Okay, go do it." Jesse went and sat at the end of a table, letting the shotgun dip toward the floor.

Silas went behind the bar and took a bottle off the back shelf. He pulled the cork with his teeth and spit it aside, then tipped the bottle and drank in long, deep swallows. Lowering it, he coughed harshly, bent in pain. Catching his breath, he said, "The Lord is a cruel master sometimes, Ross. Was never a man liked his whiskey more, but it works on my belly like a wolf works on a new-born calf anymore."

"You going to bandage that hand?"

"Naw. Whiskey will kill the pain and I'll chew up some 'baccy later that'll draw out the poison."

He lifted the bottle, shook it enticingly. "Want a slug?"

"You ought to sew the flesh back over that stub. It'll look better if you did. Probably heal quicker, too."

"You shot the sonofabitch off, now you gotta worry about how I fix it?"

Jesse shrugged. "I don't guess it matters to me. Did Quint pay you for the cattle?"

The question surprised the old stationkeeper, but he replied. "Quint paid me twenty dollars. That's cheap beef."

Jesse lowered his head and shook it. "That's expensive for stolen cattle."

Silas looked confused. "Didn't you know you was stealing 'em when you left here?"

A whip popped outside, followed by the sound of horses and creaking thoroughbraces, and a driver's gravelly voice whoaing a team. Jesse looked at Silas, who said, "The midnight stage from St. Lou, and I'm surprised they ain't no later than this. Callahan must be handling the lines."

"Callahan a good driver?" Jesse asked for no special reason.

"Callahan's a goddamn fool, otherwise he'd have holed up down the line and not worn good horses to a frazzle bucking last night's storm."

"Well, there ain't any accounting," Jesse said. He pulled the caps off the shotgun and set it aside.

"You leaving?" Silas asked hopefully.

"Reckon. Are you going to bury Curly for me?"

Silas shook his head. "Nope, ground's froze and my finger is starting to throb. Be easier to just wrap him up and send him on to Jeff City for someone else to worry about. Any reward on him, do you know?"

"I never bothered to ask," Jesse replied. It seemed a peculiar conversation, all things considered, and he walked to the door, wanting to put it behind him. "Sorry about the finger," he said.

Silas shrugged without concern. "Could've been my whole hand, I guess."

Jesse didn't know what to say to that, so he just let it drop. He went outside and pulled the door shut after him. In the yard a beefy man was climbing down from the box of a fancy Concord stagecoach. Six matching sorrels blew frosty clouds and stamped nervously, but they were worn too, pulled out. The shotgun was a short, hard-eyed man in a bulky bearskin coat, with bearskin mittens that buttoned to the coat's sleeves. He paused in what he was doing, hugging his short-barreled Greener close, but Jesse only nodded and gathered the buckskin's reins. Curly's horse was still hitched at the rail and Jesse knew he should bring it along, and Curly's guns too, but he was beyond caring now. He was tired and half sick and he'd just killed a man he knew, and all he wanted to do was to go home to the caverns along the Current River and sleep.

He rode back along the trail he'd made coming in, tickling the buckskin's ribs with his spurs and lifting him to a jog. The sun was halfway toward noon now and he could feel its touch on his face, but it didn't warm him. He didn't think the sun would ever warm what was cold inside of him.

CHAPTER 10

Dewey reined the sorrel into a copse of slim birch trees and slid quickly from the saddle, unbooting the heavy Sharps rifle as he did. Down the trail he could still see the soft green of the meadow, carpeted in lavender and blue and yellow flowers that bobbed and swayed in the breeze. He couldn't see the deer from here but he wasn't worried; he had caught only a glimpse of it nibbling at the tender shoots at the lower edge of the meadow before pushing the sorrel into the trees, but he was sure he hadn't spooked it. He glanced behind him, up the trail, for the others— Gil and Pete and the new kid, Tim O'Rourke—but they weren't in sight yet, and he decided to chance a stalk. He moved quickly through the sparse grove, pausing often to look and listen, still distrustful, even this close to winter quarters.

They had been on a scout, the four of them, six days gone and only now returning to the Current River valley. It had felt good to be on the move again, to feel the sorrel clipping smoothly under him while the sun broke the lethargic grip of a wet spring and the land burst suddenly into bloom. But surprisingly, it felt good to be coming back, too. It was as if the caverns along the river had become a home of sort, a place both comfortable and familiar after last year's long, grueling summer.

Dewey slowed as he approached the edge of the woods, dropping to a crouch and advancing from tree to tree. He could see the deer now, a little spike buck more red than brown yet, although he'd be changing soon enough. Lowering the Sharps's breech, Dewey fingered a paper cartridge from the pouch on his belt and slid it into the chamber, trimming the end with his knife to expose the coarse black grains of powder rather than risk alerting the buck by slapping the trigger guard loudly into place and slicing the cartridge that way. He capped the nipple and gently lifted the rifle to his shoulder, sighting carefully and squeezing without pause.

The Sharps bucked and roared; the breeze picked quickly at the heavy veil of powder smoke and swept it away in tatters. At the lower end of the meadow the buck lay on its side, motionless.

Dewey lowered the rifle, satisfied with the

shot, knowing even from here that it had been a clean kill. Done enough, a man got to where he could tell a bad shot from a good one even as he squeezed the trigger.

Fetching the sorrel, he led her across the meadow and hobbled her on good grass. From the trail he had just abandoned he could hear the murmur of conversation, and a short time later Gil and Pete and Tim rode out of the trees and loped toward him.

"How," Gil greeted and, eyeing the deer, smacked his lips. "Liver tonight, by God. Wish we had us some onions to go with it."

"And fry bread," Tim added.

Next to Pete, Tim was probably the youngest man rangering with Slaughter. He was sixteen—or sixteen and a half as he occasionally emphasized —slim and wiry with straight blond hair and blazing blue eyes and a kind of cockiness that never became overbearing. Tim had wandered in out of an April downpour, soaked all the way through and near starved, toting a heavy single-shot muzzleloading pistol and a squirrel rifle almost as tall as he was, but with an empty powder flask. He hadn't made much of an impression, Dewey knew, but Slaughter talked with him for a while and fed him and the next day took him to Howes Mill and traded the rifle and pistol for a good filly only green broke. Dewey knew the kid had been disappointed in receiving a rank horse, but there had been a certain logic to Slaughter's choice of horses too; the whole company had taken them both under their wings, helping Tim with the filly and the Colt Armies the Colonel had issued him.

"I'm about half-starved for a good venison steak and fry bread toasted on a grill," Tim said. "Beef's too greasy for my taste."

Gil grunted, affecting a pained expression. "That sounds like a stump-puller talking to me."

Tim grinned and ducked his head. "Yeah, I reckon," he said, then reached out suddenly and flipped Gil's hat off.

Dewey grinned and pulled his belt knife. With Pete's help he quickly skinned and butchered the small buck, while Gil and Tim lounged in the grass nearby and exchanged friendly barbs. Dewey was wiping his knife clean in the grass when a small sound reached his ears, a clank, as of metal against metal, and Dewey's heart began to beat a little faster. Gil sat up, scowling, and Pete stood and walked quickly to his horse.

"Riders," Gil said, and scrambled to his feet. Dewey belted his knife and began to drift toward the sorrel. A tic jumped in his cheek. "A bunch of 'em," Gil added.

Looking confused, Tim stood and looked toward the far end of the meadow. "What's that rattling?" he asked.

"Get your horse," Gil said stiffly.

Dewey could see movement in the trees now, the splotchy colors of horses and dark Yankee blue. "Federals," he breathed, and bent swiftly to pull the hobbles off the sorrel.

The soldiers came out of the woods in haphazard formation, gathering in a group that continued to grow. Less than two hundred yards, Dewey thought desperately, but so far none had drawn a weapon.

"They don't know who we are yet," Gil said.

"They will if we make a run for it," Pete replied.

"They will soon enough whether we make a run for it or not," Dewey added. He stood beside the sorrel, ready to swing aboard if necessary, but not wanting to rush the Yankees' response either. They were in a sort of stand-off now, but balanced precariously.

Pete was mounted and Gil and Dewey stood ready, but Tim was fumbling with his hobbles, the filly shuffling uncooperatively. About fifty Union troopers had gathered at the far end of the meadow by now, with more straggling in all the time, but the only officer Dewey could see was a lieutenant.

"Cut the goddamn hobbles," Gil ordered. "They're coming."

Across the meadow the knot of soldiers began to break apart, spreading, flowing. Here and there among them Dewey could see a carbine or drawn revolver, and he glanced anxiously at

Tim just as he sliced through the rawhide hobbles.

"Let's go," Dewey barked, grabbing the horn and swinging into the saddle. Gil and Tom followed, and Pete snagged a revolver and tried a far shot.

A ragged volley answered and Dewey heard the dry rattle of lead among the limbs behind them. Pete's horse whinnied shrilly, rearing and throwing its head before collapsing in a heap.

Gil had already spurred his bay toward the woods and Tim was close behind him. Neither saw Pete's horse fall, nor heard his choking cry.

Dewey forced the sorrel close. Pete climbed to his knees, pulling his second revolver; he began firing rapidly toward the advancing cavalry.

"Get up, Pete," Dewey shouted, kicking his boot free of the near stirrup. He was firing too, but on the plunging sorrel his shots were all going wild.

"Get out of here," Pete yelled. "Go on, before it's too late."

"Pete!"

One hundred yards now, then seventy-five. The air was thick with buzzing lead. A bullet nicked the brim of Dewey's hat, another clipped the sorrel's mane. Sixty yards then, and the lieutenant's mount stumbled and fell; a sergeant pulled his horse aside, forcing the others to give way too, and a private on the other side began to swing wide. On one knee now, Pete screamed in wild delight. "Come on, you Yankee bastards! Come and get a bellyful of Confederate lead!"

The wedge started with the lieutenant's horse began to grow, their advance to falter. Dewey could hear firing behind him now and knew that Gil and Tim had returned, adding four more revolvers to the fight. Dewey's sorrel lunged past Pete and he forced her back with his spurs. Pete saw him coming and holstered a revolver, grabbing the saddle horn as the sorrel passed and letting the momentum pull him up behind Dewey.

"Hang on," Dewey shouted grimly, and now he spurred for the timber, though swinging wide so that he wouldn't interfere with Gil's and Tim's covering fire. They were almost into the trees when Pete suddenly grunted and jerked forward.

"I'm hit," Pete said with a touch of surprise, and Dewey looked back just as he belched a splatter of bright blood over Dewey's shoulder.

Dewey couldn't stop, he couldn't even slow down. He forced the sorrel into the trees and cut toward dense timber, hoping to throw pursuit that way. He could still hear Gil and Tim firing, but he had a wounded man now, and only one horse; he had to keep going.

He came to a trail after a while, narrow and twisting, little more than a trace, but he put the sorrel onto it and let her have her head, picking her own path over the fallen logs and slanting trees. Alone, Dewey might have stayed with the path. The sorrel was fleet and sure-footed and he didn't weigh enough to give her any trouble, but Pete clung to the cantle like a sack of oats, swaying and lurching, all but dead weight. Dewey tried to call to him once but Pete didn't answer and Dewey couldn't look back—the path was too treacherous for that, so as soon as he could he slowed the mare and struck off toward a low saddle in the east. On the far side, in a sort of hollow, Dewey finally halted.

With their flight stopped, Pete leaned forward until his head was resting against Dewey's shoulder. Dewey tried to twist around to see him but Pete was too close. He said, "Pete, can you hear me? How bad is it?"

When he didn't reply Dewey lifted a leg over the horn and slid to the ground. The sorrel sidled away and Pete swayed and tumbled limply into Dewey's arms. Dewey pulled him a few feet away from the sorrel and laid him out upon a bed of sweet-smelling honeysuckle. Pulling his hand away, his mouth tightened at the smear of blood and the pink froth of a lung shot.

"Pete, can you hear me?" Dewey asked gently.

Dewey leaned close, putting his ear close to Pete's mouth, but all he heard was the shallow rattle of his breath. Dewey sighed and leaned back, looking around at the dense, shadowed forest. Nothing showed, not even a trail now. He wondered how far behind the Yankees were, and if they still followed. He couldn't hole up here for long, he knew; a lung shot wasn't always fatal but it would be if he didn't get Pete some help quick.

A branch cracked on Dewey's right and he swung in that direction and put his hand on his revolver. His gaze searched the thick brush and probed among the trees but he couldn't see anything. It might have been a squirrel, he knew, or even a deer, but he didn't think so. An uneasy silence hung over the forest and he stood slowly, pulling his pistol but keeping the muzzle aimed at the ground.

"Who's there?" he called. "Speak up, or my pistol will."

Crackling laughter soared among the treetops, startling a flock of blackbirds into flight, echoing, but sourceless.

Dewey fought a shudder, cocked his revolver. "Show yourself," he demanded.

Silence now, like a shroud, and then a chill did pass through his body and raise the hair along the back of his neck. From the corner of his eye he saw the sorrel watching a clump of huckleberry about twenty-five yards away. "I didn't come to fight, but I will if I'm forced to it," Dewey called.

After that the silence seemed even deeper, but it was short-lived. "Reckon ye'd make b'ar bait was ye ta try," a shrill yet masculine voice cracked. "Want me ta shoot ye now? Huh? Do ye?"

Dewey took a deep breath and weighed his reply. Then he said, "I'd rather you helped me with my friend. He's hurt pretty bad."

"Why should I?" the voice demanded.

Gambling, Dewey replied, "Because there's about fifty Yankee soldiers looking for him, and if they find him they'll find you."

"Won't!" The single word came clipped, defiant, and the hair along Dewey's neck refused to go down. The man was touched, a crazy like some Dewey had seen wandering the streets of New Orleans, talking with God or Satan or George Washington. A wrong move could set him off, and Dewey didn't doubt that he had a rifle; it was a rare man in Missouri that didn't carry a weapon. But that didn't change anything, it didn't shake the Yankees from their trail. Crazy or not, Dewey needed help.

"I want you to hide my friend," Dewey called. "I want you to hide him so the Yankees can't find him."

"What be in it fer me? Huh?"

"What do you want?"

"A thousand dollars and a white mule." The demand came without hesitation, as if he'd been sitting there all spring waiting for someone sick or wounded to fall in front of him and ask the price for doctoring.

"I haven't got a thousand dollars," Dewey answered. He thought he was probably wasting his time, but he couldn't just turn his back on the man, not without risking a bullet in it, and he thought there was a good chance the man lived with someone who might be more reasonable.

"What 'ave ye then?" the crazy snapped.

"About five dollars and a good Sharps rifle that throws center to four hundred yards."

"One of them new-fangled breech-loaders?"

"Yes. It's in the scabbard on the far side of my horse. It's yours if you can take my friend to someone who can help him and hide him."

"Don't want it," the crazy snapped. "Got ol' Centerpunch here, and she be good enough fer me."

"My friend needs help." Dewey didn't know what else to say, could imagine himself standing at this same place tomorrow, pursuing the same argument.

The leaves on the huckleberry stirred as if touched by an unfelt breeze, and an old man slowly uncoiled from its center, white-haired and stoop-shouldered, one cheek bulging with a wad of tobacco. He held a long, slim muzzleloader casually in one gnarled hand, aimed only imprecisely at Dewey. "Do it fer two dollars, I will," the old man cracked. "That what a fancy whore up to St. Louie still costin'?"

"Yes," Dewey replied, feeling a kind of relief now that he could actually see who he was talking to. He didn't know what the price of a prostitute in St. Louis was but doubted if it really mattered.

"Put the money on the boy's chest where I kin see it," the old man instructed. "I'll see he be gettin' better, I will. Or beeried, whichever needs be."

Dewey frowned. "I want to come along and see where you take him. I'm not going to just walk—"

"*No!* Ye can't and I twon't be havin' it. He'll live or die whether ye know of it or not, but I don't want me no strangers a tromping in my woods, I don't. Now leave ye that money and get on with ye. Get, now."

Dewey felt trapped, started to refuse, paused when a voice came faintly along his backtrail, the words unintelligible, but eager.

The old man grinned. "Best ye be a humpin' it, sonny, 'fore those soldier boys ketch up."

"How can I find you?" Dewey persisted.

"Ye can't. Not if I don't want to be found. Now get, 'fore I decide ta just leave him fer the Yankees. I will, too, ye don't be forkin' that red hoss of yers."

Dewey didn't have any choice. He dug two silver dollars from his poke and laid them on the ground next to Pete's head. "I'll be back," he promised grimly, but didn't know if Pete could hear him or not. Swinging onto the sorrel, Dewey turned her south, creating quite a racket through the brush and trees in an attempt to draw the trailing Federals away from Pete and the old man. It didn't seem like much, as long as he'd known Pete. It didn't seem like much at all.

There had been a narrow path along the base of the cliffs that held the four big caverns where Slaughter had bivouacked his men for the winter, but constant traffic had broadened it, hardening the spring mud into a solid, lumpy road.

Gil pushed the bay at a lope. He could see patches of the Current River on his right, tinged with silver by the afternoon sun, and the silhouette of rangers here and there, working with their horses or fishing or just loafing in the unaccustomed warmth. Horses on short picket lines cropped the new grass hungrily, and perched atop the fallen slabs of chalky stone along the face of the cliff, men repaired gear or cleaned their weapons. There was a kind of harmony to life here that they all recognized, Gil thought; he hated to bear the news that would end it.

The Colonel had abandoned his marquee last summer but had rigged a canvas shelter inside the largest cavern as a sort of field office. Gil rode there first, forcing the bay up the gentle incline and straight to the Colonel's shelter. There was always a little knot of men around the shelter— officers and orderlies and such—and Gil pushed through without dismounting, calling loudly.

Slaughter stepped out immediately, his cold gray eyes snapping. "Yes, what is it, Banks?"

"Federals, Colonel. About fifty or sixty cavalry jumped us four or five miles back. Seems like they were heading this way."

"Seems like?"

"They was."

"And the rest of your journey?"

"Ain't seen nary a uniform until today."

"Where's Lieutenant Harker?"

There had been quite a few promotions since Cow Creek, but they hadn't really changed anything; Gil still called Dewey Sarge, as did most of the others.

"Couldn't rightly say, Colonel. We got separated and me and Tim run a pretty jagged course coming back, hoping to throw our trail if possible. I was hoping he'd be here by now."

Slaughter looked grim. Calling to Borden—promoted to Major, if anyone cared—he said, "This could be a planned raid, James. Federal forces couldn't ignore us much longer. If that's true, they'll follow. I want you to keep them off our backs for an hour. Give us that long. I'll send Banks and O'Rourke along as scouts. We'll rendezvous at Howes Mill, as planned. Understood?"

"Yes sir," Borden replied, and turning, grabbed the arm of an orderly. "Go find Miles and have him back here within two minutes."

"Yes sir," the orderly said, scampering out of the cavern at a run.

The Colonel was barking quick orders to those around him, and orderlies and officers were scurrying away from the shelter like ants. Gil pulled the bay away from the confusion and rode to the base of the incline where Tim waited, bug-eyed at the spreading excitement, his filly high-headed and blowing.

"I guess the fat is in the fire now, huh?" Tim asked.

Gil nodded and quickly related the Colonel's instructions to accompany Borden back to engage to Yankees. Tim nodded once and licked at lips suddenly gone dry. Gil knew the feeling, but he lounged back and put his elbow against the bay's rump and cocked his leg around the saddle horn as if he were only waiting for some of the boys to go fishing. It amused him to no end that everyone thought of him as such a cool customer. He could never understand what blinded them to the facade of his courage when it was so plain to him. He knew of course that his reputation had been built upon Cow Creek, and that was funny too, that they hadn't seen that the bay had bolted forward on her own. Sometimes he thought it was a good thing; had he not been in the lead there they would have seen his fear and known him for what he really was.

Gil had never felt fear in Kansas, hadn't felt much of anything in fact, but he'd picked up a heap of it after coming to Missouri, and his biggest fear of all was that someday he'd let it all show. He could remember a hog butchering he'd seen as a boy, his first, he thought. It was a spotty memory, nearly erased by time now, but the way the intestines had spilled onto the ground when they'd slit its belly was still vivid in his mind. That was the way he sometimes envisioned his fears revealing themselves someday, just spilling into the open for everyone to see.

A rider appeared from downtrail and Gil felt a surge of relief at seeing Jesse on the big buckskin. He had thought he and Tim might have to scout alone for Borden, and the prospect frightened him. They'd only seen fifty or sixty troopers, but something inside told Gil that there had been a lot more still in the woods.

"How, Gil," Jesse said, pulling the buckskin down beside his bay. Coming close to Tim's gray, the buckskin lunged without warning, his yellow teeth sliding off the filly's hip with a sharp *pop* and exposing a patch of bare, pink flesh. "God-damn you," Jesse hollered, and pulling his hat off, slapped the buckskin between the ears. Wasted effort, Gil thought; there was a streak of meanness in the buckskin that punishment would never cure.

Tim's filly squealed and jumped sideways, but Tim reined her back without trouble. He glared at the buckskin as if he wanted to kill him.

"You hear?" Gil asked.

Jesse nodded. "Where's Dewey?" he asked.

"I don't know. Pete's horse was shot from under him, and he and Sarge took off for the trees riding double. Me and Tim came on back."

"My horse," Tim said accusingly, shifting his glare to Jesse.

"Are you taking Borden out?" Jesse asked.

"Me and Tim. Come along."

Jesse shook his head. "Slaughter wants me to scout the back door. I think the old bastard's afraid it might be a trap."

"There's a chance," Gil agreed, and felt his stomach lurch. He hated himself for his fear but didn't know of any way to quell it.

"Seen Dan Black or Bob Wilkes?" Jesse asked. "I want someone to ride with me."

"Ain't seen either one," Gil answered.

"Your goddamn horse bit my filly," Tim persisted.

Jesse just grinned. "Yeah, he's bad about that." To Gil, he said, "Gotta ride, pard. Watch yourself."

Gil gave him a small wave and watched him ride away. He could remember when Jesse had been as green as Tim was now, but he couldn't ever remember Jesse looking frightened. It was what he admired about him most, the ability to ride calmly into danger.

"I hate that damn buckskin," Tim said.

Gil didn't reply. He was watching Ted Miles assemble Borden's command of twenty-odd riders in front of the farthest cavern now. He could dimly hear the bark of Miles's orders, the hoots and jeers of those who good-naturedly resisted. They were looking forward to the coming battle, Gil realized sinkingly, were anxious to grapple with the enemy again.

"Ready, Banks?"

Gil turned and straightened in the saddle. Borden sat his horse a few feet away. "Anytime," Gil said.

But Borden didn't push on past. He stared at his small command for a moment, short and stout and worried-looking, a frayed cigar gone cold in the corner of his mouth. He said, "What are we facing, Banks? Is this only Federal luck, or have we stayed here too long?"

"Hard to say," Gil replied. He had wondered the same thing on the ride back.

"You know what I think?" Borden asked. "I think they jumped the gun, running into you boys. I think we've stayed too long and now they've slipped a noose around our necks. That's what I'm thinking."

"Could be," Gil replied nonchalantly. That thought had also crossed his mind. He hadn't realized until today how vulnerable their position here was. Crowded between the river on one side and the steep, passageless bluffs on the other, there were only two ways out. It made their camp an easy bottle to plug.

"Yeah, could be," Borden said darkly. "Well, you know what to do, Banks. You and O'Rourke swing into it. We'll be close behind."

Gil watched Borden ride away, then looked at Tim and forced a grin. "Let's go, partner. It looks like summer is about to commence."

CHAPTER 11

From time to time as Jesse loped south along the river trail he would throw a longing glance toward the bald knob on the opposite side of the river and wonder what a view from its crest would show him. They called the knob Eagle's Nest, although no actual nest existed there, and Jesse had climbed it a time or two over the past winter and knew a man could see a good little piece from it. But it was on the west bank of the Current and he was on the east bank, and he wouldn't ford the river now, not with the possibility of Yankee snipers about.

There were two trails leading away from winter quarters, one going north and the other south, both keeping close to the river, but the one going south forked about a mile below the caverns, and that was the one Slaughter wanted Jesse and Dan Black to scout. But upon reaching it, Jesse halted unexpectedly.

Black came up from behind. "What's wrong?" he asked.

Jesse shook his head. "I don't know," he said with honest confusion. He looked down the branch trail, scanning the dense border of trees, then lifted his gaze to the steep hills where the trail led, the jumbled end of the sharp bluffs that housed the caverns. He saw thick forest freshly green and here and there the dark bark of a tree trunk, or a sunny patch of grassy hillside, but nothing threatened and the buckskin pawed impatiently at the ground.

"Hear something?" Black asked.

Jesse shook his head. Birds sang in the woods and behind them the river murmured softly, but that was all.

"Hell's getting ready to break loose back there," Black growled suddenly, urging his horse past Jesse. "We can't sit here forever."

The far-off *crack* of a rifle surprised them both. Jesse eased some in his saddle, sliding a hand down to the butt of a Walker. Frowning, he said, "Where'd that come from?"

Black looked at him bewilderedly, his face oddly pale, and said, "I been hit, Jesse," then crumbled, slipping off the near side of his horse.

Jesse jumped off the buckskin. Another *crack,* from the northeast, and this time he saw the puff of powder smoke from the branches of a tall, sprawling hickory about halfway up a hill several hundred yards away. The bullet kicked up dust in the trail a couple of yards away and ricocheted into the low bushes beside the trail. Jesse bent over Black, rolling him onto his back. Black's eyes rolled and came slowly into focus. "Goddamn," he whispered, dragging the word out.

"Where you hit, Dan?"

Black shut his eyes. "Inside. Feels like I'm on fire inside."

Another bullet whined overhead and smacked into a nearby tree trunk, and the buckskin snorted nervously.

"Can you ride?" Jesse asked.

Black grunted an affirmative. "Just get me on my horse," he said.

Black's horse had danced off some distance, head high and nostrils wide, with only the buckskin's marginal calmness to keep him from spooking completely. Jesse approached slowly, swore gently as the horse backed away, but kept after it, whispering sweetly of his disgust with the animal's foolishness. Catching a rein, he hauled the horse back to Black's side and helped him stand. Another bullet whistled close by, cutting a tiny path through the brush, then a fifth kicked up dirt close to Black's horse just as Jesse was boosting him into the saddle. For a moment Jesse thought the horse might bolt, but Black tightened his grip on the rein and spoke sharply and the horse settled down. With Black mounted, Jesse quickly swung onto the buckskin. But he paused before turning away, staring grimly at the green hillside where the tall hickory stood. Slaughter had been right, it seemed. The Yankees had slammed the back door in their faces.

Gunfire broke out in the north, sporadic at first, but waxing steadily. Slaughter seemed to flinch at the first scattered reports, his eyes flitting quickly to the cavern's mouth, then back, astir with something unfamiliar. Uncertainty, Jesse realized with a start. He had never seen that there before, had never known Slaughter to hesitate or question, and was surprised to discover that seeing it there now was a blow to his own confidence. Somehow, it had never occurred to Jesse that even Slaughter sometimes doubted.

But it was a brief thing—the uncertainty—there and gone, and Jesse's own relief was immediate. He remembered the look on Black's face when they'd first come in and Eli Davis, now a lieutenant in Prescott's command, had announced the wound was serious but far from fatal. That's how Jesse felt now, the way Black had looked when he found out he wasn't going to die.

Slaughter suddenly lifted a pair of yellow calfskin gloves and brought them down loudly against his thigh, his eyes snapping with a decision made, his face set with determination. To

Prescott, standing nearby, he said, "Charlie, we're going north."

"To relieve Major Borden?"

"Yes, and then on through. I'm convinced Union troops have set up an ambuscade on the trails south of us, and that only a token force advances from the north."

Prescott looked doubtful, but he nodded obediently. "How soon?" he asked.

"Immediately. Have Sergeant Boone detail some men to care for Black and whatever wounded Borden may have suffered."

"Yes sir," Prescott said, and turned to his tasks.

"Bring my horse," Slaughter curtly ordered an aide.

"Yes sir," the orderly replied, hurrying away.

Alone with Jesse, Slaughter regarded him silently for a moment, then said, "Your opinion, scout?"

Jesse was taken aback by the question. Slaughter had never asked for his opinion before, only the facts, and Jesse remembered once more the uncertainty he had seen deep within the Colonel's eyes. "Reckon it's a gamble either way," Jesse replied vaguely.

"Aptly put," Slaughter replied, as if pleased with Jesse's answer. "There are hardly enough facts known to assess the odds of either direction, but I don't believe an experienced sniper would miss so often with so many shots. I think it was a ploy, Ross, a trick to halt your advance without scaring you away. Do you agree?"

Jesse shrugged. He saw a lot of holes in Slaughter's theory, but had no better explanation. He had told Slaughter it was a gamble either way, but he only now began to realize how much of a gamble it really was.

At the cavern's entrance the orderly appeared leading Slaughter's big gray, riding a shaggy mount of his own, and beyond him Prescott's forty-plus men were climbing eagerly into their saddles, anxious for the coming fray. In the north the rattle of gunfire seemed to swell and draw closer, as if Borden had begun his retreat. Sighing, Slaughter said, "Well, Ross, shall we ride to battle?"

They walked to the cavern's entrance and Jesse stepped into the saddle. Slaughter was like a rock again, a keen-edged bastard, and riding close, he ordered crisply, "Take one man and ride ahead, Ross. Set a brisk pace."

Jesse nodded and glanced at the front rank of men, settling finally on Harvey Quint. Jesse didn't care much for Quint, had changed his opinion after the incident at the roadhouse, which he somehow felt was Quint's doing, but he knew Quint was a good man on the trail, probably more qualified than he was. "What about it, Quint?" Jesse asked. "Feel up to it?"

"Born to it," Quint said dispassionately.

Wheeling, Jesse put the buckskin into a lope along the sun-dappled trail, leaving his own doubt and worry at the caverns, feeling in its place a cleansing sense of anticipation. For Jesse, there was a simplicity in battle he had never found elsewhere, a purity, so to speak, in its basic element. Gone, then, were all the trappings of civilized life, the fears and uncertainties and the dizzying array of choices that could turn a man old quicker than any battlefield. In battle a man soon discovered his true worth, Jesse thought, and he either became better for the knowledge, or worse. Riding swiftly toward an approaching enemy, Jesse could forget the qualms he'd felt at seeing Slaughter's own doubts and concentrate solely upon the coming fight.

The crackle of gunfire became louder as they drew closer, but broken by long moments of silence now, and he thought Borden must have begun his retreat in earnest. Slaughter had asked for an hour, Jesse knew, and Borden had given him that.

Rounding a bend about half a mile north of the caverns, Jesse spotted a lone rider galloping down the trail, and he pulled the buckskin to a halt and palmed a revolver. Then he grinned widely, and Quint, who had halted behind him, grunted and said, "I figured he was dead."

"Huh, not likely," Jesse replied. He holstered his pistol and rode forward at a walk, meeting Dewey in the middle of the trail. "How," he greeted.

"Jesse," Dewey said, and nodded to Quint. "Where're you bound for?"

"North. The Colonel thinks the Yankees have set a trap to the south, and he aims to bull right through whatever is coming from your direction."

Dewey swore, looking past Jesse to where Slaughter had suddenly appeared along the trail, followed closely by Prescott and his forty. "There's a heap of Yankees north of us yet," Dewey said worriedly. "Woods are full of them."

Slaughter halted the Rangers some distance back and quickly trotted forward alone. Relief was clear on his face when he recognized Dewey, which gave Jesse something else to wonder about. Until today he couldn't remember ever seeing much more than anger on Slaughter's face.

"Lieutenant," Slaughter greeted. "I'm glad you found your way back."

Dewey nodded, said, "I'm surprised to see you, Colonel. Borden thought you were riding south."

"We go north, Lieutenant. Down the throat of the federal cavalry. Surprise and chaos will open our path."

"Colonel, there's more than just a squad of cavalry out there," Dewey replied urgently. "Me and Gil Banks scouted them some and there's at least four hundred regulars coming down this trail."

Jesse's mouth went dry and Quint swore in awe.

"Infantry?" Slaughter asked.

"Yes sir."

"And their position now?"

"Marching, Colonel. Major Borden has engaged an advance of cavalry and is falling back from them. There's near about eighty horse soldiers to his twenty."

Slaughter nodded, his eyes bright. "Then they won't expect an attack. Surprise and confusion will still open that trail, Lieutenant."

"Lord, Colonel, there's foot soldiers strung out for a mile, and supply wagons bringing up the rear. The trail is blocked."

"So are the trails to the south of us," Slaughter snapped. "Unless you can suggest an alternate route, Lieutenant, we have no choice but to go on."

Jesse looked at Slaughter but held his tongue. Dewey had estimated nearly five hundred Union troops on the trail ahead of them, yet they had no proof of anything more than a solitary rifleman to the south, and a poor shot at that. It would be the bitterest irony if Slaughter were wrong, Jesse knew, if it had been no more than a bounty hunter perched alone in the hickory and the trail was open.

Dewey shook his head. "We're fair bottled, Colonel, unless we can build stairs up these bluffs or a bridge across the river."

Slaughter's smile was wry. "Hardly, Lieutenant.

We shall proceed northward then. Take Quint with you, locate Major Borden and inform him of my intentions. I'll want him to bring up the rear as soon as we open a corridor. Have him ready what wounded he has along the trail. It will be a reckless dash forward and we won't have time to spare for any man who falls."

Dewey nodded glumly and turned away. Quint followed. Slaughter watched them out of sight, then looked at Jesse. "You are familiar with the terrain north of here?"

"Some," Jesse said.

"I'll want you at my side then, Ross. Once we break through we'll have to ride hard and fast to lose pursuit."

Jesse nodded.

Slaughter twisted in the saddle and called to Prescott. "We shall engage the enemy within the quarter hour, Major. Prepare your men."

Prescott nodded and returned a dour salute. Jesse knotted the buckskin's reins and dropped them against the gelding's neck. He drew both Walkers and checked the caps. Then he looked at Slaughter, who was slipping a spare revolver into the waistband of his trousers. Meeting his stare, Slaughter smiled gently and said, "Take us to battle, scout."

CHAPTER 12

For two weeks the rain fell steadily, sometimes in slanting sheets that tried to bowl a man from his saddle, and at other times in a drizzle so fine it was more felt than seen. But it never stopped. Day and night it fell from low, slate-colored clouds, warm at first, but then chilling as it soaked through a man's clothing or saturated his boots until they felt as heavy as lead. It put a thin coat of rust over weapons that were forever needing cleaning, and permeated bedrolls until sleep became impossible. Dry wood disappeared and when a fire was struck it was a miserable thing, smoky and with little heat.

But despite all that, Dewey welcomed the rain. It closed the world down, making it smaller and easier to manage, shutting out the searching eyes of Union scouts and washing away the indented trace of their passage. With the June rains came the first peace Slaughter's rangers had known since the raid on their winter quarters more than a month before, and it was the peace that Dewey was grateful for.

It turned out that Slaughter had been right about the Federals splitting before them. They had done that readily enough, but the battle along the Current River had been only a temporary victory. Union cavalry followed, and now the slim strands of telegraph lines also became their enemy. Slaughter had led them toward Rolla with the intention of striking whatever federal forces they found there, but the Federals struck first, inter-cepting them about thirty miles south of their destination and bending their course to the east, straight into a third cavalry unit. They'd gone south for a while then, skirmished with those regulars that had attempted to lock them beside the Current, then swung back to the northeast. Luck had eased them past a fourth cavalry unit sweeping down from St. Louis.

Overwhelmed at last, Slaughter had driven due east, to a point just north of Chester, Illinois, with the intent of driving straight across that state and into Kentucky, before circling back to Missouri. But the ferry at Chester had fallen into federal control, and there weren't any others available.

For a while then, with their backs to the mile-wide Mississippi, things had seemed as desperate as they ever had before. Slaughter kept Dewey and Jesse and Gil and Tim O'Rourke in the saddle almost constantly, reconnoitering at least four advancing troops of cavalry, with a company of infantrymen bringing up the rear. Some of the men had wanted to build rafts, Dewey knew, but Slaughter had become abruptly leery of Illinois.

He suspected a trap, he claimed, and refused to cross.

"It's the damn telegraph," Slaughter had muttered once, sitting their wearied mounts atop a small hill overlooking the Mississippi. "It would take at least twenty-four hours to construct the rafts we'd need to cross a river this size, and by that time they could have troops waiting for us there."

On the far side of the river Dewey could see the road leading south to Chester, a straight scar across green fields of corn and hay, but empty. Still, it was possible. There was a ferry to the north of them yet, at Ste. Genevieve, that gave Slaughter's worries merit. But the alternative had been a headlong rush straight at the enemy, a tactic Dewey wasn't convinced would work twice.

But Slaughter disagreed. "That is precisely why it will work," he'd argued.

It had, too, but not without casualties. Three dead and six wounded, two of them seriously, and the Federals had dogged them since.

Their route back toward the Ozark's interior had been erratic, a sinuous course between rolling hills and through tangled bottoms as wild as swamps, dodging towns and roads and, when possible, small Yankee patrols. On the run, Slaughter had given up the offensive. They needed food badly, and medicine and time to rest their stock and repair their equipment. They needed rest themselves, too; by then it had only been about three weeks since they'd left winter quarters, but there hadn't been much letup in that time and most of the men looked half dead from fatigue. Near Sikestown the two men most seriously wounded on their flight from the Mississippi's shore died, and some grumbled that death wasn't so far away for them all now. But that night it had clouded over and the next day it began to rain. Shortly after, they had finally shaken their pursuers.

Still in retreat, Slaughter led them slowly into Arkansas, to a long, narrow meadow along the Eleven Point River, where they set up a crude camp. Here, he fanned parties out in search of food, gunpowder, and supplies. The wounded were taken to a nearby farm and loaded into a wagon to be taken to Jonesboro for care. And he sent Dewey and Jesse and Gil and Tim back into Missouri. "Copeland should be in Poplar Bluff by now," Slaughter said in a wasted voice. "Either there or on his way to Rolla. Find him. Find out what the hell's going on."

Dewey didn't ask how he knew Copeland would be in Poplar Bluff. Slaughter wouldn't have told him anyway. Somehow, the Colonel had put together a network of informers that only he knew the whole of, which was maybe as it should have been. Dewey got his horse and went to find the others.

That was two days ago, and now they rode out of the dark, dripping forest and halted their horses in the middle of the road, staring down the long hill into town. Lamplight gleamed from opened windows and doors, spilling like rumpled yellow sheets onto the muddy street, and horses stood with drooping heads at the hitchrails in front of a solitary saloon. The only traffic Dewey saw was a mule cart climbing the road toward them, flanked by a squat, slope-shouldered man lost in the billowing folds of an oilcloth slicker, leading the mule on a short rope. He could faintly hear the tinny music of a player piano and now and again the coarse shout of a drinker, but that was all. Not even a barking dog added its mournful voice to the lonely sounds of the saloon.

"It doesn't look like much, does it?" Tim observed. He sounded almost disappointed, Dewey thought, and wondered what he'd expected.

"That's the Timberman Saloon," Gil said. "Some say the Timberman has the best whores outside St. Louis, but its a monied place, not for the likes of a peddler. Best place to try is the Bucket of Blood Saloon, near the river."

Dewey laughed. "You sound like an official guide," he said.

"Hell, we used to freight into the Bluff all the time," Gil said.

"Good enough for me," Dewey said. "Lead the way."

They started down the muddy road with Gil in the lead. As they approached the cart the man leading the mule forced it to the side of the road and stopped to let them pass. As they drew closer Dewey saw that he was an elderly black man, broad-faced and wrinkled, with cottony hair kinked out from beneath a cheap wool felt hat. Dewey nodded as he passed, then suddenly jerked on the sorrel's reins, bringing her sharply around. The old man looked up, wide-eyed and frightened, and took a shorter grip on the mule's lead. Dewey stared into the old face, filtered by the dusky light, and whispered, "George," with his voice snagging in his throat. "Dancing George? Is that you?"

The old black man slowly shook his head. "No, Mister. My name's Ward."

Dewey settled back, taking a deep breath and letting it free. The voice was wrong, too high-pitched and drawling; he remembered the gravel of Dancing George's old, timeworn voice, and the way the words had seemed to rumble up slowly from somewhere deep inside. The wrong man, but for a moment . . . Lord, he thought, but it had been a long time. Thirty years or more, and he wondered how so much time had passed. Was George still alive? Could he be, after so long? He remembered that George had seemed old even then, but had that only been through the eyes of a youth? *Why haven't I ever gone back?*

"Mister," the old man said. "Mister, I gots to be going."

Dewey looked up, blinking, pulling his thoughts back to Missouri and the old man he had frightened. "Yes. Go. I'm sorry. I thought you were someone else."

"No sir, jus' me. Jus' ol' Ward." He let out a little rope and tugged urgently at the mule's lead, anxious to be gone, Dewey thought, away from this crazy white man. He wondered how long it had been since he'd thought of Dancing George, then realized with something of a start that it hadn't been that long. Even after all these years he had never let go completely.

Gil rode back, looking puzzled. "You okay, Sarge?"

"Yeah," Dewey said shortly. "I'm fine." He pushed past Gil, down the road. Near the bottom, he twisted to a final look, but the old man was gone, swallowed by the darkness.

Rain popped loudly against Dewey's India-rubber poncho and ran in a steady stream from the broken-down brim of his hat, making a small waterfall past his left eye. Mud sucked loudly at the horses' hooves, splashed as high as their bellies. They glanced warily at the horses hitched to the rails in front of the Timberman, and Dewey bent slightly to peer inside, but no one said anything until Gil led them into an alley a couple of blocks away.

"Yankees," Tim said excitedly. "Did you see 'em?"

"We saw them," Jesse replied in a vexed tone. To Dewey, he said, "What I want to know is, what the hell are they doing here?"

"Maybe Copeland can tell us," Dewey said. "Where's the Bucket of Blood?" he asked Gil.

"This way," Gil said. He led them through the alley and onto the street below. Here he turned toward the river, toward the dank odor of rotting wood and dead fish and river trash, all of it made sharper by the rain.

The Bucket of Blood was a low, box-like building of sun-warped board and batten perched close to the lapping waters of the Black River. From a two-by-four that extended above the saloon's single door a wooden bucket creaked rustily at an angle from wire ties, while an old piece of sodden red rag hung limply from its lip.

There were no windows and the door was closed, but there was no mistaking the Bucket as anything but a saloon. Up close, the raw smell of tobacco and alcohol was stronger than even the river, and the voices inside were loud, occasionally obscene. There was a mule hitched alone at the rail in front of the saloon and Dewey rode in beside it and dismounted, sinking past his spurs in the mire.

"We'd be in a hell of a fix if there was Yankee in there," Jesse observed quietly. He'd held the buckskin back some, as if afraid even to come close. Towns, Dewey remembered, always made Jesse nervous.

"A soldier isn't likely to stable a horse to come into a place like this," Dewey replied, but he knew Jesse had a point too. If there were Federals inside, they'd likely be in for a rough time. Still, there was no way around it, and he hitched at his gunbelt, taking comfort in the thought that Yankee gunpowder wouldn't be any drier than their own.

The Bucket of Blood was a small, single room with a bar down the right-hand side and eight or ten tables scattered throughout the rest of the room. Brass spittoons gleamed like tarnished buds from the gummy sawdust on the floor, and deer and cow skulls grinned back from the walls. Maybe a dozen men leaned against the drinking-side of the bar, and there was at least that many others at the tables; a lone, potbellied barkeep with a handlebar mustache and slicked-down hair tended business.

Everyone looked up when they entered and conversation drifted off. Dewey nodded to the room and took a place at the bar, the others following, falling in beside him. Tim started to shut the door, but the barkeep called, "Leave it open a spell. It'll blow some of the stink out of this joint."

A few men laughed and a couple others added their opinions on the stink and the conversation gradually built up again. The barkeep came down the sober-side and stopped opposite Dewey. "I'd leave the door open permanent but the damn hogs and dogs and chickens want to wander in out of the rain. This ain't the fanciest saloon in the Bluff, but it ain't a goddamn barn, either. What'll you have, gents?"

"Whiskey all around," Dewey said, drawing a dollar from his poke and tossing it on the bar. "We want the bottle, too."

The barkeep ambled off and Dewey put his elbows on the bar. He had spotted Zachariah Copeland almost immediately, but hadn't yet acknowledged him. Now he let his gaze settle on the lanky peddler, noting the worn cuffs and collar, the stringy hair peppered with gray, the gray stubble of his beard. It looked to Dewey as if times were tough all over.

The barkeep returned with a bottle and four glasses, setting them up and pouring carefully. Corking the bottle, he set that and Dewey's change on the bar beside his glass. "Strangers around these parts, ain't cha?" the barkeep asked amiably.

"More or less," Dewey replied. He turned around and lifted his glass.

The barkeep looked at Gil, recognition plain on his face, along with a reluctance to push on without invitation. Gil noticed the barkeep's hesitation though, and raised his glass in a kind of toast. "Howdy, Vern."

"Howdy, Gil." Vern looked uncommonly pleased at the recognition. "Ain't seen you in a spell. Or your pa."

"Pa passed away a couple of years ago," Gil said carefully. "Respiratory problems."

Vern looked genuinely saddened. "Hell, I'm sorry to hear that. I always liked your pa."

"Yeah," Gil said, and threw the whiskey against the back of his throat.

"I don't see a lunch counter," Dewey said, glancing around the room. They hadn't eaten regularly the past few weeks, and it seemed like he was always hungry.

"Took it out," Vern said. "Had too many tramps coming in and eating without buying a drink. Hell, I don't mind feeding a paying customer, but a man could go broke feeding all the bums wandering the country the last few years."

"War brought 'em out of the woodwork, has it?" Gil asked.

"Has for a fact," Vern answered emphatically. "But if you're wanting a decent meal at a fair price, I'd recommend the Ozark Palace Hotel."

"Where's that at?" Jesse asked casually.

"Hill Street, the top road. About half a block down from the Timberman Saloon. That you can't miss."

Dewey remembered the hotel, and the way his belly had rumbled when they'd passed through the aroma of home cooking wafting from it.

"Got a good cook there?" Jesse asked.

Dewey took his drink and wandered away from the bar, leaving Jesse to fish for his information alone. Jesse had his own reasons for coming to Poplar Bluff, Dewey knew.

Dewey walked over to Copeland's table and hooked a chair out with his toe, settling stiffly. Copeland offered an acknowledging smile. "So, we meet again."

"Small world," Dewey said. He leaned back, glancing briefly at Copeland's hat, sitting on the table near his elbow. It was the same hat he'd worn that day near Jefferson City, the two small holes near the crown patched with flannel of a matching color, but it had received further damage along the way; a palm-sized area along the left side was chewed and frayed, pocked by a dozen tiny holes. "Dog get a hold of it?" Dewey asked with an easy smile, indicating the hat.

Copeland smiled sadly. "A shotgun, I fear. Perhaps I should have taken your advice and stored this away until Mr. Lincoln was elected from office, but stubbornness knows few bounds."

"How's the peddling business?" Dewey asked, just to make conversation.

"My horse died. Do you remember her, the light-colored sorrel?"

Dewey nodded.

"That was last winter, in St. Louis, and I was forced to cut the traces and flee before the police arrived, as I didn't have money to afford the carcass wagon. What might have ailed her? She was old, but had appeared in wonderful health."

"I wouldn't hazard a guess," Dewey said.

"No. No, I suppose not. I wouldn't either, and I was there."

Dewey smiled patiently, without speaking.

After a while, Copeland sighed, something of a habit with him, Dewey remembered, and said, "Your Colonel Slaughter has made something of a reputation for himself among the rural population."

"Is that a fact?"

"Oh, quite, I assure you. Daring cunning, his running the federal gauntlet along the Current River that way, and again, upon leaving the Mississippi. The stuff of legends, I suppose, but it does little to better his position with Schofield."

"Schofield?"

"General John Schofield, placed in charge of the Department of the Missouri, replacing Curtis."

Dewey nodded. He hadn't heard about Schofield, but leadership changed hands so often in Missouri it was hard to keep track of who was in charge.

Copeland suddenly leaned forward, his face child-bright, eager. "Is it true," he asked, "that the federal gauntlet stretched for nearly a mile, and that the Yankees fell quaking to their knees as you dashed past, firing your horse pistols right and left?" Copeland lifted both hands, extending the index finger on each and snapping them from side to side.

"Why don't you holster them fingers before you shoot someone," Dewey said wryly. At the bar a couple of men in checked shirts had turned to watch Copeland's antics with a curious eye.

"But is it true?" Copeland persisted, lowering his fingers.

"Maybe about half," Dewey said. He didn't remember seeing anyone quaking on their knees. What he mostly remembered was the confusion, the squeal of horses and the acrid taste of powder smoke blown back in his face and the tremendous feeling of relief he'd felt in passing the last wagon unscathed.

"Yes," Copeland said after a pause, leaning back and sighing. "Most tales are only half." He studied Dewey for a moment, his gaze probing. Then he said, "Do you know a man named Pete Bottoms?"

Dewey's grip tightened imperceptibly on his glass. "Yes, I know him."

"He was brought into Rolla some time back and turned over to the federal authorities there. Seriously wounded, I understand, but expected to survive."

"Brought in by a crazy old coot?" Dewey asked softly.

"By a hermit, some say. He collected a five-hundred-dollar reward on the young man and disappeared back into the wilderness."

"Christ," Dewey muttered. The old man's treachery shocked him; he might have expected a lot of things from the old fool, but he hadn't expected to be double-crossed.

"He was taken to a St. Louis hospital, and rumor is that if he cooperates he'll be given ten years in a Yankee prison, but if he doesn't, they'll hang him. A difficult choice for young Bottoms, but hardly unpredictable."

He'd talk, Dewey thought; there were some among the rangers who wouldn't, but he figured Pete would, and Dewey wasn't so sure he could blame him, although he knew there would be plenty who would once word of his betrayal got out.

"They'll want names, naturally," Copeland went on. "Of course, they already have quite a few. Yours, for instance, and Josiah's, maybe twenty-five or thirty others." He reached inside his coat and brought out a long broadsheet, weather-worn but still intact. He pushed it across the table. "I pulled this off a telegraph pole outside Sikeston last week. You might recognize some of the names."

He did. The broadsheet was a general wanted poster for crimes against the state and people of Missouri, proclaiming murder, robbery, arson, and rustling as the offenses, with a five-hundred-dollar reward for the capture and conviction of any man listed along the bottom half of the dodger. Dewey grunted, spotting his own name halfway down the second column of names. Jesse's name was on the list too, as was Slaughter's, and Gil's and Harvey Quint's. Curly Barnes, who Jesse had killed up near the Missouri River last winter, was also listed. Dewey recognized about half the names on the dodger, but the rest were strangers.

"Other raider bands," Copeland explained. "Operating mostly along the Missouri and Kansas border."

"Burning barns and crops?" Dewey asked with disgust. There were those among the rangers who had wanted to be a part of that, Dewey knew, who saw Kansas as Missouri's threat, but Slaughter had refused to be drawn into the smaller picture. He hadn't organized the rangers to make war on farmers, he claimed.

"Mostly, it would seem. But had Slaughter confined his activities to such acts, Schofield may not have singled him out."

Dewey frowned. "What do you mean, singled him out?"

"It has been common policy to ignore as much as possible the various raider bands, to treat them merely as bullies and ruffians, largely at Mr. Lincoln's insistence, it's said. But Slaughter has persisted too diligently in harassing federal forces and Schofield cannot ignore him any longer. Every successful raid by a band of irregulars leads to more unrest among those still loyal to the South."

"And Lincoln's opened the door to martial law?" Dewey almost smiled. Fremont had briefly imposed martial law early in the war, and critics said that if Lincoln hadn't vetoed the act guerrillas wouldn't be a problem today. It was a possibility, Dewey thought, although he wasn't sure Fremont would have been the commander to pull it off.

"Quite the contrary," Copeland said, bursting the bubble of Dewey's speculations. "General Schofield is acting upon a policy begun by General Curtis, a sort of covert operation to rid Missouri of raiders once and for all. But Lincoln is not openly involved. The question, I suppose, is whether Mr. Lincoln *is* involved clandestinely, or if Schofield is placing his neck willingly upon the chopping block Curtis left him."

"What do you think?" Dewey asked.

Copeland smiled, shrugged. "I wouldn't hazard a guess. But I will tell you this, if Lincoln does support Schofield, I wouldn't want to be in your boots."

Dewey lifted his whiskey, sipped slowly. It answered a lot of questions, he thought, added logic to what had only been confusion before. But it wasn't good news, and he was already wishing it wasn't him that had to ride back to Eleven Point and tell the Colonel what he'd learned.

Copeland said, "The only bright spot is if

Schofield is acting alone on this, he won't be able to keep his troops out indefinitely. Sooner or later he'll have to account for his men, or the South will make another feint toward St. Louis, and he'll have to pull the pressure off you."

"If Lincoln isn't involved, Schofield is carrying out another general's plan against the expressed wishes of his commander."

"Not a very bright spot at that, is it?"

"No," Dewey admitted, "it isn't." He stood, paused, staring down at Copeland's frayed suit. He hadn't expected to feel compassion for this paradoxical traveling merchant, but suddenly, he did. He said, "Are you going to be okay, Copeland? If you need a loan . . ."

Copeland smiled, waved away the offer. "Worry about yourself, Mr. Harker. No man deems my carcass worth five hundred dollars."

There wasn't much Dewey could say to that, so he just nodded his good-bye and walked back to the bar. Jesse lifted the bottle in invitation as he approached but Dewey shook his head. "Let's ride," he said curtly, taking the bottle from Jesse's hand and walking with it into the rain.

He paused next to the sorrel, staring up the street, but all he saw was a wet dog shaking itself under a street lamp. Jesse and Gil and Tim came out after a while and climbed into their saddles. Dewey led them about thirty yards away and stopped them in a pocket of deep shadow.

"What's up?" Gil asked.

"Just curious," Dewey replied. He was watching the Bucket's front entrance, and his hand kept sliding back to the butt of his revolver.

"Vern was telling us about our ride through Crawford's forces," Gil said. "Damn impressive."

"Who's Crawford?" Dewey asked.

"Major Jack Crawford," Tim answered. "He was the sonofabitch that damn near cornered us along the Current."

"Looks like Slaughter was right about those southern trails," Jesse said quietly. "Word is that Crawford had set up a tight ambush south of the caverns. I hate to give the old bastard credit, but I guess he made the right move that day."

"I'll be damn," Dewey said softly. So the real threat had been behind them all along, and not with the nearly five hundred they'd dodged on the northern trail. It told Dewey a lot about the size of the operation against them.

A figure appeared suddenly at the saloon's entrance, paused, then hurried out. Dewey took a sharp breath, then gigged the sorrel into the light. Seeing him, the man stopped, flinching, then turned and hurried back to the Bucket.

Jesse said, "Shit, that's the guy in the checked shirt whose partner slipped out about five minutes before we did."

Dewey looked at Jesse. "We ought to get out of here ourselves," he said.

Jesse shook his head. "Uh, uh. You go on and I'll catch up."

Dewey sighed. He was sure they'd been recognized as raiders, and that the man in the checked shirt had gone to alert the Yankees. Could be there was a unit mounted against them even now. Hesitating could lead only to trouble. But he knew what was holding Jesse too, so he said, "All right, damnit, but we'll have to be quick about it. Let's go."

CHAPTER 13

Jesse paused in front of the big, three-story brick building just down the street from the Timberman Saloon. The lobby was empty, save for a clerk snoozing behind the desk, and only dimly lit despite the relatively early hour. Beside the desk an arched entryway led to the dining room, a square room crowded with round tables covered with blue gingham, but empty too, and nearly dark.

Tim rode close and said, "There's an empty lot beside the hotel with a light coming from a window there."

Jesse nodded and looked at Dewey. "We'll wait out here and keep our eyes peeled," Dewey said.

Jesse nodded again and guided the buckskin

around the corner and back to a small, wooden porch. Stepping down, he wrapped the buckskin's reins to the porch railing and climbed the steps. His stomach felt fluttery all of a sudden, the way it sometimes did right before a battle, but he tried not to think about it, or the man in the checked shirt. He lifted a fist before the door, rapped sharply with his knuckles, waited then, listening to the whisper of rain and the hammering of his heart.

It was his ma who came, dressed in a gown and robe, her hair done up and mostly hidden beneath a nightcap, although she didn't look like she'd been to bed yet. She waved a curtain aside and peered out the window at him, then cautiously opened the door. "Yes?" she inquired.

She'd changed, Jesse saw, and felt a small wretching of his heart at how much. The fringe of hair visible beneath her cap was mostly gray now, and her face sagged with deep wrinkles. She'd put on weight, too, although she'd always been prone to it. She looked old, Jesse thought with something of a start, old and haggard, as worn in spirit as she was in body.

"What do you want?" she asked, an edge of worry in her voice now, and she started to shut the door without waiting for his reply. Jesse reached up and removed his hat, holding it at his side but not speaking. She gasped then, and clutched at the throat of her nightgown. "Jesse?" she whispered, as if uncertain yet. Then, "Oh, Jesse," and she reached out and pulled him against her, all wet and dripping and cold.

She stepped back after a while, looking him up and down, her eyes moist, her lips trembling. She said, "Jesse," again, and hugged him once more, quicker this time, and gentler, then stepped back. "My Jesse."

"Hello, Ma."

"You're soaked through and through, and hungry too, I'll bet. Come in, come to the table."

She led him inside, around a short partition to a small table set close to a fireplace. There was a mound of cobbler sparkling with sugar already on a saucer there, and a tumbler of creamy yellow milk beside it. "Peach," she said. "It's last year's harvest and a little dry, but I just took it from the oven."

Jesse's mouth watered. He'd almost forgotten what it was like to have such treats, pies and cakes warm and fresh, and cold milk to wash it down with. Time was short, he knew, but the temptation was too great. "Have some with me," he said.

"Of course," she said, and went to fetch a saucer and tumbler from the cupboard. Jesse dropped his hat on the floor and shucked out of his slicker. He considered removing his spurs and gunbelt, remembering a time when he would have, but things had changed since then and he sat down with them on. He poured milk for his ma from a blue crock, added a generous amount to the cobbler. Sitting opposite him, his ma said, "Gray sent a letter about a year ago that you were all right, and that you'd joined an old friend of his to fight the Yankees. He said you were offered a chance to go to California, but that you refused."

"Missouri's my home, Ma. That's why I didn't go east to find Tom and Eddie."

"That's what Gray said, and I want you to know that I'm proud, Jesse, just right proud that you stayed to fight for your home. I'm not belittling Tom and Eddie—they did what they thought was best at the time, but you did what was best for now. We'll show those Yankees they can't walk over Christian folks like they was clods of dirt in the field. You'll show them, Jesse. Show them what good, honest, God-fearing Missourians can do."

"Reckon I'll try, Ma," he replied around a mouthful of cobbler.

"There are soldiers in town, Jesse. Some of Jack Crawford's pack of rabble, they're saying, and bent on taking Colonel Slaughter's Rangers. I say they won't. I say no Yankee will ever take Josiah Slaughter's Rangers."

Jesse grinned, spilling a little milk from the corner of his mouth that he wiped away with his sleeve, but it was a false grin, touched with sadness. It struck him that his ma didn't really have much of an idea of what war was really like, for all that she lived in the middle of it, had, in fact, lost her home to it. He wondered if she ever would, or even should. It seemed to Jesse that she had suffered enough in her life, all things considered, and he didn't think her fantasy of good Missourians and evil Yankees hurt anything. But it was sad, all the same, remembering the woman she had once been.

Gently, almost reluctantly, he asked, "Ma, where's Pa?"

The question seemed to catch her by surprise, and she put her spoon down and looked away, "I thought . . . I thought you knew."

The cobbler in Jesse's mouth turned suddenly doughy, as tasteless as wood, and he got it down only with effort. "No," he said. "I don't know."

"Your pa went up to Illinois, Jesse. Right after they took Zeb. We haven't heard from him since."

"Right after Zeb? Ma, that was . . . that was near to two years ago."

Her hands fluttered suddenly, pushing her fork away, drawing her milk closer, but not lifting anything, not eating or drinking. She did that for fifteen or twenty seconds, then just let her hands drop into her lap. "I suspect he's dead by now," she said woodenly. "Ain't no reason he wouldn't have got word back to us, otherwise. Got a letter from Zeb just a month ago, first since they took him away, and he made no mention of your pa showing up."

"Didn't anyone try to find him?"

"Course they did," she snapped. "Ivan Richards went up to Jeff City hisself and found out your pa booked passage on the Belle of Missouri, bound for St. Lou. I wrote your Aunt Martha there, knew he'd stop by and pay his respects if there was any time at all, and he did, rightly enough, and went out to catch one of them trains to Chicago. But I don't know from there. Ain't nobody does, I don't reckon."

Jesse lowered his head. The air seemed suddenly thick, hard to breathe, and he had to open his mouth to get enough wind.

"Yep, suspect he's dead," his ma said matter-of-factly now, and lifted a spoonful of cobbler to her mouth.

"Zeb okay?" Jesse asked in a whisper.

"Galvanized him," she replied shortly. "He's a Yankee now, in uniform if not in spirit."

Jesse looked up questioningly.

"Made him sign a paper, they did, promising never to take up arms against the North again, on threat of death. Then they put him in a Yankee uniform and shipped him into the wilderness to fight the heathen savages. Sent him out along the Oregon Trail, somewhere."

"Tom and Eddie?"

"They were fine, last I heard. February, that was. They write fair to regular. And the twins, oh, Jesse, I wish they were here, but they're in the country with a friend. They'll be back tomorrow. Can you stay?"

"No, Ma. We've got to leave soon."

"You came with friends?" She half stood to look over the partition, as if expecting to see them standing at the door. "Well, go fetch 'em, Jesse. Heavens, where are your manners?"

"Can't. They're keeping watch."

"Watch?"

"Crawford's men, remember?"

"Scum, is Crawford's men, and they'll get no cobbler from me, not them or any Yankee. Only good Missouri buckshot to the seat of their pants. I don't hold with Yankees or Republicans, Jesse. First one we let into the White House and see what happens."

"Reckon this has been building up for a spell before Lincoln came along," Jesse replied uneasily. He looked at his ma, seeing clearly and for the first time the confused, frightened woman she had become. He wanted to do something for her, but knew that anything that might give her comfort was beyond what he was capable of.

"Your sister is married, Jesse. Did you know that? I wrote Gray, but it may have been too late to reach you."

"I didn't know that."

"Christmas last, that was, to a fine merchant from Fort Smith, Arkansas. She's happy and expecting her first in November." She laughed and shook her head. "A grandmother. Me."

"That's good news, Ma," Jesse said, and he supposed it was, but in the wake of everything else he couldn't feel anything special. It was as if Maybelline were a stranger now, as if they all were.

"Bonsall, is her name, and her husband is Geoff, with a *G* instead of a *J*. He's a fine man, Jesse, you'd like him."

"Well, maybe I'll get down there one of these days and pay them a call."

"You do that, Jesse." She reached across the table, clamping her hand over his forearm. "It's slipping away, isn't it? Everything is slipping away."

There was a knock at the door, and they both jumped. Jesse half-drew a revolver and looked at his ma. "You expecting anyone?" he asked.

She shook her head, rose, and went around the partition. Jesse eased into a darkened doorway, slipping the Army all the way out.

"Who is it?" his Ma called.

"Gil Banks, ma'am. I need to speak with Jesse. It's real important."

Jesse stepped into the kitchen and nodded to his ma, but he didn't holster his revolver. His ma opened the door and stepped back, but Gil didn't come in. He said, "There's bluebellies running up and down the street, Jesse, and Sarge says we need to ride, *muy pronto*."

"I'll be right there," Jesse said.

Gil's hat bobbed once, and he was gone. His ma shut the door. "So soon?" she asked bewilderedly.

"I'm sorry, Ma." He picked up his hat and slicker and stood awkwardly, wondering what to say, what would make sense.

"Wait," she said abruptly, disappearing into a nearby room and reappearing almost immediately, her hands filled with Union currency and hard coin. "Take this," she said. "I've been saving it for you."

"I can't take that, Ma. Keep it for yourself and the twins, or Maybelline's baby."

"We're doing fine. We have a solid roof over our heads and plenty to eat and a little cash left over each month. Take this, Jesse. For me."

She thrust it toward him, but he closed her hand gently over the cash. "I can't take your money, Ma. It isn't right."

"Jesse, don't make me beg. Please." There were tears in her eyes again, welling up, spilling over, and he didn't think it would take much to make him cry either.

"Ma . . ."

"For me, Jesse. For a meal when you're hungry or, God forbid, medicine. Please, Jesse."

He took it, pocketing it all without looking at it. There was an incredible sadness etched on his mother's face, and the knowledge that this might well be the last time she saw him. It dawned on him then that this was the root of her fear, that it wasn't for herself, but for those she loved who had been torn away. Her world had been the farm and her family, but the farm was gone now, and her family scattered beyond reach.

Outside, a gunshot ripped apart the evening's dreary silence.

"Go, Jesse. Go with God, but go."

"I . . ." He stopped. He wanted to tell her that he loved her, but he never had before and he knew he couldn't now. It would make their parting too final. "Be careful, Ma."

"And you, Jesse. Always be careful." She stepped close, wrapping her arms around him, and his around her, and they hugged briefly, then Jesse stepped back, through the door.

The buckskin snorted and pulled back, testing the reins. Jesse hurried down the steps and swung into the saddle. Hooves thudded around him but the empty lot was too dark for him to recognize anyone. On the street Jesse could see dark forms flitting here and there, and Dewey's silhouette near the hotel's corner.

A horse thundered up from the rear, and Gil called, "There's a trail up the side of the hill behind us. I don't know where it leads but it has to be better than here."

At the front of the lot Dewey's big Sharps roared, lancing the darkness with a two-foot tongue of yellow flame and rosy sparks. Across the street someone screamed and fell silent. A rifle barked from the far side of the street, its bullet whizzing overhead. Two others followed, thumping dully into the woods behind them.

"Let's get the hell out of here," Tim cried desperately.

"Sarge," Gil pleaded.

Jesse looked once at the hotel's kitchen door, and waved his ma back. He didn't know if she saw him or not, but she stepped quickly away from the glass and a moment later the room went black.

A volley of gunfire rippled along the street, slamming into the timber to the rear or ricocheting off the hotel's bricks with a strange, whining *ping*. Dewey wheeled his sorrel, shouting, "Let's go! Go! Go!" and raced past them. Gil and Tim followed without pause. Jesse glanced once more at the darkened window, then spurred the buckskin after the others, up a steep, twisting trail to the top of the bluff, then over and out of sight.

CHAPTER 14

They rode out of the woods and halted. Before them the long, slightly curving meadow lay empty, with only trampled grass and a few scattered brush shelters as evidence that anyone had recently camped here. Along the river small tendrils of mist undulated above the current, and on the hillsides pockets of haze clung to the treetops. Gil lifted his hat and hung it from his saddle horn, then mopped his face with a faded red bandanna and draped that over his hat to dry, although he knew it wouldn't. After two weeks of spring-like rain, summer had struck with a viciousness.

"Hell," Tim said, eyeing the empty meadow.

Gil figured that about covered it. He knew they had all been looking forward to returning, to settling in for a spell and maybe swimming in the Eleven Point. He glanced at the river now and thought it looked cool and inviting, but he knew that Dewey wouldn't tarry.

"What's that?" Jesse asked quietly.

Gil followed his gaze and felt his heart cram into his throat. Low in the grass, nearly two hundred yards away, was a small, brown mound that Gil knew was a dead horse. Dewey and Jesse palmed their revolvers and, resentfully, Gil drew his own.

"What?" Tim asked. He looked quickly around, ignorant yet of their alarm, then slowly drew his own revolver.

They spread apart as they rode forward, Gil taking the flank nearest the river and from time to time his gaze would shift to it, but wary now, as if it had somehow turned traitor. It was he who spotted the second horse, lying on a gravel spit at the river's edge, and he peeled away from the others to ride close. The horse was a good-looking roan that he remembered having belonged to a ranger named John Martin. The horse was saddled yet, and in the shallow riffles nearby he spotted a huge Dragoon that Martin carried on his saddle. There was old blood carpeted with flies all over the gravel, but Gil didn't know if it had belonged to Martin or the horse.

He rode back to the others but didn't speak until they'd almost reached the first horse, the one Jesse had spotted. This was a bay, but Gil couldn't place its rider. A lot of them rode bays, and sun and time had bloated this carcass to half again its normal size. Tim wrinkled his nose and turned his face away as if to draw a breath of fresh air from behind his shoulder. Gil said, "That was John Martin's roan in the river, saddled. There was a pistol laying in the river beside it, too. I reckon it must have been a running fight or someone would've taken the time to pick the pistol up."

"Hell, this one isn't even pulled off its picket pin," Jesse said. He looked at Dewey and added doubtfully, "Crawford's men?"

Dewey shook his head. "These horses have been dead for two days at least. It wasn't Crawford, but it could have been a troop of his cavalry. There were four companies hounding us for a spell."

"Gonna run us like wolves after a horse," Gil said bitterly, yet beneath his breast he felt the first stirrings of panic. Sometimes a pack of wolves would run a horse in relays in a huge circle, most resting while a few ran the horse, then switching off so that the wolves never tired. But the horse eventually did, Gil knew.

"Slaughter's got more sense than a horse," Dewey said gruffly.

"I don't see any bodies," Jesse said. "There would have been those, or graves, if anyone was killed."

"Maybe," Dewey said shortly. He pulled away, riding his horse at a jog across the meadow, his eyes cast to the ground. The others followed, watching the grass uncertainly. About a hundred yards from the dead bay Dewey suddenly stopped and leaned from the saddle to pluck something from the grass. A hat, Gil saw, with a federal insignia sewn to the crown.

"Cavalry," Tim breathed.

Dewey said, "I was never much on reading sign, but it looks to me like there was a running fight, but maybe not unexpected. There's no camp gear scattered around, like there'd be if they were caught by surprise. The Colonel led his men north, with the federals close behind."

"We going to follow?" Tim asked.

"Not much choice, is there?" Dewey replied. He nudged the sorrel into a lope and the others followed. They rode fast for a while, the trail easy to read, but the heat and humidity soon forced them back to a jog, then a walk. Sweat darkened the horses' hides and ruffled their hair. It darkened the men's clothing, too, so that their shirts clung wetly to their flesh, transparent and chafing. They pushed their hats off to hang from drawstrings along their backs and tied bandannas around their foreheads to keep the sweat from their eyes, though it was mostly a wasted effort.

Toward dusk they came upon the site of another battle, and spied in the shade of an elm three freshly dug graves with crude wooden crosses driven into the soft dirt. Downslope from those was another grave, bigger than the others, and unmarked. From its size, Gil knew more than one body was interred there, and he wondered who they were. He would have liked to have marked it in some way, with a cross or stone or something —he figured rangers deserved that much—but Dewey was in a fret to keep moving and no one had the energy to argue.

They discovered another skirmish site just before noon the next day. There wasn't much left—a saber darkened with blood, a couple of revolvers, a single Confederate kepi like some of the rangers wore, and blood on the grass. But no graves, and there was comfort in that.

The trail ran a zigzag course through the Ozarks, more west than north, but definitely angling back into Missouri. It was a trail of flight, Gil thought angrily; from time to time they would pass discarded gear, empty canteens or winter coats, most of it from the rangers, but they never passed a campsite, not even gray firepits. The Federals were running them day and night, though losing ground because of it.

For three days they followed a littered trail, but at the end of the third day Dewey called a halt, dismounting stiffly in the middle of a small glade. "Boys," he said wearily. "We're flagging our horses and not getting any closer. It's my guess that Slaughter is riding for Kansas, and once there he'll circle south into the Indian Nations. If he does he'll circle back into Missouri sooner or later, and I'm guessing he'll swing back close to where we wintered year before last, close to Possum Knob."

"Southeast of Springfield?" Gil asked.

"Seems likely," Dewey said. "That ain't so far away from where we're at right now, and I'm thinking we might do best picking up some beef and maybe what fresh horses we can find and be waiting there for him."

"Seems chancy," Tim said.

"Hell, life's chancy," Jesse retorted.

Gil said, "There was a little chicken-scratch town west of Possum Knob called Table Rock. Some of the boys used to slip off there for corn liquor and huggin'. They said there was some right friendly gals in Table Rock."

"Huh," Jesse grunted dryly. "Just hearsay, I reckon."

Gil grinned. It was, but that didn't matter. Thinking of the big meadow where they'd camped that first winter made him want to shout. It would feel good to cut loose from the trail for a while and burrow in somewhere safe and quiet. He was sick of fighting and hard traveling, of scanty food and cold, short nights. And he was sick of horses; he wasn't cut out for it, he'd discovered during the last couple of months, and he had a new appreciation of the slow, bouncing pace of a wagon.

"Let's do that, then," Dewey said. "Swing past Table Rock and see what's available, then back to Possum Knob. If the Colonel isn't there in a week we'll come up with a different plan."

They angled south and east after that, leaving the little glade and taking their time now, stopping every once in a while to let the horses graze on green grass and to maybe catch a short nap. They came to a trail the next day that Dewey turned onto and followed that due west. Around noon they came to a sharp limestone ledge about thirty feet high, with a tiny spring at its base, and Dewey called for a short break.

They dismounted and loosened their cinches. They were on a gentle slope here, the spring creating a narrow brook that wandered off among the soft green ferns and became lost. Sunlight was patchy and the air was still; insects hummed invisibly and spider webs clung to the tree limbs. It was a peaceful place, but Gil thought it looked snaky, too, and he couldn't relax, couldn't flop back and shut his eyes like the others. He curried the bay while she cropped on the billowy ferns. It was he who first heard the faint clip of a horseshoe against stone and called a soft warning to the others.

They came to stand beside him, and Dewey jerked the Sharps from its scabbard, but nobody tightened their cinches or slipped the bits back into their horses' mouths. It was as if, after finding this spot and deciding to noon here, they would fight to stay. But Gil's mouth went dry nonetheless. He couldn't help imagining federal patrols, and sabers flashing in the dappled sunlight.

They all spotted the solitary rider at the same time, but it was Jesse who recognized him first. "Hell, that's Jubal Butler."

Butler was a Borden man, big and brawny, with long hair tinged with red and a huge beard that nearly covered his chest. He had a broad, flat face and pig-like eyes that never met another man's gaze for more than a few seconds. Butler was one of Curly Barnes's friends, and rode with Harvey Quint and John Martin and that bunch. They were a hard bunch, and since Curly's death, Gil thought Jubal Butler was probably the hardest and coldest in the bunch.

Butler was riding a chestnut with a mangled ear, bareback and bootless, his naked white feet dangling among the ferns as he rode up to them and nodded a howdy. He was unarmed, Gil noted then, gaunted some with hunger, his face and hands scratched by brambles.

"How, Jubal," Dewey said.

"Hungry, that's goddamn how," Butler replied. "I'd trade this fine horse for a steak carved off your ass right now, and likely eat it raw. You boys ain't got no food about, have you?"

Dewey shook his head. "Fresh out, but I'd rustle you up some greens, if you're hungry."

"Had a rabbit last night," Tim added innocently. "Jesse took its head off with his pistol at twenty-five yards. Cleanest shot I ever saw."

Butler slid his gaze toward Tim, then back. "Kid's got a mean streak in him," he muttered. "And no thank you, Harker. I've got a belly full of greens right now. It's red meat I'm craving."

"We're on our way to Table Rock to turn something up," Jesse said. "You'll welcome to ride along."

"Yeah, I guess," Butler replied. He tried to ride closer but the chestnut flicked its one good ear and sidled away from Jesse's buckskin. "We could eat your horse, Ross," he said then. "Nobody likes him anyway."

"I like him," Jesse replied.

"What happened to his ear?" Gil asked, meaning the chestnut.

"Goddamn Yankee minie ball is what happened to his ear. Bastards have been running our asses ragged all over southern Missouri the last six or seven days. First time we tried to rest our horses, here comes *another* bunch out of the north. That 'un caught us flat-footed for fair. I jumped this nag and lit a shuck through the brush. Leland Recker was with me for a while but we got separated next day by a Yankee patrol. These goddamn woods is full of Yankees."

Gil looked at Dewey but Dewey was still watching Butler. "Which way is the Colonel headed?" Dewey asked.

Butler laughed, spraying Tim with spittle. "Ol' Iron-ass is bouncing around like a billiard ball on a warped table, Harker. That bastard is scared like a rabbit." Softer then, he added, "Hell, I guess we all are. What the hell's going on here? It's like the goddamn Yankees know every move we make a day or so before we do."

"Bluebellies have got their hackles up and want to make an example of Slaughter," Gil said. "Maybe they figure if they can whip Slaughter the rest of us will just go on home and leave 'em alone."

"Well, about half the boys is ready to do just that," Butler said. "Ain't nobody riding with a full outfit no more. Clothes is falling off our backs,

233

and the Yankees scattered a bunch of our horses the second day out from the Eleven Point, so ten, fifteen men are riding double. Ain't hardly ate since we left Arkansas, either, but I'll give old Iron-ass credit for raiding a couple of farms. Took some hogs at gunpoint that we butchered right on the place. Goddamn, these mossbacks is tighter with grub than a preacher with a jug. Some of 'em are, anyway."

Dewey frowned. "Slaughter raided some farms?"

"That or starve, Harker. Man can't run seven days without food in his belly, though he can for three. I can goddamn vouch for that."

"We're hungry too," Jesse said curtly.

"Not like some I know, I'll bet," Butler shot back. "John Martin and Bud Gantz and Jim Brenner are waiting over at Slaughter's old winter quarters right now with bellies near stove in for want of a bone to gnaw on. That's why I was heading for Table Rock myself. Steal us a hog, if there's one to be had."

"We won't be stealing anything," Dewey grunted. "There's been enough of that."

"Well, hell, Harker, maybe we will and maybe we won't, but I'll tell you damn quick if I don't it won't be because of you. Me and some of the boys is getting tired of all this rank shit, Colonel this and Captain that. It ain't getting us nowhere that we can see."

Dewey just laughed. "Let's ride," he said.

Butler, already mounted, swung in behind Dewey, and Jesse and Tim followed, but Gil hung back a moment, digesting what he had just heard. It had never occurred to him that Slaughter might someday lose control, but he knew now that it was possible, and the thought scared him almost as much as Yankees.

Table Rock was only a couple of hours from where they'd met Butler, and they made the rest of the trip in silence, crossing at the ford downriver and coming in from the north. Gil wanted to laugh, seeing the town for the first time. He had known it was small of course, but he hadn't expected it to look so shabby, not from the tales he'd heard. Most of the dozen or so cabins lining the broad, rutted road that followed the White River were made of logs, with shake roofs and mud and willow chimneys. Ratty curtains hung lifeless from open windows, and hogs rooted in the mud under the front porches, the luckier ones chewing sleepily on the slop and garden trash dumped to the side. Only the mill, a two-story stone structure built on the north edge of town, seemed permanent. Everything else looked on the verge of desertion, as if the people inside were only waiting for the right moment to pick up and move on.

They came to a cabin with glass in one of the front windows and a barnlike lean-to to the side that looked sturdier than most, and they reined off the road to halt some distance from the front porch. There was a hog stretched out sleepily in a patch of weeds to one side of the house, and in a small pasture to the rear of the cabin a Jersey cow chewed her cud and switched her tail at flies. Gil didn't see anyone around, but there was a iron kettle of ashes and such hardening into lye soap over a low fire by the front door.

"Hello the house," Dewey called.

There was no answer, but that didn't surprise Gil any.

Jesse forced his buckskin past Dewey. "We've come to buy some food," he called. "We have money. Good hard silver."

That brought a stirring at the window, and a shotgun's muzzle appeared there. "What do you want to buy?" a male voice asked.

"Meat. Something on the hoof."

"Got that hog out there, though I ain't sure I'd sell it unless the price was right."

"I want to take it with me," Jesse said. "If that hog don't lead I'm not interested."

"I've got a yearling bull calf out of my Jersey cow and Ben Springs's Hereford bull that I'd sell for fifteen dollars."

"I would like to see that calf," Jesse said. "I've never seen a yearling worth fifteen dollars."

"Well, that's what he's worth, take it or leave it."

Jesse touched the brim of his hat and started to

turn away when the man in the cabin hollered irritably, "You must be a Kansan not to know how to dicker."

"I'm a Missourian," Jesse counted. "Best you find yourself a Kansas man if you want to sell fifteen-dollar yearling calves."

The man laughed suddenly, and the shotgun's muzzle disappeared. A moment later the front door opened and he stepped out, a man of medium height, broad through the belly and fleshy jawed. He wore homespuns with braces, but was barefoot and bare chested, save for the matt of curly hair running down to his belly. Sweat glistened on his belly, and dampened the hair on his head, and Gil figured it must be hot inside the cabin, and humid. "My name is Homer Newberry," the man said, hooking his thumbs behind his braces like that meant something. "Twelve dollars, and he's a big one."

"I'll give you five."

Newberry frowned. "Say now, that calf is worth more than that. Why, five is an insult."

"So's twelve," Jesse said, and grinned to take the edge off the words. But his impatience was obvious. Newberry wanted to dicker, was the kind of man who got as much enjoyment from the trading as he would the cash, but Jesse wasn't in the mood for it today. None of them were.

"Well now, I might come down a smidgen, if you was to come up. Say, ten?"

Jesse shook his head. "Last I priced them a yearling could be had for four dollars. Six is as high as I'll go."

"I'm thinking you ain't priced many the last couple of years then," Newberry said. "The army pays good money for beef nowadays."

"Scrip. I'm offering cold, hard cash."

"I can get eight for him at Springfield, and I'd have to go up there to spend it anyway, so the trip wouldn't matter none. Eight's final, by God. I'll keep him before I sell him for less than that."

Newberry looked half mad, but Jesse didn't argue. "I'm tired and hungry, and I find eight dollars agreeable, providing the animal is in good condition."

"He is that, sir," Newberry said, the hint of anger gone now, his eyes flashing greedily. Turning back to the cabin, he bawled, "Seth!" and a curly haired kid of seven or eight appeared shyly at the door. "Go and fetch the bull calf," Newberry said. "And be quick about it."

The kid nodded and leaped off the porch, scampering around the corner of the cabin.

"You boys look frazzled," Newberry said. "I got a jug of snakebite remedy that might help."

"Well, I reckon it might," Butler said suddenly, and slapped his bare heels against the chestnut's ribs. "Been a spell since I enjoyed a dose of the cure."

Newberry chuckled and motioned toward the porch. "Sit a spell. I'll fetch it."

Jesse looked at Dewey and shrugged. They stepped down and let their reins trail the ground. Newberry came out in short order and pulled a corncob plug from a brown gallon jug. Gil could smell the raw, heady aroma of sourmash almost immediately, and knew even from a dozen feet away that a swig of it would bring tears to a man's eyes.

Newberry hesitated, but courtesy dictated that he offer Butler the first drink. Gil wanted to laugh at the reluctant way Newberry gave up the jug. To Jesse, he said, "I ain't going to ask you boys who you are, but I reckon those pistols tell me what you are. Just want you to know that if I could've afforded it, I'd have given you that calf."

Jesse just nodded and accepted the jug from Butler, who was red in the face and having some difficulty breathing. Newberry laughed, seeing him, and Dewey said, "Friend of ours used to live here. Roscoe Hammer. Know him?"

"Sure, I knowed the Hammers real well. But they moved on early this summer. Texas-bound, I hear."

"Jesus," Jesse croaked, lowering the jug and coughing harshly.

"Did Roscoe go with them?" Gil asked, suddenly curious. He hadn't known Roscoe hailed from Table Rock.

"The cripple? He surely did. Hurt his arm fighting Yankees, they say. Had it bent up close to his body, like this." Newberry bent his fist up close to his throat. "A shame, too. He was a likely one, though reckless, they say."

The cripple. The words seemed to echo in Gil's mind, and he took the jug Jesse offered and tipped it too fast. The sourmash was like cherry coals tumbling down his throat and he choked and coughed, as Jesse and Butler had, and his vision blurred as the fumes came back up through his nostrils. He offered the jug to Dewey, who declined with a small, tight smile.

"Say, you boys ain't drank in a good little bit, have you," Newberry said. He lifted the jug from Gil's hand and tipped it. Gil wiped his eyes and stared unbelievingly while Newberry's throat worked eight times in quick succession. Lowering the jug at last, Newberry belched and smacked his lips. "That's as good as she gets, boys," he said hoarsely and corked the jug.

With a triumphant yell, Seth chased the yearling out of the bushes and into the yard. "Don't run him like that," Newberry bawled irritably. Looking at Jesse, he said, "That boy is dumber than a stump."

"He got the calf," Jesse said evenly. He dug a leather poke from his saddlebag and handed Newberry eight silver dollars, then swung into the saddle.

Dewey said, "We could use a few more head, if there's any available."

"Well now, I'd try Ben Springs," Newberry said. "Ben raises Herefords on a small scale and might have a couple to spare."

"Where does this Springs live?"

"On south, about two miles I reckon. There's a ten-acre cornfield separates his cabin from the road. Easy to find.

"Obliged," Dewey said, reining the sorrel around.

Jesse had shaken out a loop with his rope and gone to fetch the calf. Gil followed to help, loosening his own rope but doing no more with it. Jesse dabbed the calf on the first try, which suited Gil all right. He wasn't looking forward to fighting the critter all the way back to Possum Knob, and would be satisfied to keep the calf from balking by bringing up the rear.

Dewey joined them, and Butler, with a forlorn cast to his face, and they moved out slowly, heading south to see Ben Springs.

CHAPTER 15

Jesse wasn't sure if the heat and humidity had let up some or if, after its first brutal assault, he was merely becoming used to it. Either way, despite the sweat that sheened his face and dampened his clothes, he felt an energy that had been lacking only a few days before, a willingness to get on with life. They had been holed up here at Possum Knob for ten days now, and he was anxious to be on the move again.

He knew he was largely alone in his feelings. The others, nearly sixty all told, had only straggled in after Slaughter a couple of days before and they were exhausted, their horses ribby and some near death. But Slaughter's back was to the wall. The three beeves they had brought back from Table Rock were already gone, nobody wore a complete outfit that wasn't ripped or torn, and several were barefoot or wore only crude moccasins. They needed food, clothing, ammunition, and fresh horses. And they needed them desperately, because nobody believed they had completely shaken pursuit. They were out there yet, the Federals, and coming up fast; it was as if the men could smell them.

It was early yet, the sun barely cresting the

fringe of trees in the east, but a lot of them had already removed their heavy wool-felt hats and replaced them with bandannas, some pulled back like skullcaps. Most were mounted, sitting patiently atop half-starved horses that cropped hungrily at the grass, but here and there little knots of rangers stood or sat in close groups, talking quietly among themselves.

For nearly half an hour Slaughter had huddled with his officers while the men waited in the growing heat, but now he stepped away from the others, mounting his big gray horse and riding to the top of the meadow. Dewey swung onto the sorrel and rode over to where Jesse and Gil and Tim waited, his face grim, sullen, and when Tim asked him what the trouble was, he only shook his head curtly.

Slaughter stood in his stirrups, surveying those before him for a moment, then called, "Men." His voice rang across the meadow and echoed back from the trees behind them. "We have fought a mighty enemy and proven ourselves before him. We have bested his every trick and wile, and made him a fool, laughed at even by those who support him." The Colonel paused, but no cheer greeted his words, no *hurrah* lifted toward the pale blue sky. Nearby, Jubal Butler spat into the grass. But Slaughter continued doggedly. "Our sacrifices have been great. Twenty-three men have been taken from us, either killed or captured or lost in the wilderness, and we can only offer our prayers as support.

"Seven of you are without horses, many others are weaponless. All are in want of decent clothing, and our stomachs cry for food, as the little we've had has only whetted our appetites for more substantial fare.

"Men, we are an army of irregulars, an army without sponsor. No one furnishes bandages for our wounded, or cans vegetables and preserves for our meals. No wagon filled with bedding follows our paths . . ."

"Nor could, less'n they was pulled by goats," shouted a ranger from the ranks, and the men laughed.

"Men, we have fought bravely and with honor against a clearly defined enemy and with positive results," Slaughter went on. "But now we have come to a crossroads. We cannot continue as we are. Therefore, I have reluctantly decided we must enter a town and in the name and glory of the Confederacy, restock our dwindled supplies."

Jesse's jaw dropped a little and he looked at Dewey, but Dewey sat his horse in stony silence, looking neither right nor left. Beside Jesse, Gil muttered, "I ain't so sure I like this." Here and there other voices rose in protest, but they sounded small in the big meadow, and died quickly.

"There is no choice anymore," Slaughter said. "If we are to pursue our cause we must have supplies. The alternative is to relinquish our arms now and surrender." Slaughter paused, his gaze sweeping the men before him, then he abruptly wheeled his horse and rode at a walk to the top of the meadow and disappeared into the woods.

Stunned silence settled over the meadow. Men exchanged uncertain glances, looked away; no one rode immediately after Slaughter, and Jesse wondered if anyone would. Then Dewey lifted rein and urged his horse after the Colonel. Gil looked at Jesse, his eyes pained with doubt, reluctance, then he grinned weakly and shrugged and gigged his bay after Dewey. Jesse followed, Tim close behind, and Prescott twisted in his saddle to shout, "All right, fall in, goddamnit."

At the edge of the woods Jesse glanced over his shoulder at the line of men who followed, surprised to find them all there, and no one sloping toward the opposite woods. Slaughter had offered them that opportunity, he knew, a chance to cut their ties with the rangers, and Jesse knew also that there were plenty who wanted to. But given the chance, nobody took it, and he laughed a little, turning back to face the trail ahead again. Missouri stubborn and Missouri dumb, he thought, thinking of those who followed, and him too, likely, but by God, he felt Missouri proud, too.

Gil, in the lead, spurred his horse up the steep bank and halted in the middle of the road. Jesse followed, stopping close by and leaning forward with both hands on the saddle horn, stretching his muscles. "Reckon this must be it," Gil said, as if to make conversation.

Jesse just grunted, looking north and south along the broad, double-laned road. There were fresh tracks in the dust churned from last week's mud—buggy tracks, snake-thin and wobbling, and the broad, iron-rimmed marks of a good-sized freight rig pulled by oxen, but there wasn't any traffic in sight now, nor even the haze of dust that always hung like a transparent sheet in the humid air for quite a while afterward.

Corn ran away from them in even rows in the fields bordering the road, knee-high and dark green, the leaves motionless in the still air. To the south timbered hills thrust abruptly from the fields, and to the north, beyond the muddy, sluggish Osage River, high dirt banks loomed steeply over a ribbon of weed-choked bottom-land. A telegraph line followed the road, ran like bunting from one slim pole to the next, swooping close to take advantage of the single-laned wooden bridge spanning the river before climbing the dirt bank on the far shore and disappearing.

Gil eyed the telegraph wire critically, then sighed. "Sometimes I wonder who we're at war with. The goddamn Yankees or Western Union."

Jesse grinned, leaning back to prop an elbow against the buckskin's flank and cocking his knee around the saddle horn. It was the Colonel's opinion that disrupting Yankee communication did as much good as fighting, and they'd cut a lot of wire over the last couple of years; they seldom passed a line without snipping it, sometimes in dozens of places.

Gil rode close to the line and tossed his rope over the wire, drawing it close to his snippers. There was a little *twang* as the stretched wire parted and fell into the dust. Coiling his rope, Gil rode partway onto the bridge and halted. "Hell with it," he said, contemplating the next section of line. "Once is enough when it's this hot." He dismounted and draped the reins over the bridge railing, leaning over himself to watch the swirl of water below.

Jesse and Gil were alone. About a mile to the south, on the far side of the hills and about now, if everything had gone according to plan, Slaughter was leading his men into the town of Jacksville. Beyond that Dewey and Tim would have by now cut the telegraph line to Springfield, effectively isolating the small burg. It was the Colonel's plan to lead the rangers quickly into town, confiscate what they needed, and be back on the road within an hour. With luck there wouldn't be any looting or burning, no fights or assaults, and above all, no deaths. But Jesse knew that Slaughter was worried sick about something going wrong. It wouldn't take much to ruin what reputation they'd built, he knew, to dry up his sources of information and to turn away the scanty help he knew he could depend upon now.

As if sensing Jesse's thoughts, Gil said, "I wish we could have raided into Illinois, or Iowa. Hell, I'd like to get across the Missouri River sometime and drive a wedge straight into Iowa. Give them a taste of war for a spell."

"I got no quarrel with Iowa," Jesse replied. "I'd just as soon run the Yankees out of southern Missouri and let it go at that."

"You know, if the goddamn bluebellies win this shooting match, you and me are going to be knee-deep in it. They'll call us outlaws and won't let it drop because we ain't wearing a gray uniform."

Jesse didn't respond, although it wasn't a new thought. Gray Fletcher had brought up the possibility one day while they practiced with the old Walkers and it had stuck like a burr ever since. If the South lost he would have to flee the state like a criminal; for a long time he hadn't believed the South could lose, but he wasn't so sure anymore. Anything seemed possible now.

"Hear 'em down there," Gil said.

"What's that?"

" 'Skeeters." Gil looked up, squinting into the west. "Be sundown soon, and they'll come up like a million tiny leeches."

"Worse," Jesse said. He had been leeched a time or two, for one childhood ailment or another, and knew that a leech didn't leave a man scratching for a week, for all that he hated the slimy little creatures.

"How far do you reckon the sun is now?" Gil asked out of the blue.

"How the hell do I know."

"Colorado Territory yet?"

It seemed a stupid question to Jesse, the kind that Billy Bob or Zeb might have asked, but he replied anyway, as he always had with Billy Bob and Zeb, as if drawn to it. "Maybe," he said. "But no farther. Not over the mountains yet."

"You ever wonder why if those mountains are as high as they say they are we can't see 'em from here?"

"Christ, Gil, you sound like my little brother."

"Go to hell," Gil replied absently. He was still looking west, with just his eyes in the shade of his hat brim now. "How far west you ever been, Jesse?"

"Just here," Jesse answered. He wasn't really sure where he was now, other than to know it was pretty close to the Kansas line.

"I've been into the Nations some and all through eastern Kansas and up along the Platte River as far as Kearney, but I ain't never been into the real West. Not where the Indians are hostile."

"I could never figure out why anyone would want to," Jesse said, thinking of Zeb, somewhere along the Oregon Road.

"I don't know. Excitement, maybe," Gil said. "I been studying on it. I know mule skinners who have freighted into the mining camps above Cherry Creek and they say there's money to be made for a man with his own rig."

"That's what will rub you raw every time," Jesse said. "A man without his own outfit just puts his money into someone else's pockets."

Gil laughed. "I had a slew of money after selling Pa's outfit, but I let it all slip away."

"Whiskey or women?" Jesse asked, grinning, but Gil scowled and didn't reply. Jesse didn't know too much about Gil's past, but he knew some of it, that Gil's pa had been a skinner and that Gil had swamped for him. He knew that Gil's pa had been hung by jayhawkers, too, but he didn't know much beyond that, and Gil was pretty closemouthed about most of it.

"You ever consider what you'll do when the fighting stops, Jesse? Where you'll go and all?"

"Seems like you've got a powerful obsession with it, all of a sudden."

"Oh, it ain't nothing that just crossed my mind," Gil replied. "It just took a different turn this morning when the Colonel rode away like he did. Hell, for a minute I thought it was all over for the rangers, and I ain't so sure I wouldn't have sloped if the Sarge hadn't followed like he did."

Jesse nodded to himself, remembering that morning and the surprise he'd felt at seeing

Dewey ride after Slaughter. Looking back, he knew now that he had almost ridden in a different direction himself, and that only Dewey had kept him from it.

"You've got a way with animals, did you know that?" Gil asked suddenly.

Jesse scowled at the erratic course of conversation, but held his tongue.

"You get along with mules, too?" Gil asked. "Reason I bring it up is that there are some who can get along fine with horses but can't seem to handle a mule."

"Some ain't got the knack, all right," Jesse admitted.

"But you do?"

"Hell, Gil, why don't you get this conversation chewed and swallowed? I'm getting a headache trying to figure out what you're after."

Gil laughed and pushed away from the railing. "I was thinking that if things didn't work out in Missouri maybe we could go West together and freight into the mountains. I ain't ashamed to admit I'm a better swamper than skinner, but I've got you pegged as a mule man, Jesse. I'm thinking you can handle a jerk-line rig as well as any man, or better. You know mules and I know the business. What do you say?"

It was a fresh idea, and for a while Jesse didn't know what to say. Then they heard the echo of hooves from the south, and it didn't matter. Gil mounted the bay and Jesse straightened in the saddle and put his hand on one of the Walkers.

"There," Gil said, as a rider came around a bend and out of the trees, loping a big black horse toward them. "That's Boone, ain't it?"

"Looks like," Jesse said, releasing his grip on the revolver. It was Boone, all right, Major Borden's big sergeant, coming on fast but not rushed.

Boone slowed as he approached, and nodded, his gaze taking in the clipped wire and the empty road beyond the bridge. "Trouble?" he asked.

"Nary a bit."

Colonel thinks a couple of men might have slipped out before we closed all the doors, and he's worried about Yankees prowling the area.

"Ain't seen no one here," Jesse said.

Boone shrugged and pulled a square-tipped cigar from the breast pocket of his shirt. From the same pocket he dug a sulfur match and struck it alight against his saddle horn.

"Gawddamn," Gil drawled in a mocking tone. "Ol' Boone's come up in the world."

Boone laughed through a cloud of cigar smoke. "Major sent me to fetch you two," he said. "Ol' Iron-ass took us in slicker than axle grease. Me and Davis outfitted right off so we could come after you two and Harker and O'Rourke."

"What else have you got in there?" Gil asked curiously, pointing with his chin toward Boone's bulging saddlebags.

Boone laughed again, a hard sound this time, without humor. "Ol' Iron-ass tried to limit us to the three mercantile stores, but he couldn't watch us all the time. Some of us slipped into the saloons early and helped ourselves to some entertainment, courtesy of the Jacksville merchants."

"Whiskey?"

"Hell, whiskey and seegars and free lunch, but they got whores too, and some of the boys helped themselves to that. Would've myself, if Borden hadn't cornered me and sent me after you two."

Jesse slid a glance toward Gil, noted the troubled brow, and took some comfort from that. He remembered the worry he'd seen in Slaughter's face when the Colonel told them of his plan, and knew that his fears were coming true. Somewhere in the last twelve hours they had crossed an invisible line, but how far over, Jesse didn't know yet. Lifting the buckskin's reins, he went to find out.

There was a sign on a post at the edge of town that read: *WELCOME TO JACKSVILLE, pop. 937.* Three Rangers stood in the shade of a cotton-wood about twenty feet away and popped shots at the sign with their revolvers. The *O* in welcome had been mostly splintered out, but the men were half drunk and had more or less peppered the whole sign with wild shots.

"Whoa, who the hell goes there?" one of the three shouted as Jesse and Gil approached.

"Christ," Jesse muttered, and rode past without slowing or speaking.

One of the three, a little sawed-off loudmouth named LeMay, came partway into the street after them, calling, "Haul rein, Ross, or I'll plug you in the back."

Jesse didn't bother with a reply, but Gil did. Turning in the saddle, he called back, "Pull yourself in, LeMay, before someone plucks your feathers."

LeMay didn't say anything to that; Jesse didn't expect him to. Rumor had built his killing of Curly Barnes into something more than it was, and from it had sprung an unwarranted reputation. Jesse supposed he should put a stop to it, but so far it hadn't seemed worth the effort.

Jacksville was bigger than Jesse had expected, but not by much. There were about eight blocks running north and south along the Springfield to Independence Road, and three or four blocks running east and west, with a square in the center of town that sported a red brick courthouse and a grassy commons around it. Most of the businesses ran outward from the square along the two main routes, but Jesse noticed several smaller businesses along the side streets, too. He didn't see anyone on the streets or along the boardwalks that he didn't recognize, but most of the windows around town had a face or two framed in them, most of them pale with fright. Rangers galloped up and down the street, firing their revolvers into the air, but it didn't look all that wild to Jesse. It was a riot without chaos that was the Colonel's idea, and it kept the citizens inside and out of the way.

On the commons about half a dozen men were pulling down a United States flag, and Jesse smiled in spite of himself, spotting the stars and bars one of the rangers held ready to be hoisted aloft. They rode without hurry now, halted when Borden came out of a tobacco store, his face red, vexed. To Jesse, he said, "They tell me some of my men are drunk and shooting up the north end of town."

"I don't know how drunk they are, but they're shooting the hell out of the *Welcome to Jacksville* sign."

"Sonofabitch," Borden said. He bit his lower lip, studied the street for a moment. Then he said, "Well, I guess I ought to ride down there and stop them, although I ain't sure why anymore."

"Gonna upset the Colonel something fierce if you don't," Gil observed blankly.

Borden unexpectedly laughed. "Sounds like a good reason to let them go," he said. "But I guess I'll mosey on down in a while and see what they're up to."

Borden turned around and walked into the store,

and Jesse and Gil exchanged puzzled looks. They rode on and, south of the commons, found Dewey grimly sitting his horse in the middle of the street.

"Howdy, Sarge," Gil greeted.

"You're to go into Caldo's General and outfit yourselves with new clothes and ammunition," Dewey said bluntly. "You are to leave a detailed list of everything you take. Best hump it, too. Looks like a couple of townsmen slipped out, and there's supposed to be a shitpot full of Yankees camped just south of here."

"You ain't outfitted yourself," Jesse said casually.

"Just do what you're told, Jesse."

"Go on in and steal whatever I want, huh? Well, I don't guess that should bother a cattle rustler."

Dewey glanced at him, then away. "Nobody's holding you responsible for what you take today. Nor the cows you and Quint brought back from the Missouri, either."

"I ain't doing it, Dewey. I ain't stealing no more if you ain't." Jesse could feel his stubbornness rising, and clenched his fists. Goddamnit, it wasn't fair; Dewey was setting himself above the rest by refusing to participate, was announcing by his dissent his feelings on the matter.

From down the street the sound of breaking glass came faintly to their ears. Slaughter's control was slipping, Jesse knew; if they didn't leave soon it might vanish altogether. He didn't like thinking about what might happen to Jacksville then.

"Just do as you're told," Dewey said harshly. "Consider it an order."

"Order?" Jesse laughed.

"Hell, Sarge, Jesse feels the same way you do," Gil said earnestly. "It cuts him cross-grained to do this."

Dewey's face reddened, then, abruptly, it faded. With resignation, he said, "Go get us some powder and ball at least, Jesse. Leave the rest, if that's the way you want to do it."

"Come with us," Jesse urged.

Dewey shook his head, his mouth drawn into a thin line.

Gil said, "But you'll take some of the powder and lead, right, Sarge?" He looked at Jesse. "Hell, Jesse, we can take that much. They owe us that much."

"Nobody owes me anything," Jesse said sourly, but he could feel his resolve sway. There was logic to Gil's words, no matter how distasteful, and even to Slaughter's raid on Jacksville. He remembered the meadow, early that morning, and Slaughter's only alternative: surrender. "Goddamnit," he gritted, jerking the buckskin around roughly and spurring to the nearby store.

Gil followed uncertainly, but Dewey remained in the middle of the street, his face set. Leland Recker, who had been separated for a while from

Jubal Butler before Butler found them outside Table Rock, met them on the boardwalk wearing a new broadcloth suit between new boots and a new hat. He grinned, seeing Jesse, and flipped the loose ends of his string tie. "Not bad, eh, Ross? They got some more in there; go get yourself one."

Jesse brushed past him without speaking, hearing Recker's startled exclamation and Gil's muted response. He stepped inside, stopped dead, shocked at the ruin around him. The store —Caldo's General—was a shambles. The aisles were heaped with spilled clothing and unwound bolts of material, with dented airtights of meat and fruit, and boxes and bags and broken glass. Wire-frame mannequins lay like wounded among the rubble of crushed hickory splits baskets and stiff, white straw hats.

"Wickedness," hissed a small, bald man in a clerk's apron. He stood with two or three others— customers—against the back wall, under Bob Wilkes's watchful eye. "Satan's work through border bandits. Are you another of Satan's sons?"

"He talked like a regular human being until some of the boys got a little rough with the merchandise," Wilkes said. He was sitting on the counter with a pistol in his lap, eating cheese and crackers.

"Goddamn," Gil said with honest awe. "This looks like what a tornado did to Willow Grove, Kansas, one time."

"Jayhawkers," the clerk pronounced. "The trash of Kansas."

"Shut up, old man," Wilkes said, scowling. He looked at Jesse and added, "The Colonel said not to hurt anyone unless it was absolutely necessary, but this yahoo tries a man's patience for a fact."

"What happened here?" Jesse asked softly.

"Oh, Butler and Recker and some of that bunch. I was going to stop them until Pops here turned religious."

"Satan's path leads to hell," the clerk whispered.

"Where's the powder and lead?" Jesse asked.

"Under the counter," Wilkes replied.

Jesse walked behind the counter, stooping and picking up six pounds of powder and fifteen pounds of lead and several tins of caps. He made a little pile of it all on the counter and for a while then just stared at it.

Wilkes said, "There's jeans and shirts and such along the far aisle. Most of the boys are just packing their clothes with them until they can take a bath sometime. That's what I'm doing."

"Guilt eats at you, doesn't it, son?" the clerk said, grinning like a wolf at Jesse. "It won't get better. It won't wash off in the river like good earth. The Lord will punish those who have done evil this day. He will ride behind your saddle and whisper admonitions in your ear. He will lie beside you at night and haunt your dreams with visions of eternal fire. What you have—"

Wilkes lifted his pistol and snapped a shot into the floor, the report thunderous in the confines of the room, and the clerk squawked and jumped, and an elderly woman screamed briefly, while a potbellied man in a good suit gasped, "My word," and swayed back against the wall as if contemplating fainting. Wilkes looked at Jesse and grinned, but Jesse couldn't see any humor in the situation, felt only a suffocating sense of deception, as if he'd stepped into a trap and only just now reached the end of its chain. Coming around the counter, he gathered everything into his arms and went outside. He was stowing the powder in his saddlebags when Tim loped up.

"Where's Sarge?" Tim asked. "I can't find him anywhere, and the Colonel's wanting him."

"He'll show up," Jesse grunted. He felt suddenly tired, drained in a way he hadn't felt since his early days with Gray. The little bald clerk's warning came sharp to his mind, and he angrily thrust it aside. Damn Slaughter for all of this, he thought, but he knew also that Slaughter had offered them a choice that morning, and that he had ridden into Jacksville anyway. But did accepting blame change their position in any way? A man had only to look at his partners to see the hunger and nakedness that plagued them all, to see the horses standing half dead from weariness, and the leather falling apart on saddles and boots.

Why are we fighting, if those we fight for won't even clothe us?

The question came unbidden and without answer, and with a small exclamation of anger he jerked the reins loose and swung into the saddle.

From the south a rider pounded up the street, bent low over the horn with his hat pushed off the back of his head and kept from blowing away by only a drawstring. Eli Davis, Jesse saw, and felt a touch of concern. Hadn't Boone said Davis was watching the southern route?

"Must've stirred up a hell of a hornet's nest," Tim said casually.

"That's what I'm thinking," Jesse said, trying to ignore the hollow pounding of his heart. Davis raced past without slowing or acknowledging those who hailed him, his spurs raking his horse's ribs every other stride.

Gil came out of Caldo's then with his arms laden with powder and lead, and clothing, too, his face flushed from embarrassment, but when he saw Davis he dropped the clothing and jumped into the street, shoving his ammunition into his saddle-bags. Jesse spurred after Davis without waiting for Gil, and Tim followed. From up and down the street others began to appear, uncertainly at first, then with increasing panic, abandoning whatever they were doing and getting on their horses to follow.

Jesse found Slaughter on the north side of the

commons with about forty men, Davis among them, leaning forward until he was nearly standing in his stirrups and talking excitedly. Jesse couldn't get close, but had no urge to. He held the buckskin back, away from the crowd, and studied Slaughter's face, watching its flatness of expression, and its slow transformation. There, again, he saw the brief flare of panic, the wild swing of his gaze. It was gone then, the panic, disappearing as swiftly as it had that day on the Current, but this time Jesse sensed a restlessness among the men and knew that others had seen it too.

Slaughter turned away from Davis then, spoke quickly to Prescott, called across the crowd to Dewey, half hidden among the others. Dewey rode close, listened, then pulled away, forcing his sorrel through the crowd and to Jesse's side.

"What's up, Sarge?" Tim asked, his eyes big with a fear unlike any Jesse had ever seen there before.

"Yankees," Dewey said in a clipped tone. "Coming up the Springfield Road and no more than five minutes behind. The Colonel's going to leave Davis behind with ten men to slow them down. Tim, go with Jesse, scout the Independence Road. I'll stay behind with Gil."

Jesse nodded, wheeled the buckskin and spurred up the street with Tim close behind. He tried not to think about what Dewey had just said, the implications of it. He and Gil were staying behind, ten men against who knew how many Yankees.

The afternoon was waning by now, the sun hidden by hills and forest, but it was hot yet, the air thick and damp against their lungs, and by the time they'd cleared the hills and halted at the edge of the big cornfield bordering the river, their horses were lathered and blowing.

Jesse expected to see Boone on the bridge. What he did see puzzled him for a moment, as if his mind refused to register what his eyes saw. Then his throat constricted. In a line across the bridge, carbines drawn, sat a dozen federal soldiers.

CHAPTER 16

They heard the jingle of bits and spurs and the dry-limbed rattle of sabers for quite a while before the first federal officer appeared at the far end of the street. Dewey's hand tightened on the sorrel's reins and beside him, Gil began to curse, a low, steady monotone of meaningless obscenities. In advance of the Yankees by several blocks, a solitary Union scout rode forward at a walk, a tall, bony figure, shirtless in the heat, riding a stubby Indian pony. He carried a carbine butted to his thigh, and pistols belted high around his waist. His head swiveled slowly but steadily, and Dewey doubted if much escaped his notice.

"This is it, boys," Davis said so softly that only those closest to him heard, but when he cocked his revolver, everyone else followed.

They waited in the entry of the Jacksville Livery, far enough back within its shadows to remain invisible, yet with a clear view of the street to the south.

Opposite Caldo's, the scout finally halted his pony. Cradling the carbine in his arms, he stood in his stirrups and called in a loud, mocking voice, "Slaughter . . . Josiah Slaughter. Where are you hiding, Josiah?" In the thickening shadows the scout's broad, reckless grin gleamed like a target.

"Well, goddamn that bastard," whispered Bud Gantz, one of those who had wandered alone into the meadow below Possum Knob to await the Colonel's return from Kansas and the Indian Nations. "I could shoot him out of the saddle from here."

"Save your powder," Davis replied. "You'll use it soon enough."

The federal forces were advancing at a shuffling walk, kicking up a cloud of dust that clung to within a couple of feet of the ground. Dewey tried to count them, made it as high as two hundred and gave it up. Gil's cursing had lowered to a mere mumble now, but it continued without interruption, and perspiration beaded his face, dripping from the end of his nose.

The scout nudged his pony into a walk, still

standing in the stirrups, still goading with his voice. "Come on out, Josiah," he called. "Don't be bashful." He laughed and lifted his carbine, firing it into the air. Then he did a curious thing. He levered the trigger guard, cocked the hammer, and fired into the air a second time.

"Jesus Christ," Davis exclaimed; others echoed his sentiment. Gil looked at Dewey and his eyes widened. "A repeater?"

"Looks like," Dewey admitted. He had heard of such weapons of course, had known they were in production even, but this was the first one he'd ever seen.

By now the Federals had drawn even with Caldo's; the scout rode his pony onto the grass of the commons and disappeared behind the courthouse. The Jacksville Livery was on the northeast corner of the commons, less than two blocks from the front line of troopers, and Dewey threw Davis a puzzled glance. Time was running out and there wasn't a rear exit, only a large, high-railed corral behind the stable.

"Just a little closer," Davis whispered.

Dewey took a deep breath. The sorrel shifted under him, pawed once at the loose dirt and straw on the floor. Sweat trickled down the side of Dewey's face, tickling. Suddenly, the door to Caldo's swung open and the little bald-headed clerk ran onto the boardwalk. Dewey couldn't hear the words, but when the little clerk lifted his hand, the finger seemed to point straight at his heart.

"Sonofabitch," Davis said, then slapped spurs to his horse and burst from the livery, loosening a shrill rebel yell to coincide with the first loud burst of their gunfire.

The Yankees' horses erupted into a panic as ranger bullets stung or buzzed among them; a few ducked their heads and went to pitching. Here and there gunsmoke blossomed along the line of blue, but they were caught largely by surprise.

For a while it seemed almost too simple. They put their first rounds into the knot of officers and non-coms at the head of the column, wounding a couple and raising havoc among the horses, so that those troopers to the rear were left momentarily without command. But that changed quickly. While Davis led his men swiftly around the south end of the commons and swung back toward the north, a burly sergeant with a handlebar mustache drew a dozen men to the side, had them dismount, and from kneeling positions, ordered three quick volleys before the rangers were able to slip behind the protection of the courthouse. Four ranger horses galloped with them as they pounded north, toward the edge of town, saddles empty and stirrups flapping.

They were free then, or nearly so. Only the bare-chested scout remained in their path now, and he pulled his little Indian pony broadside to them and started to lift his repeater, but then his nerve broke and he spurred to the side. Dewey didn't bother with a shot; too many others did, and he watched the scout jerk and twitch in the saddle as if stung by hornets, before toppling to the ground.

As they rode out of town Dewey risked a backward glance, but they were alone yet, the road behind them empty.

Jesse didn't turn at Slaughter's approach, but he watched it in his mind, seeing there the look of surprise that would cross the Colonel's face as he halted his men, the quick flash of panic when he spotted the federal soldiers on the bridge, and then the growing anger as he approached alone. Jesse felt no surprise when Slaughter appeared at his side.

"What is the situation here, Ross?" Slaughter asked tersely.

"What you see, I reckon," Jesse replied. "Bluebellies on the bridge and no sign of Boone."

"Sergeant Boone?"

Jesse nodded. "Was Boone that came to fetch me and Gil." The sound of gunfire shattered the stillness behind them, faint with distance. It flared momentarily, then almost immediately began to fade. Davis's men, Jesse knew; that meant they had engaged the Federals approaching from the south and were on the way now. Coming at a gallop, it wouldn't take them long, either. Only time would tell how quickly the Federals followed up.

Slaughter pulled a pair of binoculars from a case attached to his saddle horn and studied the bridge for some time. He let them drift then, moving slowly downstream, then back up. After a while, perhaps a minute all told, he slipped them back into the case. "Twelve," he said calmly. "A dead man lies in the ditch along the road. Sergeant Boone, I would presume." Turning, he motioned for Major Borden to come forward.

Jesse studied the twelve soldiers facing them and felt his uneasiness grow. "They ain't running, Colonel. There's only a few of them and better than fifty of us, but they ain't running."

"I am aware of that, Ross, but that doesn't subtract from the numbers to our rear."

Borden rose close. "Sir?"

"Major, twelve Yankee horse soldiers hold that bridge. I intend to charge it with my entire command, and I want you to lead. Understand, I have spotted twelve, but in all likelihood others await in ambush."

Borden scowled. "Goddamn, Colonel, if you suspect an ambush let's just ride around the bastards."

Slaughter's face reddened slightly, but his voice remained calm. "I do not intend to flounder through the bush like a wounded bear while

Yankee hunters complete a surround, Major. Nor do I intend to allow my orders to be questioned in times of emergency, do you understand?"

Tight-lipped, Borden said, "Then why don't you let Prescott and his boys lead one, *Colonel?* Frankly, me and my men are getting a little goddamn tired of always being the first to face the Yankees."

Slaughter's eyes flashed. "You will lead your men in charge, *Captain* Borden, or tomorrow I will see you before a firing squad."

Borden's mouth tightened into a thin line, and he gritted, "Yes sir," and wheeled his horse. "Miles," he bawled. "Get the men into line. We're gonna open another goddamn trail for the others to follow."

Softly, Slaughter said, "Do not push your luck with me, Captain. I will not allow it."

Borden looked at Slaughter, his whole face working, but he didn't reply. Slaughter rode back to Prescott's side; Jesse stayed with Borden. Miles brought his men forward, his voice loud in the gathering shadows. Dusk was near now; in the west the sky blazed with a color like blood, and the corn looked black. Riding forward then, Miles said, "Ready when you are, Major."

"Then let's go take that goddamn bridge," Borden said.

They broke into a gallop, lifted that to a run. Jesse had already drawn one of the Walkers, now he dropped his reins over the buckskin's neck and drew the second. A rebel yell rose tentatively from one of Borden's men, soared then from a dozen voices, then broke loud and strong across the fields, a rising discord of swelling anger. Jesse rode low, the buckskin's mane in his face, and it was one of his Walkers that belched the first shot.

On the bridge the twelve horse soldiers turned and fled, forcing their mounts off the road and into the weeds. A wild, crazy cheering erupted from the men, laced with triumph. They thought the Yankees had run, leaving the road before them open, but deep down, Jesse knew they were wrong. He looked at Borden, riding close, and knew that he sensed it too, but before either could shout a warning, a huge cloud of gray smoke mushroomed from the brush atop the dirt bank across the river, and lead grape whistled through the air around them. The buckskin squealed shrilly and jumped to one side, almost unseating Jesse. Ted Miles screamed and flipped off the back of his horse, the side of his face blown away. Four others died with him.

"Howitzer!" Borden shrieked from the dust, his thigh cherry red. Tim O'Rourke's gray filly was down too, her big eyes liquid with pain and confusion, and Tim swayed on his hands and knees, his face chalky, his eyes glassy.

Unable to stop in time, Slaughter led his men into the melee of rearing, lunging horses, screaming men, death and blood. A volley of rifle fire from the high bank cut half a dozen raiders from the saddle. Slaughter's gray went down, rose, and Slaughter scrambled after it, clutching comically for the reins. Terror was their only leader now, and it reigned with an iron fist.

Jesse jerked the buckskin around, back to the road. To the south a small band of riders pounded out of the trees, Davis leading, Dewey and Gil close behind. Jesse expected them to halt, seeing the chaos before them, but they only slowed and veered wide around the confusion, and Jesse figured pursuit must be close then. They had to get across the bridge now, and he whipped the buckskin around and drove his spurs savagely into the gelding's flanks.

Others followed. Jubal Butler forced his chestnut onto the road beside Jesse, with John Martin and Leland Recker and Harvey Quint coming up side-by-side right behind him. Another little knot of riders broke from the swirling dust where Borden's charge had been abruptly halted and joined them as Davis's bunch swung back toward the road. Nearly thirty men, almost half of Slaughter's command, made another hard drive for the bridge.

Minie balls whined sharply through the air, striking flesh, tearing leather. John Martin howled and clutched at his stomach as he spilled off the side of his horse, and Leland Recker's face paled suddenly and he bent forward, grabbing desperately for his saddle horn.

Hooves against the plank bridge created a hollow thunder, and on the far bank the twelve soldiers who had retreated into the weeds began to retreat even farther. Quint yelled, a wild, rising, heart-pounding cry that half a dozen others immediately echoed, and Jesse knew there was no stopping them now that they had the bit in their teeth and the bridge was theirs. He cut loose with his own shout then, letting fly right and left with the old Walkers. From the dirt bank another gray cloud of powder smoke spurted toward the river, but the grape went high.

The bridge was crossed then, but still not won. The soldiers, those not dead or lying wounded, had fallen back to a clump of saplings with an old, sun-bleached tree trunk to take shelter behind. They'd abandoned their horses and now scrabbled in the dirt, but they were returning a withering fire.

Jesse reined the buckskin to the side, Quint and Butler with him. Eli Davis and his small command were still on the bridge, halted there and returning fire, but despite its lesser numbers, the enemy was too well protected to be routed.

For a while then, they were stymied, brought up short by those unable yet to follow, capable only of firing their revolvers and being fired at in return. Slaughter was mounted again, hatless now, his hair a wild mane as he moved among the men, trying to bring order to the pandemonium, urging them onto the bridge. Far beyond and indistinct in the rapidly fading light, swept the first wave of Union cavalry from Jacksville.

That much Jesse saw clearly. Then, from the little grove of saplings, a Yankee minie ball reached out and plucked him neatly from the saddle.

CHAPTER 17

Dawn brought a gray, diffused light to the marshy patch of land within the fork of the Osage and South Grand rivers, but little else. Gil had hoped for more, a return to reality, perhaps, after the long, reckless flight of the night before. He found only a smoky fire surrounded by a handful of exhausted rangers, their horses standing hipshot nearby, spattered with mud and blood, saddled yet, and worn out.

Dewey called a halt and slid wearily from his saddle, hobbling painfully to a sycamore that leaned toward the South Grand and sinking beside, his wounded leg thrust stiffly before him. Gil pulled the bridle off the bay and hung it over the saddle horn; he didn't bother with hobbles, the animal was too tired to wander far. He went back to help Bob Wilkes lift Jesse from the buckskin's back and stretch him out on the ground. The entire left side of Jesse's shirt was dark with blood that had already dried and crusted. He looked pale, feverish, but Gil had examined the wound briefly around midnight in the light of a sulphur match and knew that as long as infection didn't set in he would recover.

Wilkes led the horses away, but Gil stayed with Jesse. He wanted to pull Jesse's shirt off, to wash his wound with water and bandage it with something clean, but he doubted if there would be time. They had lost their pursuit when night fell, but Gil knew the Yankees would be pushing on already. They were on the run again, and there wouldn't be much letup for the next several days, to Gil's way of thinking.

"Hell of a night, huh?" Jesse croaked dryly.

"Yeah," Gil said. He touched Jesse's shoulder gently. "How are you feeling, pard?"

"Felt worse, I reckon. Better too, though," he said, and laughed a little, until a spasm of pain choked the laughter off. "Jesus Christ," he whispered.

Gil patted his shoulder but felt too helpless to attempt anything more. From the thin fog more horsemen straggled in, halting uncertainly when they spotted the small campfire and the scattered rangers. Gil saw Eli Davis among them and went forward to greet him.

"How," Davis greeted, sliding from his saddle. "What's up?" he asked. "Why has everyone stopped?"

"River, I reckon," Gil said. "We ain't gonna ford this one without some swimming, and there's wounded that ain't up to it."

"Where's Colonel Slaughter?"

Gil shrugged.

"Who's in command?"

"Well, Dewey Harker's here, but he took a bullet in the leg and he's fair whipped. Reckon that makes you the man in charge."

Davis said, "Shit," with feeling, and walked toward the South Grand with Gil beside him. He stared for a moment at its dark, swirling waters, then said, "We're going to need a boat." He paused, then added, "Unless you just want to give up."

"There's some that would, I'm thinking."

"Probably," Davis said, and hitched at his belt. "But I ain't, so why don't you and some of the boys try to scare up a boat or canoe or something? Take King and Johnson, they're good men."

Arliss King was a Prescott man from the early days and something of a friend until Gil had started riding regularly with Dewey and Jesse as a scout. King had partnered with Woody Johnson sometime after that. Gil didn't know Johnson well, but figured if King had stayed with him this long he was likely a good hand.

Gil said, "Okay," and went to get his horse. On the way he stopped next to Dewey and hunkered down beside him. "Howdy, Sarge," he said.

Dewey looked up sleepily and cleared his throat. "Gil. Riding out?"

"Yeah. Davis wants me to scare up a boat of some kind."

Dewey smiled and shut his eyes, half out of it, Gil thought. "How's Jesse?" Dewey asked.

"I don't reckon he'll die, but he ain't gonna keep up for long if we can't shake the goddamn Yankees."

"We could all use a break," Dewey said in a faraway voice. He shut his eyes and for a second Gil thought he was sleeping, but then he said, in a voice still soft and unfamiliar, "We took a hell of a beating yesterday, Gil. Hell of a beating. I don't think I've ever seen so many dead friends in one place before."

A shiver ran up Gil's spine and his scalp crawled. He stared at Dewey, saw a stranger instead.

"The worst part is knowing that most of them wouldn't have been there if not for me," Dewey continued. "Did you know that, Gil? I didn't, until last night. I did a lot of thinking last night."

"Hell, dreamin' is more like it, Sarge. That's fever talking there. It was Slaughter they followed, and of their own will, too."

Dewey laughed softly, a sound barely heard. "I

told myself that once too," he said. "But I don't believe it anymore."

Gil didn't know what to think about that, didn't know how to react to Dewey's sudden shift of character. He could understand a man blaming himself for something, but Dewey had gone beyond that. He said, "Sarge, it ain't your fault no more'n it was mine. It's just a goddamn war, and you can't take that upon your shoulders. It's . . . it's just like . . ." His mind struggled for comparison. "It's just like a branch tossed in a river, Sarge. It gets drug here and there, but it ain't the branch's fault."

Dewey opened his eyes and chuckled, a familiar sound, and Gil wanted to laugh himself, hearing it. Dewey said, "You won't find a boat sitting here."

"I ain't even gonna look until I know you're all right."

"Hell, I'm all right. Just worn-down sleepy is all. Light a shuck, Gil. We need that boat."

Gil hesitated. Dewey seemed fine now, but he wasn't convinced yet. The stranger's voice, his pain, still haunted him. He remembered Kansas then, and the stranger he had become for a while.

Leaves rustled, a branch cracked. Looking up, Gil found Arliss King and Woody Johnson staring at him. King said, "Howdy Gil, Sarge," and added to Dewey, "How bad you hit, Sarge?"

"Nothing a little sleep wouldn't cure," Dewey replied.

"Could use a little myself," King admitted. "But I reckon we gotta put this river behind us first." He looked at Gil.

"You going to be okay, Sarge?" Gil asked. "Want me to take a look at that leg for you before I go?"

"Naw. Hell, I've been hurt worse than this falling off a horse."

Gil didn't know whether to believe him or not, but he thought time was running short, so he just nodded and swung onto the bay. He rode out of the trees and halted again in a weedy clearing. King and Johnson followed. Gil said, "Reckon we'll go north a ways, along the South Grand."

"You remember that farm we passed about half a mile back?" King asked.

Gil did, vaguely. It had still been dark then, but he remembered smelling cattle and hogs and the strong, musty odor of corn.

"It was just turning light when we came past," King continued, "but I remember looking at the river and seeing something like a pier, maybe, with a boat or something pulled up on the bank. I ain't sure, mind you. It was still pretty gray then, but that's what it looked like to me."

"Worth checking," Gil said. "Lead the way."

King turned away, Johnson behind him and Gil bringing up the rear. They kept passing others along the trail, riding singly or in pairs, or in small bunches of three or four or five riders, but none bigger. About every third man sported a wound of some kind, surrounded by old blood that was already drawing a few flies. Nobody said much; a few barely looked up. Among them all Gil sensed an air of surrender that seemed almost overwhelming. They had been harried by Yankees into a frantic, erratic retreat for weeks without end, had briefly, hopefully, believed they had finally eluded pursuit, only to ride into their worse defeat yet.

They were beaten, Gil realized sickly, crushed in spirit as well as body, dead but not fallen. He remembered the only buffalo he had ever seen, a cow along the road to Fort Kearney, shot in the lungs by a meat hunter from the post. But even half dead, she had refused to drop, had stood instead with her legs braced and her bloodied nose brushing the ground, until the hunter pulled her over by her tail. That's the way he saw the rangers now, waiting for someone to grab them by the tail.

The farm Arliss King mentioned was about where Gil remembered, set back a ways from the river, though, with broad fields of corn and beans and tobacco between. But no pier jutted into the Osage, and no boat lay overturned on the bank. There was only a boy's crude raft pulled half out of the water, and an old broom with its bristles nearly gone to serve as a paddle.

King shook his head. "Goddamnit, Gil, I thought it was a pier and boat. I thought sure as hell it was."

"It doesn't matter," Gil said, but he thought it probably did. At best they had about a ten-hour lead, but he knew they couldn't count on that. If the Yankees had pushed on through the night, instead of camping . . . If they had telegraphed another troop garrisoned closer . . .

Gil studied the raft. It was small and would probably be awkward to handle, but he thought it might carry two at a time, maybe three if they were careful. "It'll work," he said quietly. "And it's handy."

"Banks is right," Johnson said. "We could ride all the way back to Jacksville without finding anything better."

King shrugged doubtfully. "Maybe," he said, "but I ain't floating it. It doesn't even have sideboards."

Gil laughed, then sobered. He looked at Johnson and Johnson shook his head emphatically. "Not me," Johnson said.

"Well, somebody's got to ride the damn thing," Gil said. He eyed the water distrustfully. He was only a moderate swimmer, and deep water frightened him.

From the trail above them a voice called derisively, "What's the old bastard up to now? Thinking of starting a navy?"

It was Borden. He sat an unfamiliar black horse, hatless, one sleeve of his shirt ripped and stained with blood, his eyes red-rimmed and hollow-looking. Bud Gantz and Jubal Butler and the Dye brothers, Charlie and John, sat their horses with him.

"Got us a river to cross," King returned. "Maybe that'll put the Yankees behind us for a spell."

"Didn't do much good last night," Borden said flatly.

King frowned, looked at Johnson. Charlie Dye leaned forward in his saddle. "You're a smart man, Arliss. You ought to be riding with us."

"Riding where?" King asked.

Charlie laughed; so did Jubal Butler. Borden said, "Come on, boys. The hay ain't quite cured yet."

Borden gigged his horse and the others fell into line behind him. When they'd passed from hearing, King whistled softly. "What was that about?" he asked.

"That was trouble brewing," Gil said quietly, staring after Borden and his men. Then he shook his head, turned. "Come on," he said. "Let's get this raft into the river. If I can figure out how to rein the sonofabitch, I'll ride it down."

Across the South Grand and then north, the Yankees still nipping, but without teeth now, just little patrols they dodged when they could and fought when they couldn't. Hazy days and black, muggy nights filled with the moans of the wounded and the ghosts of those killed or left behind. Of the nearly sixty men who left the Current River with Slaughter that spring, only thirty-four remained. Most died crossing the Osage outside of Jacksville and during the wild flight downriver to the fork with the South Grand. The numbers had been staggering at first, unacceptable to some, who surreptitiously watched their backtrail for friends who never appeared. But animosity gradually grew, spread; there was muttering in the dark, and resentful glares. Borden's popularity flourished as Slaughter's waned. There was talk of mutiny that never came to anything but never went away, either.

It was three days from when they crossed the South Grand on a clumsy raft until they returned once more to the Osage River. Sometime within those three days Josiah Slaughter's Company of Missouri Rangers died; no one mourned its passage.

CHAPTER 18

Jesse sat up slowly, one hand held gently, experimentally, to his side, but the pain was slight, and except for some lingering dizziness he felt nearly whole again. Across the gray ashes of last night's fire, Dewey lifted his head from his saddle and grinned. "Ho, boy, you're looking some better."

"Feel it," Jesse conceded, glancing around at his surroundings. Nearby, the Osage murmured faintly, its surface rippled now and again by feeding fish. It was early yet, foggy in spots and damp all over, the tall grass along the river bent by a heavy dew. At the far end of the strung-out camp a couple of men sat by a small fire that trailed a wispy banner of smoke, but most of the men were asleep, oblong bundles, still as death.

Dewey pushed his blanket back and jackknifed into a sitting position, his gaze questioning. "Okay?" he asked.

"Yeah," Jesse said, but he wasn't sure if he meant it. He was hungry, ravenous in fact, but when he tried to remember his last meal he drew only a blank picture. He tried to think back to his last clear image and saw the bridge outside Jacksville drawing near, heard the hum of bullets passing close, remembered the wild, choking sense of exhilaration as they thundered over it. But everything between then and now came only fuzzily, fragmented scenes of mumbled words and looming faces, and in between a kind of enveloping darkness in which only a faint and lancing pain resided.

Dewey shook his boots out and slipped them on. He stood and stretched and threw Jesse a skeptical glance. "You're sure you're okay? Not going to puke again?"

"Again?" Jesse's mind reeled.

Dewey grinned and said, "I guess you'll be okay. Hungry?"

That much he could answer. "Near starved, it seems." He toed the *mochilla* on his saddle and remembered the aisles of tinned foods he had refused in Jacksville.

"Gil ran a trout line last night," Dewey said. "I'll go see what's on it."

Jesse watched Dewey limp away, then walked in the opposite direction, stooping carefully to collect firewood. Slaughter's camp stretched for a good little distance along the river, the horses picketed here and there on scattered patches of grass between the trees. He walked slowly, stopping now and again to just stare or take note. He felt as if he'd just awakened from a long sleep to discover himself in a strange house.

Dewey returned just as Jesse got back with his second load, toting three big catfish and a turtle. They gutted the fish and cut the heads and tails off and tossed them into the weeds, then spitted them on slim green branches and propped them close to the flames. While the fish roasted Jesse fixed coffee and Dewey rolled a cigarette. The turtle cowered in the grass beside Jesse's saddle and watched with unblinking eyes from the cover of its shell.

Gil stirred as the aroma of roasting catfish slipped beneath his blankets, and he pushed them back to squint speculatively at his breakfast. "Damn," he said. "Three for three, how's that for luck?"

"And a turtle," Dewey said, lighting his cigarette with a twig from the fire. "What do you aim to do with it?"

Gil sat up and knuckled an eye. "If I had some barley I'd make soup. Best soup I ever ate was turtle, down at a little roadhouse in Arkansas."

"Huh," Jesse said. "I can see you hunkered down here watching a pot of soup while Slaughter's waiting to pull out. He'd have your ears."

Gil looked at Jesse, then away. He said, "Hell, I thought I'd sleep 'til Christmas if I ever got the chance, and it ain't hardly past dawn."

"Be moving soon anyway," Dewey said. He leaned forward and rotated the fish a quarter turn.

Here and there around the camp men were rising slowly, stiffly, stretching and tramping off into the woods or to see their horses. Jesse could see Slaughter some distance away, standing with his fists tight against the small of his back. He was hatless yet, his hair tangled, with a leaf caught in a cowlick. He wore boots and trousers, but no shirt over his partially unbuttoned uppers; Jesse couldn't remember ever seeing Slaughter so unkempt, not even during winter quarters when they all relaxed a little more than normal.

"He's some, ain't he?" Gil said scornfully.

Jesse frowned, looked at Dewey.

Dewey fussed with the fish for a moment, knocked the ash from his cigarette, then sighed. "How much do you remember of the last few days?" he asked.

"Not much. Hardly anything."

Dewey contemplated the end of his cigarette for a moment, as if debating where to start, then said, "We're a split camp, Jesse, and it's getting worse. I guess it's been building up since we left the Current. Or maybe it's always been there. But Borden's turned on Slaughter and he's got about half of those left ready to side with him. He hasn't done it yet, turned I mean, but it won't be long, and Slaughter, damn him, isn't doing anything to stop it."

"Well, I'll tell you one thing," Gil said. "I ain't riding with Jim Borden. I threw my lot in with Slaughter and when he quits, I quit."

Tim wasn't there. That fact struck Jesse unexpectedly. He rose and walked to the river, putting his shoulder against a slanting hickory and stared at the brown water. He remembered Tim as he had last seen him, kneeling in the dust beside his dying horse, his eyes dazed, uncomprehending, and he wondered how he could have forgotten. Then he tried to remember the last time he had seen Pete, and couldn't, and with a low, drawn moan, he bent forward and vomited.

Boots in the grass, and Dewey's voice comforting above him. "You'll be okay, Jesse. Your belly is empty, come on over and put something in it."

Dewey's hand squeezed his shoulder, a gesture Gray had often made. Jesse straightened and leaned into the hickory once more. He had been famished a few minutes before, but he wasn't now. He wondered what had happened to him, that he could forget Pete. Was he dead? Had he lived? And would Tim slip as easily from his mind? Was death and loss that commonplace now, life that expendable? What kind of man had he become?

Gil called, "Hell, the coffee's hot. Come and have some of that while the fish finish."

"We can take you to a doctor if it's your side," Dewey said.

Jesse shook his head. "I'm fine, Dewey. Maybe I could use some food." He let Dewey lead him back to the fire, but it wasn't food he was thinking of then, or even Tim or Pete. It was himself, and the emptiness he felt inside, now that the old anger was finally gone.

Texas Crossing lay like a dead thing along both sides of the broad lane that passed for a main street. Breakfast smoke rose lazily from several of the dozen or so buildings that made up the town, while a couple of small shoats rooted in a mudhole next to Kerwin's General Store. There was a saddle mule hitched at the rail in front of the Osage Emporium Saloon, and a single red rooster pecking in the dirt beside a ramshackle billiards hall with boarded windows. On Kerwin's porch a lanky man in a gaudy plaid suit was sloped into a cane-backed rocker with a pug hat tipped over his face, but there was no one else that Dewey could see, and if not for the blue columns of chimney smoke it would have been easy to imagine the town deserted.

It was that air of serenity that bothered Dewey. It was too quiet, even for Texas Crossing.

Slaughter sensed it too, and for the last couple of minutes had held his men back while Jesse and Gil made a quick scout through the woods surrounding the town. Dewey wished he could slip across the river and talk with the Cap'n, but he knew there wasn't time. They'd jumped a Yankee patrol that morning that had been too quick to retreat, and everyone feared retaliation from a larger force.

At the mudhole beside Kerwin's one of the shoats squealed loudly over some prize its mate claimed and the lanky man on the porch jumped and sat up. He stood then, rubbing his eyes, and walked to the edge of the porch. He spotted the rangers almost immediately, but didn't show much surprise.

Brush crackled on their right and Dewey's fingers twitched, but he didn't move. It was Gil, and coming up beside them, he announced, "All clear as far as I can see."

"Did you go all the way to the river?" Slaughter asked.

Gil nodded, looked away, his expression bored. Like so many others, Gil had lost respect for Slaughter, Dewey knew, but he hadn't yet spoken of mutiny, or drifted to Borden's camp. Yet it illustrated the problem as Dewey saw it, which wasn't so much Borden's defiance as Slaughter's refusal to deal with it.

"What is it, Lieutenant?" Slaughter asked Dewey. "What halts our advance when Captain Fletcher's ferry beckons so invitingly?"

"I couldn't say, Colonel," Dewey replied, glad that he didn't have to, that the decision to advance or retreat was Slaughter's alone. He hadn't always felt that way of course, but something had changed for him the night he learned from Copeland of Pete's fate; following Slaughter away from Possum Knob, knowing that others stayed only because of him, had only compounded the problem. He felt weak, vulnerable, as if some invisible shell had fallen away somewhere and exposed him to feelings he had never experienced before. A decision now was like a piece of himself pried loose and tossed away, and he knew a man couldn't do that for long without eventually losing himself along the way.

To their left now, Jesse's big gelding bulled its

way through the bushes and saplings with a loud racket. Coming onto the road, Jesse shook his head to Slaughter's unspoken question. "I saw a seven-foot black snake, but no sign of Yankees."

Slaughter looked at Dewey and said, "If I wasn't so certain the Federals were approaching from the rear I'd order a retreat." He paused as if waiting for a reply, but Dewey remained silent. Sighing then, Slaughter said, "Lead us into town, Lieutenant."

Dewey lifted the sorrel's reins, touched her with his spurs. He rode into town at a walk, keeping his free hand back and high on his thigh, close to his revolver. The mule lifted its head at their approach and brayed loudly, but no one appeared at the Emporium's door; only the lanky man in the plaid suit showed more interest.

Near the center of town Dewey turned aside from the others and halted in front of Kerwin's porch. "Howdy," he said.

The lanky stranger nodded a reply.

"Lazy day," Dewey offered then.

"Hot, for a fact," the stranger responded. He was watching Slaughter and the others, and when they reached the edge of the pier and stopped, he took a deep breath and exhaled it slowly.

A prickle of fear ran up Dewey's spine when the stranger looked directly at him. Dewey let his gaze slide right and then left, but nothing had changed, and he swore softly. He said, "This is the most uncurious town I've ever ridden through. You'd think a bunch this size would've drawn a face to every window in town."

The stranger smiled. "Oh, I think there are plenty of people watching you."

"You ain't Kerwin, are you?" Dewey asked bluntly.

"I understand that Mr. Kerwin left some years ago, but that no one has bothered to change the name. My name is Jonathan Douglas, Captain, United States Army, on detached service. You have led us on quite a chase, Mr. Harker."

Dewey grunted and drew up some, but he was careful not to move his hand any closer to his revolver. Beyond Douglas he could see shadowy forms flitting through the store's dark interior. He considered a denial but let it go without an attempt. It was too late for that now.

Douglas was watching the rangers again. Riding partway onto the pier, Slaughter drew his revolver and fired it once into the air. "Fletcher won't come," Douglas said, rather sadly, Dewey thought. "I sent three men over last night to subdue him."

"You were expecting us?"

"Here or a couple of other places. A company was left here just in case."

"Lucky you," Dewey said flatly.

Douglas's brow furrowed. "My sergeant urged ambush, Mr. Harker. It was his contention that even if you were offered a peaceful termination, you would still fight. I had hoped he was wrong, and that we could avoid bloodshed, but you seem to take the situation somewhat lightly."

Dewey looked toward the river, where Slaughter sat his gray alone on the pier. Jesse and Gil, with King and Johnson and a few others, sat their horses close by, but off to one side Borden waited within a knot of his own followers, nearly equal in size to Slaughter's. It struck Dewey as funny that the Yankees should finally get the drop on them now; given another few days, a week at the most, and they would have likely disbanded anyway. Was that why he had stuck around this long, he wondered suddenly? Had he only wanted to witness the end?

"Mr. Harker, do you realize the seriousness of your situation? We have commandeered this store and the livery across the street, and from these vantage points we now have your entire band under our sights. There is no escape, Mr. Harker. None."

Dewey considered that for a minute, but looked ahead, too. "Tell me, Captain," he asked. "What happens if we surrender? That is, if the Colonel can talk the boys into laying down their pistols, which I'm not at all convinced he can."

"You will be escorted on foot to Jefferson City and from there sent to St. Louis, where I assume you will all stand trial for crimes against the

Union and the state of Missouri, plus whatever civil charges might be brought against you."

Dewey chewed reflectively on his lower lip, remembering the list of names Copeland had given him in Poplar Bluff. Jesse's name had been on that list, as had Gil's, and in his mind he saw them both hanging limply from a gallows, their arms bound tightly, immorally, behind their backs. What had their crimes been, he wondered, except to fight against the injustices waged against them and their families? Did Douglas's mother cook in a hotel because her property had been destroyed by invaders? Or had Douglas ever awakened to find his father hung unceremoniously from a cottonwood limb? Dewey took a deep breath. He had wondered from time to time about his own justification for joining Slaughter's rangers, but he had never doubted Jesse's or Gil's.

Dewey looked across the river, to its far shore, and grinned hugely. "How many men did you say you sent across the river to—was it *subdue*—Cap'n Fletcher?"

Douglas followed Dewey's gaze and his face darkened. On the far bank Gray Fletcher was humping it down the slope to his ferry.

"What we have here, Captain," Dewey said amiably, "is what the Texas Rangers used to call a Mexican standoff. What that means is if I make an untoward move, your men will probably shoot me. But, Captain, if you so much as peep like a chick, I'm going to draw my pistol and blow a hole in your belly big enough to read through."

"By God, sir, I should have listened to my sergeant."

"Probably," Dewey said flatly. "Because as far as I can see all you've offered us is a chance to rot in a damn Yankee prison until you got around to hanging us. I'd just as soon die today, with a pistol in my hand."

"I will try my best to arrange for that," Douglas said grimly. But he didn't alert his men, and on the river Gray was already edging his ferry into the current.

Still, it wasn't a perfect setup. Douglas's men wouldn't immediately open fire without orders, but Dewey didn't think they'd allow the Rangers to escape, either. Sooner or later someone within either the livery or the store would grasp the situation and give the command to fire. It came to him then that there would be no way out for him, that no matter what would happen he wouldn't survive this day. It was an odd thought, and it gave him a funny, punched-in-the-gut feeling.

At the door behind Douglas a broad-faced man with a dark, coarse stubble over his cheeks suddenly appeared. "Captain, something went wrong over there. The old man's bringing the ferry across."

"I am aware of that, Sergeant. Give us one minute here," Douglas replied.

"Ain't so sure we've got a minute, Captain," the sergeant said, but he disappeared anyway.

Dewey said, "Hell, Captain, Colonel Slaughter and his boys ain't worth it anymore. They've been shot to hell over the last six weeks and if you'd just leave them alone for twenty-four hours they'd likely fall apart on their own."

"They are still criminals."

Dewey shook his head. "They aren't criminals, Captain. Most of them are still boys. Let them go now and they'll be back on their farms within a week."

Douglas looked at him for a moment, then shook his head. "You are lying to me, Mr. Harker. But it doesn't make any difference."

Dewey's mouth went dry. There was a touch of regret in Douglas's voice that had been absent earlier, and he knew that he had lost. Slowly, he began to lift his legs away from the sorrel, spurs poised.

The sergeant appeared at the door again, his voice urgent. "Captain, the old man's almost docked. In another minute they'll all be aboard and on the way back."

Dewey wanted to look, to see how close the ferry really was, but he didn't dare take the pressure of his gaze off Douglas.

"Captain, I can shoot this man dead before his hand ever touches that pistol," the sergeant offered.

From the river, Slaughter called, "Come along, Lieutenant. We're ready to load."

Douglas sighed, fingered his clothes. "I am an officer in the United States Army, Mr. Harker, dressed this way only to initiate negotiations for surrender. I would hate to die in these clothes, but I'm afraid duty transcends all else."

"I'm sorry to hear that too," Dewey said, and drove his spurs into the sorrel's flanks. The mare grunted with both surprise and pain, and lunged forward, nearly jumping onto the porch before Dewey got her turned. He palmed his revolver as he did and shot Douglas square in the chest, slamming him backward into the sergeant. Douglas's hand fell limply from inside his gaudy suit and a small pocket pistol bounced onto the porch. The sergeant had been drawing down on Dewey with a carbine, but Douglas's body knocked the barrel aside and he shot a lantern off the wall instead, spilling kerosene over the porch.

Dewey pointed the mare toward the nearest woods but she'd hardly settled into her stride when her front legs buckled and she collapsed. Dewey fell hard, the wind knocked from him, but he scrambled up anyway, impelled into blind action by the drone of bullets kicking up the dust around him. He drew his second revolver and shattered a pane of glass in one of Kerwin's windows, then splintered the door frame just as the sergeant poked his head out for another shot. Diving first for the protection of the fallen sorrel, Dewey quickly rolled under the shelter of the porch, sprawling there for a moment with his face in the dirt, fighting for air while around him the world seemed to explode with gunfire.

Dewey had expected the worst, but when he lifted his face from the dust the sound of gunfire continued unabated, the rangers returning fire from the river's edge with a vengeance. Across the street the livery was wreathed in gunsmoke, but the old, dark lumber was pocked with fresh scars of yellow innerwood, too, and Dewey laughed and thought that maybe it wasn't finished yet.

He crawled to the rear of the porch, hoping to find an entry to the crawlspace beneath the store, but the board and batten continued all the way to the ground. He rested on his elbows for a moment, contemplating his next move. He needed to get out of here, and he needed a horse. Then he smelled the kerosene and the panicky urge to escape slipped away entirely. Crawling on his belly, he came to the spot where the kerosene from the broken lantern had run through the floorboards, staining the light-colored wood dark. It still dripped a little, catching in a little pile of wind-driven leaves, and Dewey grinned and fumbled a match from his pocket. He scratched the match across a dry board; the sulfur flared, fluttered, threatened to go out, but caught then, steadied, and he lowered it carefully to the litter of kerosene-soaked leaves, rolling back at the rush of yellow flames.

The fire caught quicker than Dewey would have thought possible, the flames biting hungrily into the dry, splintery wood and climbing rapidly. The response came almost immediately. From inside the store someone yelled, "Smoke," and a moment later a second voice added, "Fire! The place is on fire!"

To Dewey, it sounded like a brawl above him. Furniture crashed to the floor, glass shattered, men yelled and cursed, and a moment later a rear window burst outward in a thousand tiny pieces. Soldiers jumped from the window, sprawling, lurching to their feet, falling again as others jumped on top of them, a wild, tangled melee that slowly disengaged to become something more than two dozen stumbling, scurrying legs. Laughing until the tears rolled down his cheeks, Dewey hurried them on with his pistol.

Dewey decided it had been a hell of a plan, but within minutes he discovered its obvious flaw. Smoke rolled like gray cotton, filling Dewey's low shelter, stinging his eyes. He could feel the heat of the flames on his legs and rolled toward the outer edge of the porch, but that only exposed him to the rifle fire from the livery. The men within the livery had ignored him at first, content to concentrate on those along the river, but the smoke and fire soon drew their attention, their bullets.

He was trapped. There was nowhere to run. He coughed as the smoke thickened, the flames spread. He couldn't stay here much longer, he knew, but couldn't leave either, and he laughed again and loudly at the hopelessness of the situation. But it was a laughter without regret, too, for he had bought those trapped along the river some time, had given them a chance, no matter how slim. A man could ask no more of his death than that.

Clutching his revolvers tightly then, he rolled out from beneath the porch and onto his knees. He lunged to his feet, snapped a shot, another, then cried hoarsely as a rifle ball shattered his chest.

The world, sight and sound and smell, disappeared, and in its place was a swirling crimson edged in black. It was a brief thing, the red shrinking rapidly, pulling into itself, a faint glow, and then nothing.

CHAPTER 19

Gray Fletcher tried for a while, but work was impossible and after a couple of hours he put aside the partially-mended harness and walked slowly to the edge of the porch, hands buried in his pockets. His gaze was drawn to the Osage's far shore, as it had been a dozen times already that morning. Tendrils of gray smoke still curled from the ruins of Kerwin's store, gutted in yesterday's fire. He could see a solitary figure prowling leisurely among the ashes and fallen timbers, searching for souvenirs perhaps, but the distance was too great for Gray to make out the man's features. Swearing softly, he lifted blunt, suddenly clumsy fingers to the fragile wire rims of his new spectacles and pushed them higher upon the bridge of his nose. Still, the stranger's face did not take shape. Gray sighed and let it go.

His vision had started to fail last spring and he had grudgingly and with much complaint ordered a pair of spectacles from St. Louis, but they hadn't helped much, and he was beginning to think nothing would. He hadn't told Irene, though; he hadn't wanted to worry her. He didn't know if he was fooling her or not, and sometimes he suspected she knew a lot more than either one of them was willing to admit. He had dropped a sight of weight since spring, more than a man should have, eating as he did and working in the fresh air every day. But it kept slipping away nonetheless, and his strength too, until some nights, undressing for bed, his fingers shook from the effort. He wondered occasionally if he was dying, but it was a thought he didn't dwell on. It was funny in a way, this sudden fear of death after all he had faced in life, but he hadn't laughed about it, or much else over the last few weeks.

He removed the spectacles and folded them carefully, slipping them into the little hard-shell case they had arrived in. He knew death would be less frightening to him if Irene was married to a good man. But she showed little interest in those who came to call, and Gray suspected her heart had already made its decision, whether she knew it yet or not.

Without the spectacles the Osage lost form and motion, becoming only a flat silver sheet. He stared at the river a lot anymore, seeing in its passing waters lands he had never visited and adventures he had never known. But there was no sadness; his life had been full and eventful and, in its own way, satisfying. If there were things he had missed there was also much that he had seen and done, and there was Irene, and what mattered after that?

Dewey. Gray's shoulders slumped a little,

thinking of his old comrade. Last night he had tried to remember the first time they met but he hadn't been able to bring the scene to his mind. It was as if Dewey had always been a part of his life, a friendship that was like the warmth of summer, gone for long months at a time, sure, but always returning. Yet if it seemed a lifetime for him, it actually was for Irene, and she grieved terribly; Dewey's friendship had been about the only thing of substance that she had been able to salvage from her years in Texas.

Movement across the river caught Gray's attention, and he fumbled the glasses from their case and put them on. The far shore didn't come into focus immediately—he had to concentrate on it a few seconds—but he didn't feel any surprise in seeing what he did. In fact, he had half expected them yesterday. He backed off a few paces, calling softly, "Irene, come here."

He spoke calmly but Irene was no fool; she came immediately, armed. "What is it, Papa?"

"Across the river, daughter. Horsemen, but are they soldiers?"

Irene gasped. "Yankees," she breathed.

"How many?" To Gray's blurred sight it looked as if the whole shore bristled with men.

"Hundreds, I'd guess. They're motioning for you to bring the ferry."

Gray could hear them now, shouts made faint by a small breeze. Tonelessly, Gray said, "I want you to go into the woods. Go to the McClearys and stay with them until I come to fetch you."

"No!"

Gray turned, his old eyes flashing. "Do as I tell you, and do it now!"

There was a large splash in the river and Gray turned back, squinting toward the far shore.

"Papa you can't even see!"

"How many?"

She came to his side, studying the river. "Three. They're swimming their horses over."

Gray laughed harshly. Douglas had sent three men over, too.

Irene looked at him, her eyes big with fright. "No," she whispered. "Papa, please."

Gray's voice hardened. "Irene, you're near to nineteen and too old to be belted, but by God I will if I have to." He curved his hand threateningly over his belt buckle.

"But you can't win, Papa! It won't change anything!"

Gray's voice shook, his hand trembled. He could hear the splash of swimming horses now, the shouts of encouragement from the far shore. "I am your father and I order you to leave. Now damnit, Irene, go. Go!"

Tears welled in Irene's eyes, rolled uncharacteristically down her cheek. She whispered, "I love you, Papa."

Something inside Gray twisted, tore at his

heart, but he steeled his voice, held it in. "Take the shotgun and slip out the back door. Keep out of sight. I'll likely come for you tomorrow."

Irene blinked, started to speak, then clamped her mouth shut. She was a Missourian, and a Texan before that, and she wouldn't give in to frivolous sentiment. She went to the cabin's door and slipped inside without pause.

Gray took a deep breath and closed his eyes. This was a plan he had worked out a long time ago. The McClearys were old friends, and they would care for Irene as they would their own.

He went back to the chair where he had earlier tried to mend the harness and lifted the old Hall carbine he had carried in Texas. It was a breech-loader, bulky and awkward compared to the newer models, but familiar, and graceful because of it. From a pigskin bullet bag he dipped out a handful of linen cartridges and laid them on the seat of the chair like fat grubworms awaiting a hook. He counted them slowly, those and the others in the bag yet. Nineteen. That wasn't many but when he considered rolling extras he realized sadly that nineteen would be enough, one way or the other.

Gray flipped the breech open and inserted a cartridge, snapping it shut as the three Yankees rode their dripping horses up the near bank. He fumbled a small copper percussion cap from the bag and fitted it quickly over the carbine's nipple, half expecting the three to approach the cabin.

But they didn't, and Gray swore when they led their horses onto the ferry. He should have expected that, should have cut it loose yesterday to drift downriver, or tried to hide it, but he hadn't been thinking clearly, caught up in his own grief and fears.

He scooped the rest of the cartridges back into the bag, debated sniping a shot at the three on the ferry and decided against it. Despite what Irene thought, it wasn't death that Gray looked for, merely dignity. This was his home and he wouldn't be chased from it like a common criminal.

With two men handling the cable it didn't take long to cross the river. A detachment immediately came on board and within minutes the ferry was again slicing through the Osage's waters. Gray lifted the heavy carbine to the crook of his left arm and let his right hand curl around the lock, thumb planted on the hammer. His heart hammered in his chest and his breath quickened, but it wasn't fear that caused it, and he smiled suddenly, unexpectedly. He hadn't felt this way in a long time.

Gray was still waiting at the edge of the porch when the detachment of cavalry thundered up the wooden pier and onto dry land. They advanced at a trot, perhaps a score of men with rifles in hand. When they came closer Gray saw that they were led by a major.

The major halted his men in front of the porch and fanned them into a shallow crescent. He was a stocky man, not fat or even heavy, but well built, with silver hair and the pronounced slump of old exhaustion to his shoulders. "Would you be Gray Fletcher, sir, operator of the Texas Crossing ferry?" the Major asked.

"I'm Gray Fletcher."

"I am Major Jack Crawford, Mr. Fletcher, United States Cavalry under detached service to the state of Missouri. We are in pursuit of the border raiders known as the Missouri Rangers. Are you aware of these men and their identity?"

Gray nodded.

"And did you, sir, knowing full well the status of these men as outlaws, and of Captain Jonathan Douglas's intent to capture these men and return them for trial, overcome three of his soldiers and assist in the escape of said outlaws?"

Gray wanted to laugh, but didn't. "Major," he said, "as far as Missouri is concerned, you and your men are the outlaws."

Gray might have expected anger, but Crawford's face remained unchanged. "Did you assist in the escape of the men known as Missouri Rangers, Mr. Fletcher, and were you aware of their status as outlaws at the time?"

"Yes, Major, I did."

Crawford studied him silently for a moment, then said, "May I ask why, sir?"

Gray smiled. "Why, to further the cause of the glorious South, you pompous sonofabitch."

Crawford's face finally reddened, if only slightly. "I would be entirely within the law to hang you here," he said stiffly. "But Missouri has enough martyrs. I will not give it another. You are under arrest, Fletcher. Lay your weapon aside immediately."

Gray cocked the Hall, the sound loud in his ears. There was a hurried rustling among the men behind Crawford, silenced quickly by a young, wide-eyed lieutenant with a face full of doubt. "Come and get it, you Yankee bastard," Gray said.

"It is tempting, it is truly tempting," Crawford whispered thinly. He looked behind him, at the lieutenant. "Townsend, arrest this man." Crawford reined his horse around and started back toward the river.

For a minute it looked as if Townsend might swallow his tongue. His eyes, already big, widened even more, and his mouth gaped a little. Behind him a couple of the older veterans snickered. Gray cursed loudly. "Come back here, Crawford. My quarrel is with you."

Crawford didn't stop, didn't even look back.

Townsend reluctantly urged his horse forward. "Mr. Fletcher, put your rifle down, sir."

"Get out of my way, sonny," Gray spat angrily. "Show me Crawford's yellow back."

"Please, sir."

A few of the men behind Townsend came forward, their faces grim in the shadow of their hats. Gray's shoulders sagged. He didn't want to shoot this kid, nor did he have a bone to pick with any of the privates behind Townsend. It was Crawford he wanted, but Crawford had turned his back, had made him impotent. He was on the verge of surrender when a gray cloud of smoke erupted from the cabin window on his left with a deafening roar, and Crawford's horse squealed shrilly and dropped dead beneath him.

"God*damn!*" Gray shouted, shouldering the Hall and snapping a shot that bowled Lieutenant Townsend from his saddle. He leaped back, slammed his shoulder against the cabin door, and stumbled inside just as the quickest of the soldiers behind Townsend fired their first round. Bullets plopped hollowly into the door frame; on his knees, Gray slammed the door shut. He lunged up and slapped the bar into place just as another half dozen or so minie balls thudded like angry wasps into the thick planks. Then he whirled, glaring at Irene as she calmly reloaded the shotgun.

She looked up defiantly, matching his anger with her own, but neither spoke; there wasn't time. Gray quickly fingered a second cartridge from his pouch and reloaded. He cracked a shutter open just as a soldier leaped onto the porch with a drawn revolver, and sliding the rifle forward, he squeezed the trigger. The soldier disappeared into a billowing cloud of smoke, but Gray clearly heard his hoarse, gurgling cry and knew the soldier would die. By he time he reloaded again the field was empty save for the boots of the dead soldier just visible beyond the porch, Crawford's horse, and Townsend.

Gray's ears rang from the crash of the rifle indoors and his eyes smarted in the thin haze of powder smoke that had drifted back inside. His shoulder was sore and likely bruised from that last shot, but when he turned away from the window, he felt none of that.

Irene was at the west side of the house, peering between the shutters. "They've gone behind the barn, Papa. I guess they'll think twice before trying that again."

Gray wanted to shout but forced himself to remain calm. "Why are you here?" he asked. "Why did you do this?"

"Did you think I would run? Is that the kind of woman you think Gray Fletcher's daughter should be?"

It was over, he thought dully; he was defeated, not by the Yankees, but by his own daughter, for he wouldn't fight with her in the cabin. He set the Hall aside, picked it up again. Irene had shot Crawford's horse, had likely wounded Crawford in the process. Would they let her go, or would they want to arrest her also? A shiver passed through his body at the thought of Irene as a prisoner of the federal army. He told himself that they were honorable men, but he knew they were still men and that he could never turn her over to them like a piece of property.

A shot from the woods thumped the rear door, two more from the woods at the top of the meadow rattled a shutter.

"They have us surrounded?" Irene whispered as if to herself.

"Did you think they would leave?" Gray cried suddenly. "Did you think they would be frightened off like dogs?"

A stray bullet wormed its way between a pair of shutters, shattering the glass in the window, burying itself in the back wall. Irene screamed, a quick, shrill sound, and put her hands over her mouth.

Gray sighed and shook his head. He had no choice. He walked stiffly to the galvanized sink and from a peg on the wall above it took a piece of white cotton sacking. "Give me your ramrod," he ordered.

Irene looked confused, then understanding dawned and she shook her head. "No, Papa. You want to surrender."

"I have no choice but to surrender," he gritted. "Damnit, daughter, do I have to fight you every step? Give me the ramrod!"

"Papa, they'll take you away. They'll try you for treason. No, Papa, please."

Gray swore and wrapped the rag around the barrel of the Hall. Irene leaned the shotgun against the wall and hurried to his side, grabbing an arm, but he shook her away violently and strode to the front door. He paused there only a moment, then flung it open and stepped outside, the flag of truce dangling in the sultry air. "Don't shoot," he called. "I'll—"

From the barn Crawford's graveled, "Fire!" instantly discharged a dozen rifles, cutting off Gray's surrender in mid-sentence.

Gray cried out, spun under impact, and fell roughly against the door, stumbling inside then before dropping to his knees. He could hear as if from beyond the wooden ridge a scream that he knew was Irene's, and her hands on his shoulders felt distant, too, as if felt in a dream. He hurt all over, but it was a dull pain, and bearable. In the end it was the weariness that proved overwhelming, reaching up and pulling him back. He went without resistance, desiring only sleep.

Jesse sat alone in the weed-choked clearing, his back to a half-dead apple tree that was green on one side, its boughs bent low under the weight of its wormy fruit, and gray-white and brittle on the other side, rigidly vertical, barren. Nearby, the buckskin tore greedily at the green grass, the sound loud but comforting in the still air, broken only by the music of a couple of meadowlarks and the far-off lament of a mourning dove. It was a peaceful setting here, alone and nestled low in the tall grass, the blemishes of old burns hidden from view, but for Jesse it was an elusive peace, haunted by memories of the past. He saw the clearing as it had once been, with the house and barn and all the outbuildings, and his ma hanging laundry on a cotton line while Shep nosed the basket.

Riding through earlier he had spotted the weather-bleached bones of old Sam, the gray mule, and had searched without success for those of Shep. He had felt an unreasonable anger at his failure, but it ebbed quickly, leaving in its place an emptiness he knew had nothing to do with Shep.

Everyone missed Dewey, but Jesse wondered if anyone missed him as much as he did. Jesse and Dewey and Gil had ridden alone in search of the enemy while the others had remained behind. They had shared food and shelter when it was available, hunger and discomfort when it wasn't. But now Dewey was dead—no doubt of that, even witnessed from a bobbing ferry—and he couldn't even mourn him, not the way he wanted to. Within the rangers Dewey was merely another soldier, with only the meaningless title of rank to set him apart from Tim or Pete or any of the others torn from them by Yankee bullets.

But for Jesse, Dewey was different; he was a

friend, perhaps one of the best he had ever had, and he squeezed his eyes shut and clenched his fists, taking advantage of what little time he had alone.

Hoofbeats drummed along the distant road, and Jesse lifted his head. A breeze stirred the upper limbs of the nearby trees and passed on. A tick jumped from the grass to the sleeve of his shirt and started its journey toward his shoulder, but Jesse flicked it off with his finger. The hoofbeats drew nearer, louder, a quick cadence drummed into the hard-packed road. Jesse listened intently, picturing the route in his mind, but he didn't stand until the rider left the road and started up the overgrown lane that had once led to his home.

The buckskin grazed within easy reach, but the saddle was dumped in a heap in the grass and Jesse wouldn't abandon it, not for just one rider. He drew his revolver, felt a trickle of sweat move down the side of his face and into his beard, but it was only Bob Wilkes who burst into the clearing on a lathered horse.

After crossing the Osage yesterday they had pushed hard until nightfall, coming without Jesse's guidance to within a few miles of the old homeplace. Calling a halt, Slaughter had motioned Jesse and Gil forward. "We've got to find a place to hole up for a few days," he'd said in a voice tinged with panic. "We have wounded who'll die if we don't." Jesse had reluctantly volunteered information about the cave, knowing its remoteness and his own knowledge of the country would make it a suitable, if temporary, hideout. Lost both mentally and geographically, Slaughter had jumped at the offer.

Jesse led them past his old home in the dark and onto the deer trail that led past the sink where he had hidden from the Yankees nearly two years before, and on to the cave's larger mouth, near the river. Well before dawn Slaughter had sent Wilkes along their backtrail for whatever information he could ferret out, and Jesse had ridden with him this far.

Wilkes saw Jesse and swerved toward him, bringing his horse to a plunging stop. "Where the hell's the trail to the cave?" he called.

"What's up?" Jesse countered.

"Goddamn Yankees, the dirty bastards. They've got that old man that ferried us across the river holed up in his cabin and they're punching it full of holes."

Jesse swayed, his vision blackening, then clearing. *Gray, they were going to kill Gray to avenge yesterday.*

"Where's the goddamn trail, Ross?" Wilkes shouted. "That old man risked his neck for us and he's needing help!"

Jesse pointed mutely toward the head of the trail, invisible from here but easy enough to find when a man got close. Wilkes spurred his horse forward, crashing through the brush and young saplings, while Jesse hoisted his saddle and carried it to the buckskin. He left the clearing at a gallop, spurred to a run, and never considered a final, backward glance.

CHAPTER 20

For a long time Jesse rode numbly while the world flashed dully and without note behind. Dimly, he could hear the drum of the buckskin's hooves against the road, could feel the small jolt and rock of the animal's gait, and the breeze clean on his face. He was aware of the sky above, hazy blue and littered with dingy puffs of clouds that drifted briskly to the east, and of the deep, somber forest that paralleled the winding, bucking road. From time to time he passed tiny fields of corn or beans, or narrow farm lanes that wound out of sight; once he passed a wagon pulled by a pair of scrawny, runted mules, the driver a barefoot kid in bib overalls and a chewed-up straw hat, but he didn't stop or wave or acknowledge the boy in any fashion, and it was the mules and wagon that gave up the road.

It was forty miles more or less to Gray's place, but Jesse held the buckskin to a killing pace and made it in just under five hours. Scattered rifle fire greeted him as he drew near, and Jesse felt like cheering. If the battle was still engaged, that meant Gray was still alive and fighting.

Jesse slowed the buckskin to a walk, aware for the first time of the lather that spotted his trouser legs, and of the buckskin's ragged, wheezing breath. His grip tightened on the reins but that was all the emotion he showed. A rifle cracked some distance ahead and he decided that if he had ruined the buckskin's wind it at least hadn't been in vain.

He left the road while still several hundred yards shy of the entrance to the long meadow, easing his horse through the thick woods, dodging clinging spider webs and wild grape vines that hung like ropes from the upper branches of the trees. The ground was covered with a thick, leafy mold, rigged beneath with old dead limbs that would pop sharply in the muggy air when stepped upon. Patches of dark, broad-leafed mayapple spotted the woods, and here and there, feathery limbs of pale green ferns sprouted in delicate splendor, but there wasn't any grass—with a permanent overcast of forest there was never enough sunlight to support grass. It was a shadowy world, silenced by the nearby battle and marred with acrid tendrils of gunsmoke.

Jesse knew he would stand a better chance of slipping close by leaving the buckskin behind, but he was a ranger now, a horseman all the way through, and the thought of fighting on foot made his skin crawl. So he wound his way slowly through the forest, pausing frequently to scan the terrain ahead for movement or color. The buckskin sensed Jesse's tension through the reins and stepped high, his ears perked forward, but not even the buckskin detected the Yankee soldier until he stepped from behind a tree with his fly only half buttoned, a cocked Springfield rifle grasped firmly in both hands.

"Hold it right there, Mister," the soldier commanded in a shaky voice.

Jesse fell off the buckskin, putting the animal's body between himself and the soldier, and by the time his shoulder struck the spongy loam, he had drawn and fired both revolvers under the buckskin's belly.

The soldier's face paled and he staggered backward a couple of feet, his rifle dropping unnoticed from nerveless fingers, and a moment later he sank to his knees and slowly toppled sideways.

The buckskin squealed and bucked, stung along his stomach and rear legs by the revolvers' muzzle blasts, and bolted with his head high and to one side. Jesse rolled quickly to his feet, whistling softly, but the buckskin was spooked now, and kept on running. Within seconds he had disappeared as if swallowed by the woods and, afoot, Jesse swore.

He turned slowly, the revolvers hanging by his side, the woods quiet save for the steady rustle of the leaves in the treetops, but strangely hostile too, in a way he knew had nothing to do with the nearby Yankees. Only moments before he had contemplated leaving the buckskin behind and dismissed the idea without hesitation. Inside, he knew it was the buckskin that set him apart from his enemy, and without him he felt alone and inadequate.

A questioning shout came from beyond a nearby rise, unanswered, and Jesse glanced at the soldier he had killed and knew the shout was for him. They had heard the twin reports from his revolver, would have had to have been deaf not to, but would they come to investigate or dismiss it as some of their own? They would come, Jesse had no doubts of that. Another shout from beyond the ridge, and he might have run then, if not for the buckskin's tentative nicker. Turning, he saw the buckskin advance hesitantly, pause, then come forward another two or three steps, more frightened of being alone than of the unexpected bite of the revolvers. Jesse could have shouted his relief. He hurried forward; the buckskin stopped and threw his head up; Jesse slowed, approached at a walk, let his breath escape only when he'd grabbed the reins. Mounted again, he turned expectantly toward the ridge just as a horse soldier came over the top.

"Hell, it's a raider," the startled soldier yelled to someone still behind him.

Jesse didn't wait to find out who or how many. He snapped a shot, heard the soldier's squawk, saw him clutch at his thigh, then the buckskin was running, scooting like a deer through the dense timber while Jesse ducked low and gave him his head.

They came out of the woods without warning, bursting unsuspectingly into the meadow, and Jesse set spurs to the buckskin, plans of discretion destroyed by a chance encounter in the woods.

Gunfire followed then; it raked the air around their heads, it dug shallow furrows in the dirt close to the buckskin's hooves. From the cabin a single rifle offered scant cover, but Jesse had surprise on his side and he'd almost reached the cabin before the buckskin's head dropped like a stone and his forelegs crumbled.

Jesse was thrown wide, lit rolling and came to his feet without slowing. He ran a twisted path, the cabin beckoning but the gunfire increasing too. Bullets kicked up little chunks of sod that bounced off his legs and tore long, jagged splinters from the porch as he leaped its steps. The door swung wide just as he tried to stop and he skidded inside, slamming his hip violently against the kitchen table and sprawling across it while the door banged shut behind him.

For the space of maybe thirty seconds bullets

thudded insistently at the door, as if demanding entrance, then ceased abruptly. Jesse pushed himself up, breathing hard from his sprint, staring at Irene for a moment without comprehension. "Where's Gray?" he asked stupidly.

Irene nodded toward the bunk against the far wall. Gray rested on his back there, eyes shut, his breathing slow, deep and regular. Jesse started toward him, stopped, turned back to a window. He cracked a shutter but saw only the buckskin, limping toward the barn.

"What happened here?" Jesse asked.

"They tried to arrest Papa," Irene replied in a voice tarnished with despair. "They shot him."

Jesse moved to another window. From here he could see the two dead Yankees, the farthest a lieutenant, and toward the river a dead horse. "How bad?" he asked.

"Bad," she whispered. After a pause, she added, "He was shot three times. Twice in the chest."

Jesse blinked. Was it tears that stung his eyes? He told himself it wasn't, that it was only the lingering traces of gunsmoke that made them water this way. He moved to the next window, then the next, cursing silently and without direction, and when he passed Gray's bunk he didn't look down.

When Jesse returned to the front window, he said, "I don't see anyone."

"They're out there," Irene answered dully. Jesse

glanced at her questioningly; something ate at her, something more than her pa, he knew.

A bullet came down the hill and thudded into the log wall. Irene said, "They've done that all day," and sobbed once, a harsh, gasping sound, the silence afterward like a shroud.

Gil didn't know Gray Fletcher personally, had only seen him once in fact, but it was a scene he wasn't likely to forget. They had been pinned fair beneath the shallow crest of the Osage's mud and grass bank yesterday morning; if not for the old man they'd likely still be there, or on their way to the gallows somewhere. But fate was a strange thing; it varied like the seasons, smiling here, frowning there. At the Jacksville bridge they had lost nearly twenty men in a chance encounter with federal patrols. Yesterday, in a perfectly executed ambush, they had lost only one—Dewey —plus six men wounded and seven horses either put down or scattered. But that didn't distract from Fletcher's act, didn't lessen what the men felt when they looked over their shoulders and saw him coming on in the face of Yankee gunfire, standing straight and unflinching. It made a man swell up a little inside to remember it even now, and to know a man that courageous thought them worthy of the risk. Now it was Fletcher who needed help, and there wasn't a man among them who wasn't ready to return what he had given them yesterday. Looking around him, at the others, Gil knew that for a while at least they had put all the old animosity, the strife and disappointment, behind them. They rode as one, united in a way they hadn't been since Cow Creek.

No one had forgotten Dewey, least of all Gil. They had seen him yesterday from the ferry, had guessed immediately that the fire was his work, and that without it the outcome might have been drastically different. But Dewey was dead, and it was Fletcher who needed their help now.

Jesse prowled the cabin restlessly, moving without plan from one window to another, never following the same sequence twice. From time to time he would spot a piece of Yankee uniform, an arm or part of a leg, and he always tried a shot no matter how difficult the target, rewarded frequently with a howl of pain or surprise.

But the Yankees kept up the pressure too, and no more than a couple of minutes ever passed between random shots into the walls or, more commonly, the doors or shutters. Jesse wasn't too concerned about the walls and doors—the wood there was heavy enough to withstand grape—but the shutters worried him; they were made of a lighter wood and were already showing some damage from the inside.

Jesse paused only once at Gray's bed, noting the pale complexion and the clammy brow, and he'd hurried on then, a feeling inside like nothing he'd ever experienced before threatening to rise up and close his throat. Dewey Harker had been a friend, but he'd discovered then that Gray was something more.

It was edging toward dark now, the sun nearly down and the shadows stretching long and losing their shape. It was cooler too, with a little gusting breeze that would now and again ruffle the Osage's waters and pass teasingly through the trees, bringing with it a scent of rain, and in the west the sky was turning gray. Jesse would welcome a rain. He would welcome anything that varied the monotony of the siege. The waiting, the sporadic rifle fire, Gray's shallow breath, all of it clawed at Jesse's nerves like sharpened fingernails. He told himself that something would have to change soon, that the Yankees couldn't afford to let darkness drop over this stage. Crawford had taken most of the men and retreated to the west, Irene had told him in a halting voice earlier, leaving behind only the twenty or so men who had originally accompanied the major across the river. They controlled the meadow now, but they had to realize they would lose their advantage after dark. So where were Wilkes and the others? Jesse wondered anxiously.

A voice like gravel underfoot interrupted Jesse's thoughts. "You, in the cabin. I want to talk to you."

Irene looked up, her eyes big in the flickering light of a single candle, more alive than he'd seen them since he'd arrived. "Keep an eye out the other windows," Jesse ordered gently. "And be careful. This could be a trick."

Irene nodded, snatching up the shotgun and hurrying to a far window.

Jesse put his back to the cabin wall and carefully lifted the latch that held the shutter in place. Nudging it open an inch or so, he peered outside. At the corner of the barn a burly man with sergeant's stripes and a bandage on his face stood nervously with empty hands spread away from his body. Jesse's lips peeled back and his eyes went hard. This was the man who had shot Dewey. Jesse recognized him easily, seeing him as he had yesterday, from the ferry, spraddle-legged on the flaming porch, a carbine held firmly in one hand. Unconsciously, Jesse cocked his revolver.

"In the cabin. Can you hear me?"

"I can hear you," Jesse returned, feeling a touch of satisfaction at the way the sergeant flinched.

"Give it up?" the sergeant said. "You're two, three at the most against twenty. We have a town full of food and a river full of water at our backs. You have nothing."

"We have a shitpot full of rangers on the way right now."

The sergeant paused, considering Jesse's threat. Then he said, "I don't believe you. You're lying."

"Ask him where Crawford is," Irene unexpectedly urged. "Ask why he isn't here to see the finish of what he started."

"Now ain't the time to worry—"

"Ask him, damnit," she cried, her face filled with such anguish that Jesse immediately shut up.

"Come on, Missouri," the sergeant prodded. "I won't let the sun set on this."

"Where's Crawford?" Jesse called. "I want to talk with the head man, not his flunky."

"The Major's got better things to do than waste his time here. You deal with me, Missouri, and you'd best do it quick, while I feel generous."

"The bastard," Irene whispered. She sank to a chair, her eyes welling tears that began to flow down her cheeks.

Jesse swore to himself, swamped in a feeling of inadequacy.

Where were the rangers?

"Last chance, Missouri."

Jesse considered surrender, dismissed it for the same reason Gray must have, because of Irene. He would have to fight then, alone if no one came. Across the river the sun was a red, glowing ball perched upon the horizon. There would be another hour of good light left, perhaps one more of dusky light, but before that the Yankees would attack; it was inevitable.

"I won't give up," Irene said in a choked voice. "You can if you want, but I won't."

Jesse looked at her, then he smiled softly. "No, I won't either. Ready?"

Irene stood and went to a window. Jesse's grip tightened on the revolver and he slid the barrel onto the sill, but before he could squeeze the trigger a rifle barked from the woods and the shutter slapped back against him, sending his shot wild. When he looked, the sergeant was gone.

From inside the barn, the sergeant yelled, "You just shit your own pants, Missouri. I hope you remember that on your way to hell."

There had been only silence save for the pounding of hooves and the harsh, ragged breathing of the horses, but suddenly the woods ahead of them erupted with gunfire. For a moment Gil envisioned an ambush and he grabbed for a revolver, but he realized then the firing was too far ahead, two or three hundred yards perhaps, and knew they had come at last to the sloping meadow opposite Texas Crossing.

Only a few rode with Gil now. Arliss King and Charlie Dye, Floyd Shuyler, and Jim Brenner rode before him on horses confiscated at Jacksville. Behind him came Woody Johnson and Eli Davis, but there was no one else in sight. Even Slaughter, on his big gray, had fallen behind, and Gil knew there were likely rangers strung out for five miles or more along the rugged, twisting road. They'd pushed hard for the last several hours, some more than others, and there wasn't a horse that wasn't lathered and glassy-eyed. Gil's bay ran as if drugged, her gait rough and jarring and her head bobbing like a cork tossed into choppy waters, but he knew he couldn't wait for the others. From the sudden, desperate pitch of gunfire he thought they might be too late already; surely no one could hold out long under such a barrage. With a sudden, furious rebel yell, he slammed his heels against the bay's ribs, urging her on. The others took it up and soon the woods echoed with their rage.

It didn't last long. It couldn't. There was too much behind them, too many hard-pressed miles and sleepless nights and hungry bellies to fuel their anger. They swept like Goths into the meadow, and the Yankees, scattered too thin and mostly afoot, fled before them, leaving behind weapons and mounts tethered in the trees. Only those trapped within the barn fought with any sincerity, but it was a hopeless effort and by the time the sun sank below the horizon the meadow belonged to the rangers.

Slaughter and most of the others had arrived by then and Slaughter took charge of the prisoners, but it was an empty gesture. The Company of Missouri Rangers died with the surrender of the broad-faced sergeant, their final victory too late to save the indefinable spirit that had once held them together. As dusk settled men began to slip quietly away, not as deserters but merely as men whose job was finished. Nine—Jubal Butler, Bud Gantz, LeMay, and the Dye brothers among them—followed Borden into the shadows. Only Charlie Prescott, Eli Davis, Arliss King, Woody Johnson, and a handful of others remained with Slaughter, their revolvers trained on the knot of sullen prisoners that no one seemed to know what to do with.

To Gil, it seemed an unfit ending to what had once been a noble purpose, yet beneath it all he felt an overwhelming sense of relief. It was over. Let the others make their own decisions, let them find other comrades to fight beside, other battles to win or lose if that was their choice. He was finished with it. The West beckoned like a brass ring; he was ready to grab for it.

Gil tightened the bay's cinch, checked his bedroll, his saddlebags, then swung into the saddle. The sun was long since down, its glow masked by a creeping sheet of low clouds, and a dampness on the breeze that might have been a fine mist. If not for the lights of Texas Crossing reflecting in its waters, the Osage would have been invisible. He couldn't see the ferry but he could hear its low, dragging screech as its timbers stretched and contracted above the river's caress. There was a comfort in the sound, a sort of reassurance that the way was still open and available. A silly feeling, he thought, but real nonetheless, and with an almost childlike anticipation he reined the bay toward it.

Jesse lifted his face to the breeze, the fresh touch of the misty rain, and caught, sudden and unexpected, the dank, pungent stench of old fire, of fresh, clotting blood, and the gassy odor of death. He turned away and shut his eyes, slamming a fist ineffectively into the grass. He laughed then, a small sound, full of disappointment and acceptance. It seemed like everything he'd seen or touched since Jacksville had soured for him; why should the wind be any different?

He stood, staring for a moment more at the low hump of dirt that was Dewey's grave, then turned and walked down the long slope to the cabin. They had two or three lanterns lit in the barn and he could see Slaughter inside, huddled in conference with Prescott and Davis, and beyond, the broad-faced sergeant glaring with unconcealed contempt at those guarding him. But for Jesse it was like watching strangers—all of them—and he turned toward the cabin without interest.

He found Irene alone with her father and went to her side, laying a hand gently across her shoulder as Gray had done with him so often, so long ago. She looked up, her face drained of everything except weariness, her eyes big and shadowed; then she did a strange thing, she lifted her hand and put it on top of his, a simple gesture, yet it shook him all the way through, made his breath catch and his heart pound. Forcing his voice to remain calm, he said, "How is he?"

"Not very good," Irene said. "But he seems to be resting more comfortably now, so maybe there's hope in that."

"Sure," Jesse said, but he thought Gray had never looked worse and knew it was more than just the wounds dragging him down. There was something wrong with Gray, something Jesse had noticed yesterday, on the ferry, and ignored in the shock of seeing Dewey shot down. But he couldn't ignore it now. Gray was dying, no matter what the outcome of his wounds.

There was a knock at the door, a tentative rapping, then it swung inward and Gil poked his head inside. "Ma'am," he said to Irene, touching the brim of his hat. To Jesse, he said, "Come outside?"

Jesse nodded and followed Gil onto the porch, pulling the door shut behind them. It was raining in earnest now, not hard but steady, and already dripping from the eaves.

"How's the old guy?" Gil asked.

"Bad, I reckon."

Gil said, "Damn," softly, and walked to the edge of the porch. With his back to Jesse, facing the river, he went on. "Decided to cut my pin tonight. I was almost to the ferry before I turned around." He paused as if to give Jesse a chance to jump into the conversation, but Jesse remained silent. Then he hitched at his trousers and said, "Well, hell, this was never really my fight. I ain't a Northerner or a Southerner."

Jesse grinned, his first in a long time. "You're a westerner, Gil. You've got an itch to see the Rocky Mountains that ain't going away until you get out there to scratch it."

Gil laughed softly. "Yeah, I guess," he breathed, and added, "Are you coming?"

Jesse hesitated. The question didn't surprise him, he had guessed it was coming as soon as Gil poked his head in the door, but he hadn't considered an answer, either. He thought of Colorado and California and wondered what they were like. He had never seen any mountain other than the stumps that were the Ozarks, had never traveled a desert or seen an ocean but suddenly he knew that, despite its promise of fortune and adventure, he didn't want to go. In his mind he could feel the buck and tug of a plow, the rich, black dirt crumbling under his fingers, remembered the honest satisfaction of a good meal after a hard day.

No, he thought, he wouldn't let the Yankees take that away from him. If the North won he would be a fugitive forever, but if the South won he could go home again, and he thought that was worth staying and fighting for. "No," he said. "I ain't going with you, Gil. I'm staying."

Gil turned. There wasn't enough light to see his face but Jesse guessed it was likely full of surprise. He kind of felt that way himself.

"Gray is in a bad way," Jesse explained. "Reckon I owe him more than I knew."

"You're an outlaw, Jesse, and Crawford hasn't given up. He'll be back, or someone else will."

Jesse had already considered that, but couldn't see where it changed anything. Hesitantly, he said, "I know life won't ever be exactly the same, but Ma's in Poplar Bluff and . . ." He let the words trail off.

"Irene?"

Jesse nodded, didn't know if Gil could see that in the shadows but felt incapable of anything more. Irene. How thickheaded had he been not to see that she loved him, and that he felt the same? He said, "Reckon I'll stay until I see what happens with Gray, then maybe drift on until I can find me an honest-to-God Confederate outfit."

Gil sighed, then laughed. "I wish you luck, Jesse. All in the world."

"Thanks, Gil. You too." He held his hand out and Gil took it, a brief thing, both embarrassed by the emotion they felt. Then Gil descended the steps and gathered the bay's reins.

It was raining harder now, pelting down with the promise of worse to come. Jesse rolled his shoulder, felt a twinge in his side from his old wound; he wasn't looking forward to an extended rain.

Mounted, Gil called, "If you change your mind, look me up. I'll be around Cherry Creek, I reckon."

"I'll do that," Jesse said, thinking that, if things didn't work out, maybe he would.

Gil reined the bay around and rode toward the ferry. Jesse watched until he was swallowed by the darkness, then he went back inside.

Center Point Large Print
600 Brooks Road / PO Box 1
Thorndike ME 04986-0001 USA

(207) 568-3717

US & Canada:
1 800 929-9108
www.centerpointlargeprint.com